Her
Own
Terms

ALSO BY THE AUTHOR

How Aliens Think

"A remarkabl 3 8015 01837 9218 rrative of a
young working class woman artist coming of age. It has

—Houston Post

HER OWN TERMS

A Novel

Judith Grossman

Published in the United States of America by
Soho Press, Inc.
853 Broadway
New York, NY 10003

Library of Congress Cataloging-in-Publication Data

Grossman, Judith, 1937–
Her own terms.
p.   cm.
ISBN 1-56947-289-0
I. Title.
PS3557.R66724H47   1988   813'.54   87–12123

Manufactured in the United States of America

Contents

Her
Own
Terms

I

I've never felt less like a woman—it's terribly exciting. This absolute *no*.

The fear is only to be expected; it's there, but there's no point in paying attention to it. What are the risks anyway? I have no idea. A hundred years ago there would have been nothing to be done—throw yourself in the mill-race, or on the parish. *Wragg is in custody.* It's better to catch a train to London.

And I have a corner seat, though on the corridor side because the train filled up so fast. The locals are taking a nice Friday off to go shopping. And some of the dons are beginning the Long Vacation with a hop to town; later comes Paris, or the Mediterranean. Stuart will be in Mykonos. Well, fuck them.

Some students are leaving too, but nobody I know. It was deathly quiet in the hallways when I left: most people had gone a couple of days ago, and the few who took the extra paper on the last day of Schools were sleeping late, black stockings and dusty black suits and gowns heaped on the floor with the ransacked litter of notes. There were champagne bottles in the kitchenette from Sally's party; our Constant Nymph has departed in style to seek her destined genius-lover. At the Lamb and Flag where we were drinking best bitter, Alistair hung his arms out like a Christ and said "It is finished."

The train seems not to go. That is a safe statement to make, in this place where I have learned something about safe statements. Ah, but what does it mean? Is it a bad sign? A scraping sound in the corridor gives the answer: they are going to put the crippled man whom I saw on the platform in our compartment. His attendant wrestles him out of his wheelchair and into the last corner seat, opposite me. Then she backs up into the doorway, filling it with her powerful torso and wide-set legs, and jerks down the sides of her tweed jacket.

"All right?" she asks. The man moves one bent-up arm from the elbow, and blurts something to her which I don't catch. She understands him though, and reaches down into his jacket pocket to fish out a pack of Craven As. At the sight of it his hollow face yearns forward, and his lips tremble as they receive the cigarette. Once it's been lit, the rest of us in the compartment see with relief that he can get his crooked fingers up to his mouth to carry on the operation. Now his attendant slides the door closed, pulls the wheelchair flat against the side of the corridor and goes away silently in her rubber-soled shoes. Doors slam, and the train moves. It's impossible not to look at the man one more time, he is so wrecked in body, wasted and bent, and yellowish-grey in the face. But it's unfair to look, now that he hoods his own eyes; and in any case I have the Penguin *Brothers Karamazov* on my lap, and a pressing duty to read it.

The teenaged boy and his mother in their window corners are still staring. I fix them with a mild look in the style of Alyosha, and finally they glance away—not back to the window however, but towards

4

the door. We have more company, it seems, and I recognize him at once: it is John Singleton.

But there's an excellent chance he won't recognize me. People who appear on television (though he made his name as a novelist, it's true) either have or develop preternaturally distinct faces, and Singleton's is a good example—the wide-open, prominent eyes, the incised nose and lips, the skin a tan from nowhere local. By comparison the rest of us form a pallid blur. So although I've met Singleton, I doubt he will remember me any more than the dozens of other young women to whom he's been introduced at parties where old friends have taken him to cheer him up after his divorce. Nor is this a good occasion for making connections.

I pull in my feet as he lunges past, heaves a bag onto the rack and rotates into the seat on my right. I am concentrating on the page before me, where Father Zossima is bowing before Dmitri until his head touches the floor. It is a moment of high interest and power, and I see that; but I also see it wavering before me like a candle flame under the competing blast of Singleton's irritated presence beside me. Really, the man seems to be twitching in every muscle with unspoken rage. But what's the matter? Is he annoyed at the crowding in the train—not having a corner seat? Then why doesn't he go first class, or was the divorce so terribly expensive?

"Excuse me, sir." He shocks us by addressing the crippled man. "D'you see that sign on the window? *'No Smoking.'* I must ask you to put out your cigarette."

It is the voice of a man accustomed to public discourse: strong, resonant, over-articulated. And the crippled man, who has been lost in the slow play of inhalation and release, seems unable to bring himself to the effort of an inadequate reply: he stays perfectly quiet.

5

"Let me add that I shall call the guard if you continue to smoke."

The crippled man slowly extends his arm a little way and lets the cigarette drop from between his fingers to the floor; with a careful economy of gesture he drags one shoe over it to crush the tip. We hear Singleton's quick sigh of gratification, as he sits back and taps his fingers on his knee. In the silence which follows we feel his look marching over us in triumph.

What if he should recognize me now, and speak? No—that prospect really can't be faced. I get up, dropping the book behind me on the seat, and keeping my face averted go out into the corridor.

The train is running beside the water-meadows of the Thames valley; the Oxford gasometer, last sight of the city, is already far behind. It is so lovely, the washed green fields netted with hedgerows, and the sky with fair-weather clouds scattered over it like the flounces of a Victorian wedding dress. This weather is a good sign. Now, standing at the end of the carriage I open my shoulder bag and check the money (the ten-pound note, the four five-pound notes) and the red address book. But I know the address by heart already: 26 Carlisle Avenue, three turns from Kensington High Street. My appointment is at three-thirty; I shall have hours to spare.

After all, Linda did it—that is, I believe she did it although she won't admit as much—and she survived. And the list of addresses is supposed to be reliable, coming from the radical ex-wife of the Regius Professor of Philosophy. Abortionists for all pockets, from the five-pound address at a pub to the sixty-pound doctor with a Russian name. It's really very much like buying a winter coat: you pick the best you can afford, and wear it. I would have had to take the ten-pound operation if it hadn't been for Stuart's offer of fifteen quid,

6

because that's all I had left from my State grant. Interesting that he didn't offer more, enough for the proper doctor, for instance. Of course, he isn't the father. And then Evan's five pounds made it up to thirty. Roger will pay him back when he hears about it all next week. One only hopes that Evan kept his mouth shut; if it hadn't been for those nice lunches I should never have told him, but one has to give a little.

When I counted out the thirty pounds this morning, it occurred to me that I had never held so much cash in my hand at one time. Three years ago, when Ma and I went to buy things for college, we had a twenty-five pound advance from the State: that was the previous high point. The only thing I still wear from that expedition is the black dress with thin red stripes from C & A's. I don't know how we had the sense to buy it. The other things, the olive corduroy skirt and the wool pinafore dress, I've quietly disposed of; nowadays I wear mostly black. Just occasionally colours—today it seemed important that I wear my pale yellow sailcloth dress and a china blue shirt over it, to be brave. The skirt is loosely pleated and comfortable over my four-months belly. At that, I can still wear most of my things; I'm really not fat even now, and Stuart finds it hard to believe I'm this far gone, although the doctor told me back in April. It must have been otherwise with his wife's four pregnancies, I assume.

And it seemed important this morning to make the best job possible of my appearance—to leave no flaw in the defences, no place for mortality to enter. First a slow, infinitely careful application of pancake make-up, from hairline to blended-out neckline; then powder blotted on and lightly brushed; then turquoise shadow, black mascara and pale lipstick, blotted and reapplied. I put my crinkly hair into a French roll, but remembered that I might be lying on some kind of

operating table later which would ruin the effect. So it is
tied back in a tortoise-shell clip.

I look down at my blue shoes, my best, and a
good match with the shirt: I've done everything I can.

And I'm still standing here, looking at green hills
moving rapidly past and combing each eyebrow in turn
with my middle fingernail when Singleton exits from the
compartment and comes up the corridor. It is the hair
he recognizes: hair fetishism is endemic in the literacy
world, as I'm well aware.

"Yes," he says. "I thought I knew you from
somewhere. The young poets, with all that hair between
you, after dinner at Ian's. Of course, it's Irene."

"Yes. How d'you do?"

"You were not about to say hallo to me yourself,
were you?" The tone is accusing.

"I'm not sure it would be my place, would it?"

"Balls. Your friends would've buttonholed me in
a moment."

That's true; and I'm remembering the lovely
orange pullover Sean told us Bowra—or was it
Coghill?—had given him during a train journey from
Cambridge. An improbable story: surely people did not
go about carrying large pullovers to present to attractive
young poets. Sean has a gift for provoking generosity,
however, and he couldn't have afforded the garment
himself. Now, a woman in such circumstances would
not get a pullover, even in the rare case that the famous
personage liked women at all. They seem to be all
buggers in the older generation, except for Bertrand
Russell.

But Singleton is speaking again, bracing himself
across the corridor as the train rocks over a set of points.
He is wearing a brownish suit with distinct green lines
criss-crossing it—rather a courageous choice, I think.

"Of course I know what it is: you disapproved of

8

my treatment of that man in there."

Careful now. "Oh—that?" One of the better delaying gambits I've learned in the past three years involves the note of surprise. "It was perhaps—sharp."

He clenches his fist and taps it on the window railing. "*Think* about it a moment: his situation. *You're* sorry for him, *everybody's* sorry for him—all he ever gets is *pity*. It's demoralizing. Dehumanizing, because he's considered below the standards of normal human behaviour. I simply applied those standards to him and thereby included him in the human race. Which would you rather have—a cigarette, or some recognition that you're a person like anyone else?"

"Well, but did you give him the choice?"

He doesn't answer, inhales vigorously instead.

"I think he would've taken the cigarette," I say.

"All right—I made the proper decision for him. I admit it, also that I find tobacco smoke extremely irritating. Every action is over-determined."

I see I'm supposed to concur—that there is an appeal here not to be turned down. "Of course."

At the party where I met Singleton, he lectured us for the space of several drinks on the need to break away as soon as we could from our Oxford training. A syllabus which stopped at 1830, he pointed out, omitted everything that really counted for the practice of literature in the present. The training was still a superb historical grounding, but he advised us not to suck too long at the teats of the ancient wet-nurse: hardly anyone here—his friend Ian was the shining exception—had a notion of what modern criticism should be dealing with. Even a man like C. S. Lewis, not precisely a progressive thinker, had been forced to move to Cambridge.

We knew he was right: literature was nowhere at Oxford; it was all philosophy and political history. And we admired Singleton—as the early companion of Larkin, our Master, one of the generation which after the war first challenged the hold of upper-class culture. Yet we were afraid of his message, demanding change; and Jeremy, who fully intended to stay exactly where he was, articulated our reservations later.

"As a critic, Singleton's not in the same class with Empson. As a novelist, the early Larkin was better, although one can't be conclusive since Singleton's still developing and writing. He may be seen, in the end, as the popularizer."

The next day Evan caught me on the way out of Upper Bodley, to pass on a message. "Ian says Singleton rather liked you. But he says, be careful, John plays for keeps."

I could hardly be interested, with Stuart preoccupying me and Roger coming back in early July. The only new thoughts I might have would be of Evan himself—was he, in fact, testing me?

"But I thought you said the woman in the green strapless dress was his mistress?"

"Well she is," Evan said. "But there are indications that it's temporary."

"Then he doesn't play for keeps, does he? Not that it matters; I merely observe the facts as presented."

"I believe it's understood that she's just helping him to get over Cynthia—his wife."

"What a charitable person."

Charity, to me, is the curse against which daily battles must be fought. At this present moment I have laid out a small amount of it for no good reason, and must find a way to adjust the ledger. Hence, when Singleton invites me to come to the dining car for a drink, I accept. He buys us bottles of Double Diamond, and asks about this year's examination questions, and I tell him.

"And what do you expect to get," he asks, "the poet's Third, or something better?"

"Well, I'm putting in for a First."

"Putting in?" He is shocked at the idea: probably he got a First himself, and retains due reverence for the accolade. "Surely it hasn't become a matter of declaring one's *intention*. In what sense?"

"If one learns anything in a State school it's how to take examinations. I did the optional paper, on the influence of French classical drama. My French is good. If I get a long Viva, I'll know I'm within striking distance, and I'll have to perform."

"That's fascinating," he says, pausing with glass in hand. "It's really the end of the gentlemanly approach."

We finish the first beer, and he orders a second. In twenty minutes we shall be at Paddington, where I'll pick up a cheese sandwich; in the meantime, this is a cheerful way to spend the time.

"Are you going home now—your family's in London?"

The question unaccountably puts me off balance. "Well, yes, they're near Lewisham. But actually I'm only going up for a few hours—for an appointment."

"For a job?"

"No—I'm seeing a doctor." I'm blushing.

Suddenly he is thinking hard, tapping his finger against his lips; and for the first time I'm acutely nervous. Is it possible that Evan gossiped, and with Ian, and at the wrong time? After a long pause he comes out with it.

"Excuse me. Look, I've just been putting two and two together. I think you must be the girl Ian and the other fellow—the historian—were talking about, when I was here a month ago. The boyfriend is out of the country, is that it? And she finds out she's pregnant, and can't get an abortion until after Schools is over?"

11

Fuck Evan—what a bastard he is! And all because he lent me five quid. The prick!

"I'm right, aren't I? It was you, the girl?"

"Whoever it was, none of your business." Normally I'm a more accomplished liar, but I am overthrown by Evan's breaking my confidence: it was not expected.

"I realise that," he says, and goes right on. "Still, it ought to be made clear that there was absolutely *no*—no sort of trivial malice in what was said. Only sympathy. It was in the context of talking about scholarship students; then we got on to the special difficulties of the women."

"I see."

"Evan, by the way, seemed to have a very low opinion of the boyfriend in the case. Marriage appears to be out of the question here."

I continue to drink up.

"Then I asked," he says, "if there were other alternatives—the family, and so forth—and I understood essentially that there were none."

Quite so: there are none. I am reminded that in the novel of his which I read last summer (the only one I've read), there was a pregnant girl who committed suicide, a secondary character of course. Later the heroine married the girl's bereft lover. I see no parallels.

"By any standards it's an awful situation," he says. "Anyone might feel desperate. And there's only one point about it that I would make. There are a few women I've known who have gone through with it, have had abortions, and they have all really hated themselves afterwards. My wife, Cynthia, was one. And either they punish themselves for it, or they have to harden themselves and stop caring about anything. Perhaps it isn't fair; but that's been my experience. So can you see how terrible that would be for someone like you, a poet, who *must* remain open and sensitive to the world?"

Not a respectable argument, as far as I'm concerned: why should I be confused with "women I've known"? He's clueless, he knows nothing about me. More interesting is the fact that, minute by minute, the quality of his attention has been changing. At first, clearly, he felt provoked; then he started focussing more carefully; and now the sensations I am getting from him are almost indistinguishable from love—it is as if he were *in love,* and how can one explain that? Even though I could say that in my small circle I am known as someone who's good at love, such a response is out of all proportion. Singleton must have an extraordinary capacity to summon up emotions, at a moment's notice. And then there must have been a cue somewhere which I didn't notice: what was it?

He lays one hand open on the table between us. "I do see your point here, Irene. You're ambitious, with reason; you don't want to waste your life, and you don't love the man concerned. You can't see any other way out."

"Look—you're going purely on suppositions." Suddenly it has occurred to me that what I'm sensing might be *moral* passion. He might believe that I'm doing something wicked, and actually get in my way—he might follow me and inform on me to the police. It is, after all, illegal. And for him to do that would be quite consistent with his behaviour to the crippled man. Now what's to be done? I shall have to run like hell at the station, and hope there's a crowd to be lost in.

"Now, listen," he says. "There is in fact an alternative. I am in a position to offer you—*one*—a job, and—*two*—a place to live, if you need it. I've been meaning to look for someone who could act as my research assistant—the project on Pope, you may have heard—and as a private secretary. Obviously you would

13

be an ideal candidate for the job: Ian thinks you're extremely bright, and I trust his judgment. In addition, I've got a large flat with a self-contained room to spare. So. I'm making you the offer in all seriousness: there it is, on condition you put aside this crazy idea of an abortion. You have a choice, now."

I see that he is serious, and it puts me in a panic. He means that I'd live with him, doesn't he? No mention of money, salary. What would Sean do in my place? He'd think of the wonderful connections to be made, for a start: all those writers and television people to meet. But to meet *as what?* For me, it would be as Singleton's whore — or mistress, as Evan likes to phrase it — someone to make a pass at, or to ignore. And there's the man himself, one of these people in whose presence it is impossible to feel your own state of mind distinctly: he takes over, he invades. I have simply no idea at this moment whether he is even tolerable to me; I can't tell.

But it's a golden opportunity. I don't need Sean here to recognize that; it's the kind of thing that could happen only once. I could find a bed-sitter too, not take the room in the flat. Yes, but there is something undisclosed: I feel that he wants something, some particular variation perhaps from the usual thing, and that he senses I would give it.

Out of the window we can see London closing in: we're entering the sooty canyon that leads into Paddington.

"You do understand," he says, "I'm perfectly serious."

"I do; I realise. Thank you."

"No strings, of course, as far as you're concerned. I want you to be clear on that point. And you'll need some time to think about it: how much time have you got?"

I look at my watch. "A couple of hours, about."

14

"Here, then." He takes out a small notebook and tears off a page. "My number and my address. I'll be in until about six this evening."

He hands the paper over, and I take it. Indeed, he is some kind of master, with an ability to pull a sequence of moments into dramatic shape; the encounter has received its definition. I wonder if this is, actually, the way to live.

We begin walking back to the compartment, but he stops me before we get there, in the gloomy corridor.

"Wait a moment. You aren't even going to a qualified doctor for this, are you? It's a back-alley job." How does he know that—has he become clairvoyant about me? "You *cannot* do this, Irene. It's virtually a death sentence. You will not come out of this undamaged, one way or another—*understand* that, please!"

I go on ahead of him and slide open the door. The crippled man gives me a vaguely sour look. Nothing is clearer than when two apparent strangers have been getting together in some way. I collect *The Brothers Karamazov,* and Singleton takes his case and follows me out. The train slows, jerks and stops.

"You've got my number there."

"I have."

He bends his head round, to look me in the eye, and we are both quite serious now. "All right. I count on you to use it."

Once we are on the platform he goes off at a rapid walk. That's settled, then—my suspicions to the contrary, he won't follow me. I get my cheese sandwich from the station buffet, and begin eating it at a table overlooking the main line. With my left hand, I take Singleton's number out of my bag. It is a remarkable thing: an aperture into a world where I have always thought I should belong. And it has an effective life of just two and a half hours. What a piece of magic!

It would be an adventure in itself to go through this door, take the lift up and away. Good-bye Roger, good-bye all of you two-faced shits. I'll have the kid adopted, of course. And no more of that whole tangle of existence as previously known, in which the original idea was all but lost.

Singleton will be home soon, in his large flat with the extra room. I picture white walls, and blue china in the kitchen, and new books all over. Why did his wife leave him? Evan didn't say; nor did he say if there were any children. I am suddenly quite sure there were no children. However, there was an abortion at some point. In which case—in which case it might just possibly be the idea of this child that he likes, or the mother and child together. The very fact of this thought's occurring to me convinces me that there is some truth in it. And when I call back to mind the expression on his face as he was putting his proposal, I realise that it had little of the usual edgy, excited feeling one associates with the beginning of an affair; rather, it conveyed something gentler, sadder, more carefully sustained. But is it actually possible—a man who wants a child? Men are by definition childless. So it has never surprised me that Stuart, for instance, is utterly vague about the four he has fathered, referring to them (when I press him on the subject) as "the tribe." And Roger is an only child, and dislikes children. It was he who reported to me the only description of an abortion I've heard, at second-hand from a friend who witnessed his girl's operation. "Came out just like a piece of liver," he said. "Nothing to it."

My heart jumps with dread as I recall those words, and again when Singleton's phrase echoes back: "A death sentence." They tell me these things, but they're as blind ignorant as I am, that's the worst of it.

I pick up my bag and book, and the telephone

number, which for the moment I shall keep in the pocket of my shirt. There are two hours still to run. I shall take the Underground to Kensington and walk about, and decide. "A death sentence." Is that possible? Yes, it's possible; but it would be so *unfair* to die now. I've come so far from Agathon Way, from nowhere, and I haven't had time to make sense of it all—I haven't had a chance.

II

35 Agathon Way

At six o'clock, that morning on Agathon Way, the factory siren began climbing and descending its scale to announce an air raid. Nobody stirred in the house. The siren was like an irregular alarm-clock—it did not have to be obeyed. But as it died away another voice, a growling drone, came seamlessly in as if long rehearsed. Footsteps thudded on the floor above our heads, accelerating back and forth. Then Ma came down to the back room where Heather and I were rousing from our heap of bedclothes under the iron table-shelter. The room was dark: only a chink of daylight came in under the blinds, and the heavy furniture and layers of carpeting strewn with clothes and toys made a congested burrow of the place. Still the intrusion of this growling monotone, vibrating in the stale air, denied the solidity of the barriers we had pulled around us.

High overhead the voice sputtered out.

Ma crawled under the iron ledge of the shelter, and with a grunt and a shove made room for herself next to the babies, who slept feet-to-feet with us. Sitting with her head bent (a Morrison shelter did not give

21

adequate head room for adults, not with a mattress underneath), she held perfectly still now, with her arm over the twins. Heather and I sat with our hands poised at our ears.

When? How close?

Actually, a couple of hundred yards. The detonation itself is an absence in the memory—a set of shock waves too fast and engulfing to sort out. But the next moments come back into focus, the way the body continues ringing with vibrations, and the way glass falling makes an erratic music. Now the shaken room re-formed in front of our eyes; we put down our hands and let out a satisfied breath, because what might have come had indeed come, and gone.

Someone's feet nearby crunched slowly downstairs.

"*Bertha!*" Ma scrambled out. "Stay put now—I'm seeing to Auntie."

Rolling back on the pillows, the babies looked blank for another moment, then started to grizzle. Immediately Heather and I felt bored, and annoyed, and we were starving for breakfast. Heather took baby Colin onto her lap, and amused him by pulling down his wet nappy in front and wiggling his penis.

"When we're grown up, he's going to be my husband."

I crawled across to get hold of the second best baby, but one sniff and I thought it best to leave her propped up next to me.

"Brenda smells. Smelly-muck."

She couldn't be my husband. Not unless you could count Auntie Vee and Auntie Phyl as married because they lived in a flat together.

"Find her dummy, muck-pie, and stop her noise!" said Heather.

"Suck-pie yourself."

22

When Brenda hushed, we heard Ma and Auntie being upset together in the kitchen on the other side of the wall. Sharp little cries of dismay alternated with consoling murmurs; then for a long time there were the harsh sounds of glass being swept up. Finally we were let out of the shelter and brought through the hallway—strangely cool and bright since the front door lay flat on the carpet—into the kitchen, which was still intact. The coke stove was burning up brightly, and mugs of hot cocoa were on the table. It looked like a surprise party.

"What a rotten old doodlebug!" Auntie Bertha said in her jokey voice. She picked up her cocoa, and we saw two big plasters on her right hand.

"What's that?" Heather pointed at the hand.

"Well, chickies, I'd just come out of the bathroom, had to wash my hands you know, and I was on the landing and Jerry dropped his load at the wrong moment, and the window blew in on me!" She mimed total surprise with her hands.

"Auntie's hair was *full* of glass," Ma put in. "And her clothes. It's a miracle she came off with just a couple of nasty cuts."

"But not to worry now!"

"It's enough for one day."

"*Quite* enough, thanks!"

Everyone laughed, and if Auntie Bertha's voice shot up an octave over the rest, we knew better than to think she was hysterical; it was simply that her voice rose in pitch according to her sense of the importance of an occasion—or the social status of her audience. I remember it reaching coloratura heights at Christmas dinners, and also once at the Conservative Summer Fête when she was introduced to the wife of the local M.P. (why were *we* there?—I can't imagine, for although Bertha was a Tory, Ma and the rest of us were

23

ardent Socialists. Perhaps they advertised a strawberry tea?).

Heather and I were not worried, in any case. The cocoa we were drinking was almost sweet enough, for once, and there was marmalade rather than dyed-turnip jam over our margarine and brown bread. Having Auntie to stay for the weekend took the edge off Ma's irritable temper. And in the afternoon when it was allowed we might be taken to see the crater down the road, which ranked high among the available treats in that time and place.

But we were kept inside all that day and half of the next, while Ma and Auntie tacked up heavy paper over empty window frames, and men in thick boots tramped up the path and made notes on our damage. When at last we were put into our coats and gripped firmly by the hand for our expedition, our excitement was aggravated to a furious level. We scuffed our feet and twisted our arms about in Auntie's gloved hold.

"Oh, I can't manage them!" she cried to Ma, who was pushing the pram along behind. "They're like little horses."

"All right, stop," Ma said in a penetrating voice. We turned to face her. "What's it going to be—back to the house, this minute, or behave yourselves properly?"

"Behave properly."

"Irene? I didn't hear you."

"Behave prop'ly." I slopped the words out, hating them.

"Well, see that you do. And get your finger out of your nose."

"It's got a sore."

"Well don't *pick* at it. I'm sorry, Bertha," she sighed, and we went on.

At the roped-off area there was a row of

neighbours, standing and talking. The flying bomb had hit the middle of the street, and had destroyed the adjacent semi-detached houses quite thoroughly, leaving a tract of rubble still faintly steaming in the sunlight. On the near side of the crater the Andrews' house had been peeled right open: their bath and toilet were hanging at an angle, and water cascaded down from the torn pipes. Their front bedroom was also exposed, papered in a mauve lattice-pattern.

"They were fortunate to get out," Ma said, and added in a murmur to Auntie: "That shade of mauve, though—not a pattern *I* could live with."

Her remark encouraged me to say what I was thinking. "Haven't they got a funny toilet, Ma? It's all green!"

"Stop that talk *this* minute!" Ma had flushed up even faster than she spoke. "It could have just as easily been our house. Nine people were killed here. It's time you realised."

Heather pulled a mechanical grin at me across Auntie's coat front, and was also caught.

"Take that look off your face, you. Little beasts!"

And we were left, as usual, to meditate on these impossible mysteries: nine people dead, but where were they? What was "dead"? Mashed-up, Heather thought. And then, where did shrapnel come from? So far as we could tell, it rained from heaven onto our neighbourhood during certain nights and could be discovered lying in odd corners of the garden or in the road the next morning. It was marvellous stuff: wild, twisted shapes of iridescent metal. We were not allowed to touch it—shrapnel caused blood poisoning. Later, when we went to school, there were children who claimed they had shrapnel collections at home. When Heather told them they might have died from picking it

25

up, they laughed. Apparently some were invulnerable—the lucky ones, unlike us. And they said that shrapnel came from the bleedin' ack-ack. Yes, well, but what was ack-ack? Heather was too embarrassed to ask a question whose answer was clearly supposed to be obvious.

For a time people liked to come and look at our crater: it was a neighbourhood possession to be proud of, while it lasted. But soon it was filled in, and Agathon Way was as silent as before. Other craters in the area became famous in their turn. And late in the war Ma once took us all for a long walk up Green Lane past the crossroads, to see a new crater that everyone talked about in the shops. Brenda and Colin were too big for the pram, though Ma brought it in case they got tired. So we laboured up the hill, helping Ma push it while the small twins held on to the sides. At the first turning past the crossroads we saw a policeman: this was the place. Here was the usual rope barrier, and women and children gathered at it to look in. And behind it, and behind the patrolling warden, was no heap of rubble—no, but a great hole, a clay quarry many houses wide, and deeper than I could estimate. The soil in that part of the Thames valley is stiff brown clay—heavy, greasy stuff cursed by gardeners when it has to be turned over with a spade. People who had strained their backs dealing with a few square feet of it stood here and could not imagine what kind of agency was at work to blow out a hole of this size, and to evaporate so completely what had been here: a row of brick villas with roses and hedges in front, and lawns in the back with raspberry canes and vegetable patches beyond, next to the tool-sheds and bonfire heaps. All were entirely gone.

Ma lifted Colin and Brenda into the pram, and rocked it back and forth while she chatted in a low

26

voice with the women next to us. When she was finished, and turned the pram around to go, we waited in vain for her to tell us something. Finally, at the corner, Heather asked.

"What was it? Another flying bomb?"

"Well, chicks, nobody quite knows. Probably a new kind of bomb." Chicks? That was Auntie's term of affection.

The later history of rocketry has always held a particular slant for us. But then, it was another good day, the day we saw the big crater, because Ma took us home by way of the recreation ground; for once she was not in a hurry, but sat on the green bench under the hollow elm smoking a precious cigarette, while we played on the swings and the roundabout and climbed the slide. And then she rocked Colin and Brenda on the iron horse with the many seats.

Heather had already told me that Hitler was trying to kill us. "He hates us, see, and we hate him."

Of course. The point was easy to accept, as affirming a natural state of things. Why, after all, should there be a discussible reason for Hitler's homicidal aversion to us, when Heather herself hated me in a rooted, consistent manner which was a fact about our life together? To live was to be hated (for I thought like any second-born), and the sirens at night and at dawn, and all the gifts of the sky were pledges of that covenant.

Yes, it was all right; well, it would have been *quite* all right if Ma's love for us were not so tightly rationed, like the foods we had learned by their increasing scarcity to adore: chocolate biscuits, oranges, ice-cream, chicken and meringues. If Heather's sweetest dream was that I should return to wherever I came from (under the gooseberry bush, or out of the sky like shrapnel), mine was that Heather should be more naughty than I was, so that Ma might love me more.

27

Perhaps I was dreaming this very dream that evening in the bath, as I sat in the regulation six inches of warm water and watched Ma at the basin doing some laundry by hand. Ma had a lovely shape: compact, well-proportioned and strong without heaviness. With rapid, economical movements she pulled pairs of thick lisle stockings out of the froth and squeezed them through her fingers. Then she folded them on the ledge and began reaching in for one pair of knickers after another, to be scrubbed at the crotch and squeezed out. The two curlers over her ears shook with the vigour of her scrubbing, its rhythmic energy. Absorbed in my enchantment with her, I sat relaxed in the bathtub despite harassment from Heather, who sat facing me in the water (we were always bathed two by two), trying to dig her toenails into my nearer leg; and now Ma pulled from the bubbles my favourite knickers, printed all over with tiny green watering-cans and flowers. I felt a small wave of happiness at the sight, which was echoed farther down by an unexpected flow of urine from between my legs. I looked down—Heather looked also, and caught on immediately.

"You went!" She pulled her legs up to the far end of the bath, and began dashing the water towards me with her hands.

"Stop that," Ma ordered without turning round.

Now she was dashing the water in my face, and that, all of a sudden, changed my bewilderment to rage; I got up on my knees and threw myself forward to get her left arm in my teeth. A confusion of loud noises surrounded my bulldog silence; then I felt Ma's hands grabbing me under the arms, and it was time to give up. She pulled me out, stood me shivering on the bathmat, then lifted Heather to her feet and put the injured arm in front of my eyes.

"Look at what you've done. You savage!"

Heather was wrapped in a towel, crying freely and sincerely—so far as I could tell; and Ma ran downstairs for the arnica. When she came back I was forced once more, standing cold, wet and naked, to look upon my crime—the two semi-circular imprints of my teeth in Heather's flesh.

"Look at the swelling!" Heather whimpered at the application of Ma's wet finger. "Poor child!"

I must even wait while Heather was thoroughly dried off and helped into her pyjamas before my punishment began—before I was turned across Ma's pinafore and slapped until her hand tired. And then at last I had the right to do my own bawling, to try to wake up the babies and bring on a migraine for Ma: the best I could do to complete my oral vengeance.

The final words spoken in this episode, like many others, were Ma's "I hope you have learned your lesson." To which the only candid answer would have had to be: "Well, yes—and no." My first dream was scrapped, and its successor ran something like: now I'm so bad, Heather won't mind me so much, and then she and Ma will both love me a bit, and two halves might make a whole.

This was so complicated, it might even work.

Not long afterwards we were evacuated out of London, and opportunities at once arose for showing Heather my badness. We were billeted with an elderly woman who from the outset resented this invasion of filthy Londoners into her detached Surrey villa. And when she saw four small children, she ran quickly to the antique bureau in her sitting room, drew out a sheet of paper and wrote down a list of rules for Ma to follow. The children were under no circumstances to set foot in either the sitting room or the dining room, or the three bedrooms above. They were to be fed in the kitchen only; no food was allowed anywhere else in the house.

At all other times they must be kept in the two rooms on the top floor of the house, except when they were taken out for an airing to the playground four streets away. The garden of the house was completely out of bounds, of course.

And then it began to rain, day after day. Ma obtained permission, on the grounds of risk to infant welfare, to bring the small ones into the kitchen with her while she cooked the mid-day dinner, but Heather and I were left upstairs. We had been allowed to bring with us from home only a small satchel containing crayons, a couple of books, and one other toy besides a favourite doll each. The room itself was quite bare except for the beds and a chest of drawers, and one ragged cane chair. Outside, the dripping branches of undifferentiated trees tossed back and forth in the driving rain.

Heather wouldn't talk; she was thinking. Oddly, although I could read Ma's mind by now with relative ease, I could never read even a corner of Heather's—that stern, impassive face, later to grow handsome rather than beautiful, was perfectly opaque to me.

"Heather?" Silence.

"We could play Pooh and Piglet?" Silence for two minutes or so.

"Can I borrow a piece of your plasticine?" *Long* silence. Language was apparently something Heather was quite pleased to do without. She continued to stare out of the window, elbow on sill, blue eyes unblinking for as long as I could stand to watch.

"Oh. Heather? The wallpaper's all loose over here." The eyes flickered for an instant, and resumed staring. "It's got—sort of bubbles in it. There's this crumbly stuff underneath."

Heather looked abruptly in my direction, got up

and came to examine the place. Down by the wainscoting the paper had come loose at a seam, and the plaster beneath was damp and rotting.

"Look here, Rene," Heather said, after consideration. "The lady'll be happy if you neaten up the loose bits. Take them off, see?"

"Why will she be happy?" She had never yet shown a single sign of happiness.

"Well, because she's going to have to take off all this paper anyway. It needs new paper." That was plausible. "See? It's got to be done, and you'll save her trouble if you get some off."

"Oh."

"Well, go on then. See, I'll start it a little bit." She took hold of the loose corner, and tore it very slightly: half an inch. That in itself should have been my warning, and indeed a sense of doom was on me as I began conscientiously to peel and strip, along the seam and then the bottom edge. To about two feet in from the seam it came off beautifully, and about eighteen inches along the bottom; after that I was using my nails, and it was harder going. But now came the stumbling sound of Ma and the twins on the stairs: it was almost dinnertime. And Heather leaped to her feet and ran to open the door.

"Ma! Ma! Come here and look!"

Now, of course, I saw.

During our third evacuation (we were thrown out of our first two billets in a matter of days) we were placed in a village under the South Downs, a bus ride from Worthing, in the cottage of a General's daughter. She was a splendid androgyne, with grey cropped hair and a cigarette drooping from her lips; she strode about in mud-coloured slacks and laced-up shoes, and demanded that we call her Auntie Ray (although her real name was admitted to be Vera). Here the rules were

31

reasonable, and it was Ma who insisted—had she learned oppression from our first landlady?—that Heather and I remain shut up in our bedroom for the hour and a half of the twins' afternoon nap. So every day at two o'clock we were stowed upstairs, while Ma took an Aspro and lay down with a wet cloth over her eyes.

At least this room overlooked a street, and now and then a villager would walk past to the bakery further along. There was one woman, a stately person in a fur-collared coat and veiled hat, who made a habit of going for her ration of teatime buns in mid-afternoon. Her passing below our window tended to occur just at the moment when our imprisonment weighed heaviest—perhaps fifteen minutes before its end. Whoever saw her would call the other, and we would stand at the window as long as she was in sight, and then wait eagerly for her return, criticizing her hat, her figure and her walk, and speculating on what she had in her bag for tea.

She was the shape of a post-box, we said, and her legs resembled those on Auntie Ray's bulgy table. That was the result of her scoffing all those flaky-pastry cream horns (with fake cream), éclairs and raisin rolls. The thought of these nagged at us, even though the one time we had been given an éclair as a special treat we had found the pasty insides sickening, and smeared them onto the plate.

So on one particularly tedious day, when the measured clop of those Cuban heels sounded below, Heather turned to me with a new thought.

"Bet you wouldn't say 'Fat Bum'—bet you wouldn't!"

A moment's calculation: the boredom, definite; the risk, unknown; the off chance of a little progress in Heather's good opinion, existent. "I would, though."

"No, you wouldn't."

32

"I will. When she comes back."

We opened the window wide, and craned to see her dignified entrance into the baker's. Minutes raced by while I became more and more terrified, and picked desperately at an old chicken pox scab on my forehead.

"Look," I said. "You've got to say something too. Because it was your idea, so you've got to."

"Have not!"

"I'm not going to, then, not if *you* don't." And I plumped down on my bed.

"All right," Heather said. "I'll say 'Pot belly.'"

" 'S'not very rude. Not like bum."

"All right, I'll say 'Fat Bum,' the same."

We glared at each other, testing. But here she came again, our victim, and we took our places at the window. Now she was almost beneath us, and my terror was such that I took four breaths in quick succession without managing to produce a sound.

"Say it!" Heather punched me with the side of her fist.

I gasped and took one more breath. The woman was almost past the house.

"Fat Bum! Fat Bum!" I shouted.

"Big obstacle!" Heather added from behind the curtain. And we fled back to our beds, laughing madly.

"*That* wasn't very rude," I complained, recovering.

"Actually it is, if you only—" She was interrupted by the sound of the doorbell.

We crept over to the window on our knees, and peeped over the sill. The woman was standing at our front door, and now we heard the door open, and a murmured conversation. Damn! That was the only word I knew appropriate to the moment, and I spoke it in a whisper. Heather and I did not look at each other. We got up and returned again to bed.

33

"At least *I* didn't say 'Bum,' " Heather remarked.

It was some consolation, when Ma stormed in with a coat hanger, that no one was interested in that as a defence.

Sometimes at Heather's urging, sometimes on my own I would steal flowers out of gardens, or biscuits out of tins, and even a watch off Auntie Ray's dressing table which Ma had to return in bitter embarrassment. These crimes, when discovered, drove Ma into anguished rage; by contrast Auntie Ray maintained an attitude of aristocratic tolerance.

"Hilda my dear," I heard her say from my concealment round the bend of the stairs. "they are *only* children: that's all it is."

"If they weren't such *savages!*"

I blushed for us, and for her because she never stood up for us. Never.

At the end of that summer we came home to our house on the railway line to Dartford, because school was beginning. Now we had fewer chances of being bad; moreover Heather was making new friends, and found less and less need to associate with me. The dream was losing ground. In fact, outside the home territory she placed an absolute prohibition on my speaking to her. Imagine my surprise, then, one day when *she* actually came up and spoke to me when we were walking home from school.

"Hallo, Rene."

"Hallo."

"Oh. Look at this stone over here. See?"

I stopped and looked where she pointed. "That looks like dog stuff."

"Shows how much *you* know, stupid. It's one of those stones that *look* like dog stuff. But it's a stone. You can pick it up."

"*You* can pick it up."

"Well, I will. But *you* pick it up first, then you can tell it's a stone."

"That's dog stuff."

" 'Tisn't."

" 'Tis though."

"Of all the dopes—" She fixed me with a disgusted look. I would have liked to leave this unpromising scene: the kerbside with the two of us balancing on it, and between us a pebble-sized, greyish-white, dried piece of turd. But on the other hand this was Heather, and she was talking to me.

Marion, who was in Heather's class, stopped to look. At once Heather appealed to her. "Look at this—see, this *is* a stone, isn't it?"

A rapid exchange of looks. " 'Course it is."

"There you are," Heather turned to me, justified.

"It's dog stuff," I whispered, not wanting to say the nasty word in public.

"Isn't she a cretin? Can't even tell what a stone looks like!" They laughed, quite effectively.

"Anyone can see that's a stone," Marion said.

"Go on," Heather said. "Just pick it up—you'll see."

I felt tears coming. "Well, do you cross your heart it's a stone?"

"Promise crossmyeart," Heather gabbled. "C'mon, Marion."

"Promise crossmyeart!"

"Well, promise you'll pick it up after me, too."

"Promise!"

I looked at the thing. No, that was a turd. But in the very moment of the thought, my clarity wavered, and I began to see a stone. They had promised! I felt the clamping-down of Heather's will, and now the thing on the roadside became something abstract almost: an indefinite, greyish entity. The only necessity here was that I reach down and pick it up. I took it between thumb and fingers, feeling a granular kind of surface, and lifted it, and instantly realised it was far too light and porous for any stone.

Even before I had time to drop it, I heard their peals of joy rising.

"She touched it, the daft!"

"Dog's muck, she touched it!"

"Got it on her now."

"Muck! Muck!"

I ran to the hedge, and madly wiped my fingers on the leaves and on the grass-tufts growing underneath; and they followed me along until I turned on them.

"*You* promised cross your hearts—you'll go to hell!"

"No, 'cos we didn't say 'I' in front. If you don't say 'I' it doesn't count, see, so there!"

At home, I sat on my bed for a long time thinking of ways to revenge myself on Heather—mutilate her Princess Elizabeth doll, get scissors and cut up her things, spit on her pillow. Hide things. Even as I formed plan after plan, their multiplication showed me their futility. The bondage I felt went all the way through me, pervasive like the stink of dog shit.

The stairs creaked, and Ma came into the bedroom with a stack of clean Liberty bodices and knickers. She put them away, then stood facing me with her arms folded.

"More waterworks. What is it this time?"

"Heather!" Tears spread again down my sticky cheeks.

"Well, what did she do?"

"Made me touch something—nasty."

"Oh dear. That was silly of you, wasn't it?"

More sobbing.

"Come on, don't be a cry baby. If I were to tell you half the nasty things your aunties did to me when I was a little girl, I'd be all night."

"M-m?" My tears stopped: was this the moment—my chance with Ma?

"Oh yes. So you'll get over this."

"What things? Tell me what things."

"I haven't got time. Wash your face and you can have a bikkie downstairs."

Ma did not like children when they were too clingy. It made her feel like nothing but a bone being gnawed over; or so she told me a few years later.

There are those people who love their mothers,
just so; and there are those who, out of whatever
accident of temperament have to be *in love* with them.
Heather was of that first group, which announces itself
by an utterly incurious filial devotion. She had no
interest in the person that Ma was—the history, the
states of mind, the destiny; and this was the obverse
side, no doubt, of her inaccessibility to my own efforts at
intimacy with her. Any mingling of the stories was
abhorrent to her powerful instinct for integrity and
cleanness. And yet all the more, to my own jealous
desperation, her love and true constancy were
unmistakable.

The other, the worse way, was left to me, with all
its perverse and filthy riches. So it was for me that Ma,
while Dad was still away at war, brought out the packets
of old photographs, to sort and plan their arrangement
into albums. I could never get enough of these
pictures—I wanted every detail stored in my mind.
Here for instance (a vital clue) was Ma at twenty,
dressed as a Bacchante in the annual youth club variety

show. She wore a leopard-skin tunic and a band round her bobbed dark hair, and she was dancing barefoot, with a bunch of grapes raised over her thrown-back head in ecstasy. This was certainly Ma: I recognized the firmly muscled arms and legs, and the pointed chin. And she was happy! And here she was on a rocky beach in Devon ("One day you must see the cliffs in Devon, Irene—they're quite, quite red"), in a striped maillot, with arms laid wide to the sun. And this was the St. Luke's ramblers' club on the walk to Knockholt where they found a feast of wild strawberries ("So tiny—*this* size—but so sweet and tasty!").

It was quite clear from the group photographs that Ma was the centre of all activities. How else could she, with her weak eyes and disfiguringly heavy glasses, have been matched with the handsomest boy, the blond idol they nicknamed "Apollo," who worked as bookkeeper for the Greenwich almshouses but wrote real poetry in his few free hours?

"Apollo" was absent from most of the photographs. He had a way, even then, of making himself scarce, and the war had merely helped him to continue it. There were also no wedding photographs of the two of them—why? Oh, there was a snap or two somewhere in the muddle—but it was only a Registry wedding, since his parents were dead and hers disapproved (the couple, although aged twenty-six, had accumulated no savings, and these were the Depression years), and anyway Dad didn't really go in much for parties and group occasions.

"He only ever joined in because of me," she said, turning the batch over and replacing it in an envelope. "He liked it better when we moved out here. And the group broke up, scattered."

Next came the photographs of Heather as a baby. Ma could not really believe that I wanted to see them, but I did—I needed to know everything. The best picture here had been enlarged, and for good reason: it had caught Dad raising Heather over his head in both hands, and they were laughing delightedly into one another's faces. The close-up showed the lacy pattern in the baby's tiny knitted jacket, along with the shimmer of blond hair on Dad's bare arms—his shirtsleeves were rolled above his elbows. It was altogether lovely. That was Heather at three months; and here again, being patted on Ma's shoulder, tenderly, and at six months sitting up in Ma's lap. Then comes a gap in the sequence, and suddenly here I am, lying passive and moon-faced on Ma's lap while she turns an anxious smile to the camera, and next to her on the beach blanket Dad sits cross-legged with Heather grasping tight round his neck.

Something has been too much for them: I have come on the scene too early—no, I should not have come at all.

I should never, at least, have asked about all this.

"Heather was quite a small baby still, and we'd just moved into the house here. Anyway a man came to the door and told me he was going to have to take back the dining-room furniture, within the week. He said the instalments hadn't been paid up. I was positive a mistake had been made; I even showed him where I had it down in my book that we'd paid. Anyway, to cut a long story short, your father *hadn't* paid—only pretended to. We had a dreadful time. I'd to borrow from May and Nannie to set things right. And I found out about other debts we had, too. After that I insisted on seeing to the bills myself. I had to; I couldn't leave things as they were.

"To tell the truth, I was wondering if I hadn't made a mistake altogether. Ever since we were married, he'd been getting more and more unsociable. Didn't want our old friends to come round. Now when Heather was born it was funny, he seemed to come out of his shell a bit, for her. But after the money trouble he barely spoke to me at all.

"I don't know—perhaps I might've done something. But then you happened. You've heard of the Stopes clinics, haven't you? They were pioneers in offering contraceptives to women, and I went to one to get fitted. Well, don't ask me why, but evidently the darned thing didn't work properly. So there we were!"

And so, piece by piece, year by year, our story descended on me. When in my teens I had it all, I was choked by a throng of questions that could not be uttered. Why hadn't she got rid of it—of me? And in the first place, if they were barely speaking to one another, how on earth could they have—? What kind of contraceptive was it? Never mind. For the key to my kind of love was to hold back my own demands, and rather to feel delicately, patiently, for the spring that was ready to give of its own internal pressure, its own need.

"Look—here's you again." Ma and I have moved on to the next envelope. "You were such a good baby: I could put you down somewhere, anywhere, while I had something to do, and you'd just stay put, quite happy looking round."

Indeed, the baby in the picture has wide, staring eyes.

"I haven't got much patience with children, and Heather was a handful in those days. So it was a good thing you were different."

Perhaps Heather remembered the good days, too, before Ma lost hope, before she turned into this alternately irritable and depressed drudge about the house; perhaps she bravely refused to reconcile herself to the change. The new baby, part of the catastrophe itself, had nothing different to remember; so it lived as comfortably as it could inside the cave of Ma's mind, the weather of her pain.

41

"Still, though," Ma remembered, "about once or twice a year you'd throw a *terrific* tantrum. D'you remember that one in Woolworth's?"

Yes—thank God. Not that the family, which had enrolled the scene in its collective history, had allowed me to forget the wretched child who, denied something trivial, dashed herself headlong onto the wooden floor (swept with sawdust, I remember the smell), drumming with her heels and screaming uncontrollably for ten minutes by the clock.

"We didn't dare go back in that place for months!"

Only Heather seemed to understand that the good baby was also a systematic liar, a thwarted demon, and did her best to undeceive the world on its score. Heather must have prayed at times for an hour of reckoning to strike for me, and after four years, with the birth of Colin and Brenda, it did. Where then had my role gone? Into oblivion, now that there were two babies—and excellent babies they were—right before our eyes. Colin had a perfect Churchillian face and blond hair; Brenda had auburn curls almost from birth. Born during the worst of the war and a month before Dad was shipped overseas, they were taken as a sign of life and hope; Ma became an heroic wartime mother, taken special care of by visiting nurses, and Heather was designated her helper, to share in the glory, give bottles and fold the clean nappies.

I could do nothing. Small for my age, almost a head shorter than Heather, I could not get the pram up our steps, nor was I trusted to hold a baby for more than a couple of minutes. The photographs from this year show Ma and Heather holding the twins, with Irene scowling in their shadow.

But something *must* be done!

"Ma, my hair's too dark. I think we could get

some of that stuff to change the colour, make it better."

"Oh. What colour do you think you'd like?"

"Well, I thought auburn. Mine used to be more auburn, didn't it? But it's got too dark."

Ma looked me straight in the eye. "I know what you're up to, don't I? No, no. One redhead's enough in a family."

Auntie Vee gave me another idea the following summer. She had come for the day, and in the afternoon while Ma stayed with the babies she took us for a walk to the recreation ground. The way led past our bomb site, and she stopped there with us to look at the ruined gardens: Auntie Vee had studied botany at training school.

"What a difference, in a year! Look at those thistles shooting up, and the marigolds crowding out everything. But a thistle is a handsome weed, don't you think?"

Now that she pointed it out, we thought so; and it was as tall as ourselves though still only in bud.

"It's the national flower of Scotland," she went on. "And they say that when the thistledown is ripe, the fairies take it to weave their dresses. It's the finest and softest thread in the world."

Auntie Vee specialized in nature study and fairies, and the two subjects became thoroughly mingled in my mind from then on. Perhaps it was later on the same walk, or on another, that she asked us her momentous question: "If *you* were fairies, what would your names be?"

Heather dragged her feet at that, but I knew in an instant.

"I'd be 'Little Fairy Thistledown'!"

"And that's a very nice name for a fairy," Auntie said. "You'd make a good fairy, Irene, so light on your feet. Now what about you, Heather?"

43

I watched her out of the corner of my eye: she was trailing along looking at the ground, as if to find suggestions in the kerbside weeds, and my tongue itched to suggest "Fairy Groundsel" or "Fairy Chickweed."

"I'd rather keep my own name," she said finally.

"What a splendid idea! Heather could perfectly well be a fairy's name. Did you know that most fairies are found in the west and north of the British Isles? They love the wild moors, and that's exactly where heather grows. A misty purple, as far as the eye can see—"

Auntie was off and away, developing a tale of her holiday to the Brontë country, in the undulating training-school enunciation which she had learned so well. But I murmured to myself, over and over, "Little Fairy Thistledown."

There was no difficulty in getting Auntie Vee to call me by my new name, or in getting her to accept the "fairy gifts" I discovered in the garden—the wing off a dead dragonfly, or a ferny leaf. But after she left that Sunday evening the going was harder. Ma had no intuitive sympathy with the fairy scene; she would tolerate my idiocies, because Auntie (a trained teacher, no less) had told her a child's imaginative life must be permitted for healthy growth, but permission did not mean positive approval (besides, she thoroughly disliked her sister—an intolerably domineering woman).

So I was offered crayons and paper—"Here, draw some fairies!"—and my "fairy houses" constructed in the garden out of twigs and grass and acorn cups were properly inspected—"Yes, that's a nice one"—but the name Little Fairy Thistledown would never pass Ma's lips. And sadly, all I wanted out of the whole fairy exercise was that: to *be* something different, to be Ma's fairy in the house.

44

And Heather, after much experimentation, found the weapon to destroy it all. That was on the day we came home from school and found the door locked because Ma had not come back from the shops in time. I wet my knickers while we waited, and in the long silence which followed this event Heather developed an enormous smile.

"What's the matter with you?"

"Little Fairy Piddledown!"

At least I could appreciate the perfection of the verbal move: I couldn't laugh, but such was the balance of conflicting feelings in me that I contributed no tears to Heather's satisfaction either.

During that first winter at school the illnesses came one after another—measles, influenza, whooping cough. I gave way to the habit of sickness, and no longer wanted to eat the plain, ration-book food: bowls of water-made porridge, plates dominated by heaps of mashed potato and stewed cabbage. All I looked forward to was our weekly spoonful of orange concentrate and malt (and the orange was terminated for children over six), and the scrap of red meat on Sundays. Ma punished me—kept me sitting for hours in front of my serving of congealed food—but she could not make me eat. The working of my intestines slowed, and she fought to get doses of senna tea into me. It was another losing battle. Finally I was taken to the doctor and stood naked and emaciated, with a dismal little pot belly, for an examination while Ma fumed in the background. We were all embarrassed.

There was nothing really wrong; the diagnosis made was "severely run down," and the doctor ordered me sent for six weeks to a State convalescent home.

My clothes were packed for the journey in a large brown-paper parcel, with my shoes in a separate paper bag. I was passed from hand to hand at London terminals, and at the end of the trip was taken into the vast drawing room of a Victorian country house which had been entirely cleared of furniture and ornament. Here, in the echoing space, some forty children milled about. The noise was deafening. My hand clenched on the hand that was leading me, but in the next moment it was firmly removed, and I was told: "Now you may go and play."

The door closed behind me. I backed up against the nearest wall, and stood perfectly still with my Teddy pressed to my chest.

"Here, what's this?" A pull at the Teddy. Respond or be very sorry.

"My Teddy."

"What's it got a dress on for?"

I had dressed my Teddy in a white machine-lace gown belonging to my Margaret Rose doll. Margaret Rose had long ago been Heather's doll, at which time she was called Elizabeth after the Princess of Wales; but when Heather got a wonderful new doll at Christmas from one of the Aunties, her old one was passed on to me. There had been a tantrum on this account, and although I ended by accepting the renamed Margaret Rose, I could not love her. The Christmas Teddy I had received was my favourite, so while Margaret Rose now lay wrapped in an old baby blanket at home, Teddy sported her petticoat and best dress in a Surrey mansion.

"That's its dress," I lied in a whisper, and held my breath to see if I would be believed.

"Oh. *This* Teddy's got a *dress!*"

The lie not only held good, it was a huge success. Now I must submit to Teddy's being handed about from girl to girl, but he was treated with respect, and came back to me more precious than before. Dramas were soon invented in which he played a major role, and it was my name, I knew with satisfaction, that was clearly inked on his back paws. *Irene* on one paw, *Tanner* on the other.

At the convalescent home I made progress and ate well, and I came back to Agathon Way taller and a little fatter. But before long I was slipping back again into the same routine of obstinacy at the table and inaction in the lavatory. There were long sessions of motionless waiting in front of half-eaten meals, followed by lonely vigils on the toilet upstairs, during which raw siftings of air poured down from the brick grating in the wall, down on my bare nape (Ma favoured short haircuts for all of us) and on my bare arse hanging over the toilet bowl. I would sit on and on until my lower half was stiff with cold.

When I heard Ma's tread on the stairs beyond the wall, I would call to her: "Can I come out now?"

"No. Keep trying, five more minutes. It'll come."

"It won't come!"

Silence. Then the sound of the vacuum cleaner starting up: Ma was occupying herself. Despair.

We had reached an impasse, Ma and I; we were stuck. I couldn't get what I wanted, and she seemed to have nothing more to give.

The men at the war sent officially approved pictures of themselves home. Out in the East where Dad was, they were wearing either bush hats or Monty berets, and their torsos were bare above their Army trousers. Their eyebrows had grown bushy, fed (Dad wrote) by the sweat that trickled down in the heat. They looked well, and quite happy. Dad's platoon was posed against a background of strange, oversized foliage.

Ma handed the photograph to us. "Here now—which one's your Dad?"

Heather refused to guess. Indeed, the three rows of soldiers were extraordinarily alike.

"This one?" I pointed to a figure who vaguely resembled Dad as he appeared in the youth group—blond, with a narrow head.

"Your father's never had a moustache in his life!"

Ma's headache was bad that evening, and we were put to bed early, long before it was dark. Heather pinched me—rightly—for my stupid lack of tact, and we lay in the beige twilight, curtains drawn, grizzling to ourselves.

Not all the men had gone to the war, but those

who stayed appeared to be mostly nocturnal creatures. It was at night that the wardens came round to complain of chinks in the blackout, and that Mr. Jobling two doors away went off to ack-ack duty. The Germans were night people too, coming over late in their bombers. Rarely would you see able-bodied men in the daytime, except when guarding a fresh bomb site. Yet once when we were visiting Auntie Bertha and Auntie May, the pilots of a Spitfire and a German fighter engaged each other in an afternoon chase over Woolwich. Everyone ran into the street to see the planes cross and recross the patch of sky between the houses, to see the smoke plumes bursting from them as they streaked on towards Plumstead, to crash in the river marshes. On one pass they had come so low that a pilot's head was visible in the cockpit of his plane—a tiny recognized shape.

We could not even begin to understand the nature of men's lives, or their powers. These belonged to some other dimension, it seemed. And they could fly, or drive cars and tanks, while women and children could only creep about on the ordinary ground, keeping things tidy.

Towards the end of the war groups of labourers appeared in the area to clear and rebuild the wrecked houses. They were a mixture of men close to retirement age or beyond it, and adolescents of fifteen and sixteen. When they came, the bomb sites had long been established as the favourite, secret haunts of neighbourhood children, their pockets of romantic wilderness in the tame suburb. Heart-stopping games were played in the ruined earth shelters in back gardens, until the workmen began pissing and shitting in there, and still after the workmen went home at night the children poked about the gardens for amusement and treasures: the occasional cigarette lighter or rusted blade of shrapnel. The abandoned gardens themselves went on blooming luxuriantly in summer, and we often picked the flowers, although officially forbidden to do so. Pink cabbage-roses grew tall and drooped over with their heavy heads, and ramblers soared upwards through bushed-out privet hedges, throwing out sprays of small ivory-coloured buds. Lupins and irises dominated the undergrowth, along with blue seeded-in scabious and red poppies. In this protected enclave away from the main road the mauve willow herb of the urban sites did not take over; instead, the infiltration blew in from the country in the form of cornfield weeds.

Now the workmen were on Agathon Way in force, coming up the road early in the morning from the bus and starting first on the houses that could be repaired, knocking out old window frames, clearing out old plaster and bringing in new materials. At the noon hooter they walked back past the school at the corner to the Byways Café, which became their place and no one else's; and going and coming they would pass the children, running to and from their own dinners at home.

Always they called out to us in a friendly way, and although we had difficulty understanding their broad Cockney accent, we called back softly " 'Lo, Mister." And over the months the names of the group became known: Nobby, Arold, Mac, Ole Dan and Freddie the young helper.

"Why do they always manage to spit outside *our* gate?" asked Ma. Mrs. Duckworth and Mrs. Brand asked the same thing; meanwhile they all made a point of being polite to the men, because you still might need their services yourself.

Dinner at home, at this time, was for me the crisis of the day. Approximately twice a week I could not manage to finish the food on my plate before the first school bell; if the meat was fat, or if the vegetable was

50

sprouts or cauliflower, I sat in front of it helplessly, and a war of nerves between Ma and me began. After the first bell rang, I would have to leave the table within three minutes if I were not to be late. Generally Ma gave in at the last possible moment—"Get off with you then, you baggage!" But a day came when she decided to draw the line. This time, this time she would carry her point, settle it once and for all.

The first bell rang while I was staring hard at four sprouts on my plate. I looked up as piteously as possible, but Ma was planted in front of the stove, arms adamantly crossed. We both heard children go past the front gate, for the doors were open in the warm weather. We heard coughing and hawking as the workmen came round the corner, and heard the syncopated tread of their boots.

"Made up y'mind yet? You're going to sit there till you *do* eat it, y'know."

A rising tide of noise from the school playground two hundred yards away lapped into the room, and then the melancholy clang of the hand-pulled bell in the arch of the school chimney sounded again. I jerked upright and turned again to Ma. The playground noise came to a peak, and began to recede.

"I'll eat one, then!"

"All of 'em."

I ate one sprout, heavily dashed with salt. As I swallowed, my stomach heaved; I kept it down with an effort. No, I couldn't do that again.

"I can't!"

"Can't what?"

"I'll be sick."

"*Be* sick then."

We remained still for perhaps five more minutes. I snivelled for a time, and then gave it up, resting my head hunched against the wall. Out of the corner of my eye I saw Ma shiver—overtaken perhaps by a wish to reach out and crush the nuisance once and for all. Instead she came forward and took the plate off the table.

"You'll have it tonight then, for tea." The tension in her jaws was audible as she spoke. "Get y'self to school then—tell the teacher why you're so late. It isn't my fault."

At the gate, it came to me that I did not have the courage to walk into school so late, in front of a class of fifty children, to be punished. No one was ever as late as this, not even the dirty ones from Leacock Road. Instead of turning left towards the school, I hesitated, then turned the other way, up towards the bomb site. It was hot out on the road; the tar was melting at the edges; no one was anywhere in sight. The mothers indoors would be finishing their washing-up after dinner and then sitting down with a cup of something to listen to Woman's Hour on the radio. The babies would be napping. As I stepped quietly along, keeping close under the hedges, I heard a desultory knocking of hammers at the bomb site, and a slow rasping sound, but no voices.

Here was the first of the bombed houses. Along the nearer side of it there were no windows except to the pantry and the upstairs landing; no one would see me once I was through the gap where the gate had been. The lace curtains of the inhabited house next door hung straight and undisturbed. I walked between the houses, past the outside shelter into the privacy of the deserted back garden. Here the untrimmed massive hydrangeas and the unpruned fruit trees would protect me. Under the trees the grass was long and thick—good to make a nest in like a cat; and for a long time I sat in my nest chewing stems of grass while my anxiety played itself out and I composed my scenario for the rest of the day.

The workmen would go home soon after the children came out of school; that was good. When they left, I could come out myself, go round the block, and reach home from the proper direction only a little bit late. The next morning I would need a note for the teacher, but I might try a story about Ma being ill, and put it off until she forgot about it.

As the details fell neatly into place, I leaned back, lay down and looked up at the sky through branches studded with tiny green fruit. So blue! And lots of apples, but they were always wormy. I sat up again to look for daisies out in the tangle that had once been a lawn. I made one daisy chain and a dandelion chain, and put them round my neck. The time slowed and slowed. I searched the vegetable patch beyond the trees for something to eat. By the back hedge were a few raspberry canes, but the berries were sour, unripe. Asparagus fern waved in my face; I picked some fronds and brushed them over my lips.

In the end boredom made me wander up and down, first as far as the back of the shelter mound, and later, round the side of the shelter into view of the house. There was a good patch of daisies in the grass here; I picked a bunch of them to make a second chain. And there Ole Dan who was distempering the downstairs back room saw me through the open French doors.

"Ey! You! Wotcher doing?"

A whisper in reply: "Nothing."

"C'mon overere."

Must I? Putting dinner-table scenes aside, I was not a defiant child, rather a child filled with awe at the mysteries of the encircling adult will.

"C'mon overere I said."

I had stayed frozen in one attitude from the moment Ole Dan had seen me. Now I let the stolen daisies slide quietly out of my hand, and looked longingly towards the path round the side of the house.

If he had left space enough between any two of his commands, I might have gathered up enough sense to run. But he was shrewd, and kept on talking.

"C'mon then, I won't bitecher! 'Ere. Gotta nice sweetie. You c'mon and I'll give it yer."

The words pulled me forward until I was a step from the doorsill. It wasn't the sweetie; I never liked sweeties so much as that. It was the pressure communicated by his voice, his need for me to come closer. Like a somnambulist's, my legs moved towards him.

"Wotsamatter then? Come in 'ere and getcher sweetie. Thassit."

What he was actually saying made little sense to me; I had only some idea that he was going to punish me for being in the forbidden garden and for not going to school. I supposed vaguely that he must know all about how bad I had been at dinnertime too. But the main crime was Trespassing. *Trespassers will be prosecuted,* said the faded letters on the board outside the bomb site. And I was a trespasser, caught in the act.

" 'Ere's yer sweetie, then. Thassit."

The air inside the room was heavy with the odour of distemper. Ole Dan's filthy overalls were crusted with pale blue, and his fingers, holding out a Glacier mint to me, were flaked with paint too. The room was bare and echoing; in it stood only trestles with a plank across them, buckets and a litter of rags and brushes. The space in here seemed vast and lonely. Ole Dan sat down on his plank, still holding out the mint.

The air was colder, damper than outside; I felt that, in my short frock and summer sandals. I took two sleepwalker's steps forward.

"C'mere."

He unwrapped the mint himself, reached forward to where I stood and poked it into my mouth. In the

54

next second he had me by the shoulders, and pulled me over to sit on his knee.

"Thassit. Thassit."

He jogged his knee up and down a little.

"There. Thassit."

One arm held me round the body, firmly; after a minute he shifted back slightly on the plank, then with his free hand plucked up the edge of my skirt, and pushed two large fingers, harsh with their encrustations of paint, under the elastic of my small-girl's knickers. A pause; a sigh. The two fingers worked themselves further in until they got between the smooth labia where they pushed in a rhythm, up and down, up and down.

"Like that? Like that?"

It seems as if he must have meant to offer some share of pleasure in return for what he was going to demand. But no possible notion of pleasure could reach across the absolute barrier of coercion: extreme panic had transformed me into a stiffened catatonic where I sat.

The teachers might have been proud of my deportment at that moment. No one was ever so perfectly, immovably still except the insane or the dead. Incapable of any reaction whatever, still I felt with distinctness the hands on me, unspeakably foreign, and felt the shape of the mint in my mouth and the saliva running unswallowed down one side of my chin, and I saw the room and smelled Ole Dan's tobacco breath sighing on me.

He pulled back his hand and worked open the buttons of his fly, releasing the enormous drama of his penis. Now he reached across and took hold of my left hand where it had stuck in a half-raised position ever since he picked me up, and he bent the hand over, down onto the strange column of flesh, veined and hot and not at all like Colin's had been. He rubbed my hand back and forth on himself like a rag, and I felt the heat, felt the thin matte skin under my fingers pulling over the hardness beneath. In a little while, thinking perhaps that I might have caught on to the idea, he let go of my hand, easing himself round again on the plank. But the hand, released, swung back immediately to its former position as if on an automatic spring. And again he must catch hold of it and bring it down, bending the fingers round, helping them on with the job.

Impossible to know how long he laboured at his awkward task; but time ran out on Ole Dan the slow comer, just when a certain acceleration suggested he might be near his goal. The afternoon had been passing, and now the other workmen in the houses began to call to each other and pack up their gear. A succession of hard objects thudded onto the floor of the room directly above the pair of us, and though I sat on imperviously, Ole Dan startled.

"Ey!" a voice sang out. "Ey, Danny Boy!"

Ole Dan heaved himself to his feet, tipping me off his lap but steadying me with one hand briefly.

"Gerrout!" He pulled at his fly, shook himself back inside. "Shove off!" He shooed me towards the French doors.

I didn't need it said the last time. The spell was abruptly off me—I could move, and I was out of the room like a ghost, up the side path and tearing along the road. Not towards home—no, the original plan still held in my mind. But when I got to the second corner of the block, the dreadful thought came to me that I might run into Ole Dan again that way, going to the bus. I turned left, going farther from home, alternately running and walking until I came to the paddock where the retired cart horse was kept, with its water trough at the corner. I put my hands through the wire into the greenish water of the trough, and washed them up to the elbows; then, by way of apology to the horse, I pulled a bunch of the long grass outside the fence for him to eat. Normally I was frightened of the horse, of his head-tossing and bared yellow teeth. But now I offered him my bunch of juicy greens, and he took it politely. And then I rested my head against the post, and counted up to two hundred.

Now, perhaps, it was safe. The way home was long, and filled with worry and plans because I was going to be so late. What could I say? That some boys teased me, or that the teacher kept me in. But why would she keep me in? Well, because I was late after the dinner hour.

As it happened, Ma didn't notice.

It was autumn. Heather and I were put at the dining-room table one Saturday morning, given a sheet of good stationery each and a blotter to rest it on, and told to make birthday cards for Auntie Vee. First we folded our sheets in half, then shared the four coloured pencils between us. I waited to see what Heather would draw, and watched while she did a yellow sun and a green line for the ground, and a row of yellow flowers.

"Haven't you started yet?" She reached across and took the red and blue pencils. "Here, you can have these others now."

I drew my own green line, but slanted for a hill, not level, and added three flowers growing at right angles.

"What are your flowers?" I asked.

"Daffodils," Heather said.

"So are mine."

"Well don't you dare look at the rest of my picture, because you're a nasty copycat!"

"Well I wasn't going to!"

Heather had her arm protectively round her card: now what was I going to do? These pencils were hard, too, and made a disappointingly faint mark on the paper. And it was scarcely the season for daffodils: when I got my turn with the red pencil I would turn my flowers into dahlias. Meanwhile I coloured the rest of my hill green—pale green. Heather finished her picture, opened her card out quickly so that I shouldn't see it, and wrote "To Auntie Vee, love, Heather X X" neatly across the inside. Then she took it to Ma in the kitchen, came back for her Elizabeth doll, and left. With all four pencils at my command, I added the inevitable sun, a rather indistinct blue stream running down the hill, and red petals on the flowers.

And now what? Since learning to read and write a few months before, I knew that birthday cards were supposed to have a rhyme inside them. I opened up my card, thought briefly, and began to write—

> On the hills
> The daffodils
> Open bright
> To the light.

There was another quatrain about the stream before I finished, and I was amazed at the ease with which it was done. Of course, when I closed the card I remembered that I had turned my daffodils into dahlias—now I must take the yellow pencil and try to turn them back. It was not a convincing effort. But after all, the poem explained the picture.

Ma sent off both cards without comment. And the next week a rapturous letter came from Auntie. She very much appreciated the bedsocks from Ma, and the cards were lovely, as usual, but the *poem* was quite wonderful. A talent, Auntie announced, had been revealed. The child must have got it from her father—though artistic talent ran in both families, and she herself had won awards for her still-life pastels in training school. The child must be encouraged to write more poems.

She was, and she did. *Childe Harold* never altered the terms of a life more decidedly than "On the hills." My purpose was found, my name in the family made: I was an Artist. At birthdays and seasonal events I was now called upon for verses which (good or bad, and I was quickly aware of doing both) were made much of by the recipients and my discoverer Auntie Vee. Ma warned me against getting a swelled head, but she too enjoyed the reflected credit. Soon, eager to increase the scope of my empire, I asked for and got a box of watercolours and set about illustrating my poems, after the manner of an infant Blake. Now there were two talents instead of one.

It was not easy at first to see how these assets could obtain for me a larger share of my mother. They caught me her attention, and gave me a grain of prestige, but this in itself was not much. I must feel out a way to make them work for me with her, to convert the outcome into love.

What—what could Art do for an isolated, overworked woman who saw the history of her life as a crushing disappointment of all hope, all potential? My answer was pulled uninstructed out of the air: give her the image of a child's happiness, its overflowing pleasure in the world that undamaged innocence perceives.

And what innocence, what overflowing happiness had I to offer? Well, they would be the first artifacts of my project. And I began to learn my role, and to piece together an Eden for us to inhabit from scraps of De La Mare and Auntie Vee's *Verses for the Young,* and an illustrated book on the flora and fauna of the British Isles. A little way at a time, and for moments only, Ma was seduced out of her diminished, discoloured world. The project grew, and now Agathon Way and its environs were to be redeemed for her in poetic celebration: the seepage of water on a bank beside the sports ground became a spring, and the scrubby common where we picked blackberries once a year became a forest full of dells and glades. I arranged the roadside grasses in a vase from the Labour Party sale of work, to resemble a Chinese bamboo grove; I made a painting of it for her to keep, and another of the pear tree in bloom, and another of the cat nested under the peony. The unseen net in my hands betrayed, when I pulled on it gently, the resistance of her weight within its meshes; but it was not ready yet to be drawn all the way in.

We came home from school one day to find Ma watching for us on the step.

"Your Dad's back; he's in the lounge. Go on in and give him a kiss."

We went to the door of the front room and looked in. Quickly I turned back to Ma.

"I don't want to!"

"It's your Dad. Go on, scaredy-cat—bad as Colin, you are—go on in!"

The man sat on the settee dressed in dung-coloured Army clothes and enormous boots. He had put down a newspaper and was talking to Heather, who stood in front of him pulling at her cardigan in an embarrassed way. He was an absolute stranger.

But Ma was blocking the doorway behind me, so I walked forward and gave him a kiss on the cheek, quick and light. At once he leaned over and grasped me under the arms to jump me up and down as perhaps he used to.

"Allo-allo! Have to loosen this one up, we will."

I held my breath until he let me go.

"Where have those smiles gone, Mother?" he

asked. "I can remember a time when she had a smile for her Dad."

"Pay no attention—she'll get over it."

Very well: I could tell they were settled on this being Dad. But say he was, how could he expect to belong here after all this time (it was almost four years that he had been gone)? He hadn't been with us through the bombings, or through the evacuations. He hadn't been there on the day Heather and I vowed to take care of Ma for ever and ever. That was the time she cut herself with the small discoloured knife: first she had sharpened it, throwing water on the concrete step to make an improvised whetstone, then she had begun to chop the fresh mint on the board, and a moment later slashed the blade into her index finger—we saw the blood running as eh jerked back her chair and let out a single wail.

"Of all the—Heather, get me a clean rag out of the lower drawer, could you?"

Cold water, and a tight wrapping of cloth until the bleeding slowed. I remembered that part, and then what went wrong—her putting her elbows on the table and breaking out in tears, inconsolable, while she mopped her cheeks with her swaddled hand.

"It's too much, all of it—"

Heather fetched the first-aid box in silence and put it on the table; I moved the board away to the dresser, washed the knife (with a thrill at my stomach, seeing the blood rinse off), and started to chop the mint leaves. When at last Ma sniffed energetically and reached in her pinafore pocket for a handkerchief, we sensed an opening and went up close to her.

"We'll help you," said Heather. "You've got us, anyway."

I thought we could aim a little higher. "We'll look after you," I added.

63

"You will, will you?" She was coming back to herself, with that satiric gasp.

"Always and always," Heather assured her.

"There, I'm all right now," Ma said. "Thank you, girls, you're a help."

She had said it herself: we were the help she needed.

And from the hesitancy of his movements about the house, I drew further doubts about the extent of his knowledge of Ma. Did he remember any longer where she kept her little powder compact and her stub of cerise lipstick, in behind the money box in the dresser, so that when a knock came at the front door she could whip them out—three dots on the mouth, a quick rub there and a dab round the rest with the puff—to be publicly presentable? Surely not. Did he even know, as I did, how best to approach her when she was in the usual touchy mood? She might be sitting, say, in the green armchair hunched over a piece of darning and frowning through her heavy glasses. And the first thing was to be certain you had done everything you had been instructed to do previously, otherwise you would be stopped right in the doorway with a sharp reminder: "I thought I told you to get your drawer tidied after the drying-up." If that barrier was passed, you had but a moment to measure your approach, or she would think of a new set of instructions to put you off. The best policy was directness (she detested all creeping-about): a run up to the side of the armchair, a healthy smile and hug: "Hallo Ma!" There was still an even chance that with the best technique in the world you might fail to get through, be twitched off with one of the standard formulas: "What's the matter—got nothing to do with yourself?" But at the best, she would let you sit on the broad arm of the chair with only a minor grumble—"Cupboard love, *I* know"—and you could stay there talking her into a response, and watching her pull the wool in the darn back and forth with a flirting movement of her hand.

Who had studied her as I had, these past few years, and who *saw* her as I did? I was aware of no competitors in that regard, and did not want any, either.

As it happened, Dad himself was content to come back into the household only partway, keeping his own reservations about belonging here. The best of his life was now over—he had decided that. For it was elsewhere that he had measured the height and depth of his experience. He had been in one hundred and twenty degree heat, in the south of India, where men had to fight the scavenger kites for breakfast in camp each morning: one bird dive-bombed them in front while another angled in under the elbow for a grab at the precious fried egg, bully beef and toast. He had been on leave up in Darjeeling, and seen Mount Kanchenjunga at sunset and at dawn. Then he had driven his tank against the Japs in Burma; his own camp had been overrun, and he had narrowly escaped capture; but they had won in the end. Now he had been sent back to this houseful of women who were set in their trivial ways, and to a resentful little son who had been entirely spoiled in his absence. He was thirty-eight; the best was over.

The State found him a job in the bookkeeping department of the National Health, checking the expense accounts of Jaguar-driving surgeons. An hour and a half each way on the trains, and five and a half days a week working on the hand-written ledgers and piles of forms and invoices. Early in the morning—still going by Army hours—his muffled cough was heard from the kitchen with the regularity of a woodcutter's stroke, as he drew in a puff from the first hand-rolled cigarette of the day. And he returned in the evening with the latest

65

war books from the library under his arm; to these, after he had kissed us good night and brewed himself one more pot of strong tea, he turned every evening to keep himself going—to remind himself of the great days.

He had one visitor to welcome him back from the war (leaving aside Ma's sisters, who as women did not qualify for his full attention): his older brother Bob. When Bob came, they went out together into the garden, which became in their joint presence another country, some foreign field which they explored at an inviolable distance from the house where we sat having our cuppa with Auntie Rose, his wife. Uncle Bob was a draftsman for an engineering firm (whatever *that* was Heather and the rest of us had no idea), but he was famous for his imitation of the sound of a trombone. In his teens, he had been recruited on the promise of trombone lessons for the Band of Hope temperance group, and for some years he played a horn with them on street corners outside the public houses of Woolwich. He knew the Sankey and Moody hymns well, but off duty he would play anything he heard on the radio on his trombone, and with variations.

But as Rose told us, when he married her, she wouldn't have the instrument in the house.

"Think of the racket!" she said. "I mean, *would* you?"

We looked sadly at her, thinking of Uncle Bob's permanent devotion to that sound. But she continued. "And d'you know what he said? 'Rose is worth it.' Didn't hesitate for a minute. Course, he knew I meant what I said."

Rose was a small woman, but densely packed into her smoothly pancaked skin; you would not care to be jockeying against her for a place in a queue. Ma said in our hearing that Rose was a bit common, and Dad answered that she took care of Bob all right, which was the real test. They seem, in memory, a well-suited couple—she with her heavy make-up and pointed shoes, he with brilliantined wavy hair combed back in thirties style, and a sallow, corrugated face. The corrugations increased when he geared up to produce his imitation of the lost trombone; he raised his eyebrows, brought his lips out wide and tensed certain muscles in his cheeks, while he brought his hands up as if holding the instrument and its slide, to complete the impression.

One evening, after we had had a game of cricket with the watering can as the stumps and small children placed between the trees as fielders, Uncle Bob stood by the flowering currant bush in the long twilight and gave a sonorous rendering of "Two Lovely Black Eyes" on the imaginary trombone. As he finished, an unseen listener from a couple of fences away applauded and called "Encore!"

"Thank you!" he called through the fruit trees, and facing in the same direction began "And the Band Played On."

"Look at 'im," Rose said to Ma. "Couldn't seem to get it out of 'is system, somehow. I *mean.*"

Uncle Bob died three years after the war, keeling over with a heart attack during his lunch break at work. Before he died, he said he was glad it hadn't happened at home, not to give Rose all the bother.

The men in this family seemed like garden flowers, sweet and colourful and quick to fade: ten years later, Dad like his brother would be gone. The women, by contrast, were like weeds—there were so many of them, and they lasted on and on with a minimal flowering, able to subsist on altogether less in the way of space, nourishment and hope.

Ma and her sisters shared a rooted expectation that men would in one way or another let them down.

And they did. Auntie Vee's only serious young man—years and years ago—had broken their engagement off almost as soon as it was made public; he ran away to Canada, and his father afterwards had the nerve to deny that there had ever been an engagement. Vee, he said, had imagined the whole episode. And Auntie May had been led on by her boss, who told her that his wife was dying; a decade later the wife was still "dying," having produced two healthy children and apparently leading a vigorous life out in Orpington. Auntie Bertha, the next to youngest, *had* married but her husband contracted tuberculosis from a neighbour's child and died of it within five years. And look at Ma, said Auntie Vee: her husband plants four children on her and then joins the Army to go gadding about the world for years at a time.

Auntie Vee also said that I had inherited my poetry from Dad; she even claimed that I looked like him, although it was clear from all the photographs that Colin had his light hair and blue eyes to the life. Such remarks made me uneasy. I did not like the dubious compliment of being similar to a member of a suspect class. Moreover, the only poem of Dad's I had ever seen or was ever to see was a rhyme he sent me for my last birthday before his return home, in which I was advised to be kind and good. Although there was no one at hand to whom I could make the remark, this was not my idea of a proper poem. There was no Nature in it. As for "kind and good," everyone was supposed to be that: why me particularly?

It was very difficult to know whom even to want to resemble. Auntie Vee liked painting and poetry and Nature, and she owned very pleasant things like an angora bed-jacket. And she paid extra attention to me, casting herself as godmother to my "gift" and encouraging me to write letters to her about all my observations of the beautiful things in the world. But Auntie Vee was a rabid Conservative in her politics, which was very bad, and she complained about everybody and everything, except Nature. Even I noticed that. And she spent many weekends nursing her ulcer on Benger's food; and during the week she was a primary-school teacher, which I knew from experience was an iniquitous line of work to be in.

On another side, there were May and Bertha, the aunts who lived together in a flat near Gran and Grandpa and worked as secretaries in town. Certainly they were nicer than Auntie Vee: they did not make any edged remarks and their visits provoked no rows at home as hers often did, and once a year they treated Ma, Heather and me to lunch at their favourite tea room in Blackheath. *That* was a piece of tremendous benevolence, for we never visited cafés unless perhaps it rained on the annual Labour Party charabanc outing and the picnic food became too sodden to eat. The two of them dressed alike, in patterned dresses and pale cardigans during the summer months, and in blouses, skirts and cardigans in winter; their greying hair was meticulously permed, and set once a month at the local salon because office standards demanded it. Beside them, Ma looked a little disordered and shabby, in spite of her efforts to smarten all of us up on family occasions.

We saw much more of Bertha than we did of May, who spent many weekends with an old schoolfriend somewhere beyond Shooter's Hill. One of our summer routines was to take the bus after Sunday dinner to Bertha's, and go to the heath for a walk among the gorse bushes and around the pond; we never stopped for more than a drink at the flat, since it was so small, and so bare of interest—even to Bertha, who always said as she latched the door behind her that she was glad to get out for a few hours. She would stand on the step, pull herself up tall and draw a breath into her deep bosom with satisfaction.

"Ah! The fresh air!"

On the heath even in July and August the wind could blow raw out of an overcast sky, and Auntie's strong nose became purple under its fuzz of powder, but we went bravely on along the sandy paths for the predetermined hour and a quarter, since we must not arrive at our next stop—Gran's—until the old people's nap was over at half-past four and they had got their teeth back in. For Gran would not answer the door unless they looked respectable.

The grandparents lived on the ground floor of a brick villa two streets over from the Heath. Above them were two flats; but in splitting up the house this way so little alteration had been done that the ground floor had no bathroom—Gran kept a galvanized metal bath hung in her little wash-house, and the toilet was reached by going outside the back door. While the first pot of tea was being made, Heather and I took the younger ones by the hand into the back garden. Grandpa had been allotted the left-hand half of the garden, and he had filled it up in accordance with his early training in a Kentish village—flowers close to the house, behind them lettuce, radishes and onions, then peas, beans and tomatoes, and finally as many rows of potatoes as would fit, leaving room only for bonfire heaps at the back. He never bothered with cabbages, though—cheap enough at the shops, and why invite caterpillars in on purpose?

There was a strip of grass down the middle of the garden, and another crosswise between the flowers and vegetables which led to Grandpa's one beehive, a pale blue wooden construction by the fence. We were allowed to roll, or at most bounce, an ancient tennis ball

70

along these strips, but we must never throw it in case it got lost over the fence or damaged the plants. Under these terms the game quickly became boring, and Brenda and I would drift over to the hive to watch the bees flying in and out of their tiny arched door, or steal a peapod if the season was right, and bite off the smooth peas one by one.

Tea, when we were called in to it at last, was a familiar spread of corned beef and cheddar cheese with lettuce and bread-and-butter, followed by custard trifle with evaporated milk and whatever cakes Auntie Bertha or Ma had brought with them. In Gran's house there was no talk during a meal, and afterwards the children were to play very quietly on the floor with a tray of buttons and spools while the grown-ups cleared dishes away and then chatted over the final cup of tea.

Gran's talk was concerned first of all with health, her own and that of each family member in turn, and second with food—the price of it and the quality available, and especially the tenderness and flavour of the Sunday joints of the past month. As we listened, Heather and I traded looks over her dropped aitches: we were forbidden to speak that way, but the grandparents were clearly a kind of race apart. They were, for instance, short and fat while their daughters ranged from trim to bony and were all (except for Ma, their youngest) conspicuously taller than themselves. Their faces were red and weathered, so were their hands, and Gran wore a hairnet perpetually over her little row of sausage curls; in addition, they shuffled about in cloth slippers even in the presence of company, which Ma, let alone the aunties, would never dream of doing. Grandpa had been a stoker in the Metropolitan Gas Works for twenty-five years before retiring, and a certificate on the wall proved it; so did the song which he liked to sing as his party turn at Christmas.

71

I'm a—stoker!
I'm the—joker
Wot works wiv a shovel and a poker!
The 'eat and smell
Are just like—well—
No wonder I'm an 'orrible soaker!

According to Ma, he was precisely as the song said, coming home drunk every Friday night and not above beating out his frustrations on the family at home. But someone (Gran? Vee, the first daughter?) decided that the next generation would learn its way out of the working class, through self-discipline, self-denial and the schools. And now the old man was harmless, sitting with his ear to the radio for the commentary on the weekend cricket match, or pottering down the garden, and Gran sat back satisfied with the progress made.

On every visit, it seemed, the conversation at some point came round to Vee—Victoria, as Gran alone still called her. And then, as Ma cautiously slipped out to have a cigarette in the kitchen, and Auntie Bertha's face drooped into resignation, Gran brought Heather and me into the circle to hear her reminiscences of the triumphs of Vee's youth: the scholarships, the prizes, the fine handwriting and needlework, and the special grant she won to go to the teachers' training school. We heard how Vee had always had the looks of a perfect lady, and with that fine, chestnut-brown hair that never went grey what a picture she made with it rippling over her shoulders, and what narrow feet she had so that ordinary shoe shops couldn't fit her—she had to go up to Regent's Street to get specially made pairs of shoes.

Such was Gran's heartfelt admiration of her favourite that we found ourselves responding, asking for more of the stories, caught up in that dream of success. But when, later, Auntie Bertha walked with us to the bus

72

stop the mood was altogether different. Then we learned from remarks passed above our heads that it had been May, taken out of school and put to work at fifteen, who had made Vee's training as a teacher possible; and that Ma herself had won better marks at school but was sent without matriculation to the secretarial course, at her parents' insistence.

"And after all that," Bertha said, "wouldn't you think she'd have the *decency* to be happy?"

"I know," Ma said. "You would. But it's ulcers, and neuralgia, and if it isn't that it's migraines."

"One complaint after another."

"No end to it."

"You'd think out of common decency—but no."

Vee lived in a flat off the main road just beyond Lee Green, with Phyllis, a fellow teacher. The place was as completely equipped and immaculate as any full-time housewife's: the tea set was stacked in the sideboard next to the sherry glasses, the kitchen cups hung from hooks in the dresser, the egg timer stood on the back of the stove and the dishcloth always hung over the edge of the drainer to air out. Despite the small size of the rooms, Vee and Phyl insisted on fitting in the proper amount of furniture: a three-piece lounge set with crocheted anti-macassars, as well as a folded dining table and four chairs, the sideboard and an occasional table and a hassock in the living room; and in the bedroom a matched walnut double bed, dressing table and wardrobe, inherited from Phyl's parents ("She comes," Vee reminded us, "from a very good family, in Kettering—that's Northamptonshire"). So narrow were the spaces between these monumental pieces that you barked your shins with any sudden movement through the obstacle course, but Vee and Phyl could glide with genteel ease in their eighteen-inch alleys and round their polished corners.

73

To me, they presented a different face, and I could not agree with Ma and Auntie Bertha that they were miserable; on the contrary although I prayed not to grow up to be like them (Auntie Vee had already suggested that I might follow in her training-college footsteps), I thought they had a pretty good time of it, moaning and all.

Heather and I were sent over to visit them regularly as Ma's surrogates, especially after the terrible Christmas when Auntie Vee came to stay: not content with asking for hot milk with just a dash of Nescafé in bed in the mornings, she had let fall in the heat of some random argument the opinion that childbearing and what led up to it were "animal activities"—subsequently claiming, to Ma's infinite exasperation, that she couldn't see why anyone would take offence at a statement of fact. The fourth day of the visit saw both sisters felled by migraine, lying upstairs in darkened rooms with wet cloths on their heads. Nor was the incident forgotten—communication afterwards was reduced to the necessary minimum of cards and perfunctory ritual teas, and whenever possible Ma used the twins as an excuse to back out of the latter.

Once, Ma sent us off early on a Saturday morning; it was summertime, and she was turning out the cupboards. Heather carried a shopping bag with two lettuces and some early beans from the garden, and I brought a bunch of sweet peas and mixed weeds which I had composed and wrapped myself. The garden was the only special asset our family had, with the six of us living on Dad's fifty pounds a month. When any of the aunties came over, they could afford to bring a Marks and Spencer's cake or an ice-cream brick wrapped in newspaper to keep it from melting while we munched through sandwiches first. But the lettuces were fresh, at least.

Auntie Vee was giving Phyl a home permanent when we showed up at the door.

"Well, hallo! Just a kiss, dear, no hugs because of me hands, excuse me." Vee waved her rubber-gloved hands, smelling of ammonia. "But come on in, we'll put coffee on in twenty minutes. *Lovely* to see you, oh it *is!*"

The rule in all our family encounters was hysterical happiness: Vee squeezed her eyes shut and raised her shoulders up to her ears for emphasis. In the kitchen I showed the bunch of flowers.

"It's just a few, mostly from the garden."

"Oh they're lovely flowers, lovely! Just pop them in the green glass vase, bottom shelf in the pantry, right corner." Vee paused a moment in winding up the narrow sausage of Phyl's sandy hair. "That's the one, dear."

"Yes. They'll make a very pretty arrangement." Phyl was relied upon to make the final judgements; in a muted and tactful way she was the man of the place, and it was she who wore the straight tweed skirts and thick soles, where Vee had her Cuban heels from Regent's Street and her wool dresses.

Now it was Heather's turn: she was content to let the "artist" go first, since she herself represented real, practical worth. "And two lettuces. They're home-grown, and some beans. Shall I put them in the vegetable bin?"

"Would you, dear? But I think we should put one of the lettuces in cold water, have a few leaves with our luncheon, with the cold chicken and chutney. Oh, what a treat! And it's *most* generous of Hilda, with all those mouths to feed."

We noticed that the bin already contained a lettuce, but that was just too bad. We sat down on two chairs squeezed between the kitchen table and the wall and watched while Vee went on with her work, swabbing the shiny rounds of hair done up in pink plastic with ammonia lotion. It was clear that she enjoyed the game of beauty salon: she danced around Phyl with playful gestures, fixing the rollers one last time and finally wrapping up the lumpy, squarish head in an old scarf, to cook. Meanwhile Phyl sat contentedly under the fuss: she raised her face with its weatherbeaten cheeks and wide slit of a mouth up to Vee's thin and hawk-like countenance, happiness reflecting more happiness, without a cloud in sight.

"Thank you, dear," she said, looking straight into Vee's eyes, "for all your trouble."

"No trouble at all—I like to do it."

It was the first time I ever felt the warmth of love between two grown-up people—reciprocated, tender love, and I saw that they didn't care about looking odd or being silly. Imagine that there was a feeling so strong as to erase critical considerations and to stop self-consciousness! That, perhaps, was heaven on earth. Yes, but such disgusting mannerisms as they had, Vee dropping her g's at the end of *teachin'* and *doin's,* and now look at them playing house, skipping about getting in each other's way over the elevenses! Soon they would want to gloat over the details of our latest report cards, and ask what poems I'd been writing, and then we would have to hear about the hotel they were going to near Sandown—always extremely private, they insisted on that, with an exclusive beach miles away from the trippers. They were awful snobs.

After that it was time to lay the table for lunch. Small plates were decorated with lettuce leaves and shreds of chicken, with one small tomato and a couple of radishes for colour and slices of Hovis and a scraping of butter to fill us up. Dessert was a pink junket with light gratings of nutmeg on top, easy for Vee's sensitive stomach to digest. Then it was Heather's and my privilege to do the washing-up, at the little metal sink where the job felt so different, handling the flower-painted crockery with anxious slowness. At two-thirty we must leave: Vee and Phyl were ready to go for their little lie-down on the bed, under its immense rose taffeta eiderdown.

They watched us go, holding back each side of the lace curtain at the living-room window, and waved to us just before we went out of sight. Once we had turned the corner I wiped their kisses and my polite expression off with the back of my hand: there was something obscurely terrible about all that loving display we put on. And it was a powerful relief to be outside in the wind, freshened by the grit and waste paper of the main road, while they lay back there in the close little room under the eiderdown in their petticoats and stockinged feet, with their corrugated hair flattening against the pillows.

"Does Auntie Phyl have false teeth too?" I asked Heather. We both knew Vee's were false, because we had seen her without them when she came to stay.

"I expect so," Heather said. "She had a mug on her bedside table. That's where they put them in water when they go to bed."

"D'you like the aunties—a lot, I mean?"

" 'Course, don't you? Nasty little suck-up if you don't, after they gave you two bob."

This point put my question to rest, for the moment; after Ma's allowance of one Saturday penny the aunties' gift of two shillings represented niceness to the point of magnificence. And we had better spend some of it on the way home, or Ma would make us save the lot. She was stingy, all right, and cross, and heavy-handed. But you knew where you were with her—that was the difference. Some instinct warned me that the aunties put on a front with us, as we felt compelled to put on a front

77

with them: behind their jolly weekend selves hovered the draconian shadow of their other existence—the teacher, armed with red pencil, ruler and cane.

In those schools, where the classes ran fifty and sixty children to a room, teachers saw no alternative to the exercise of tyranny, and the enforcement of obedience was their first and last lesson. It was Miss Goff who initiated us as five-year-olds, an elderly woman with slow, stiff movements but possessed of the complete technique of social control. The fifty small chairs in her room were arranged in a single large circle so that no child could be out of the line of her sight, and we must sit with our hands visible on our laps at all times. Silence was the next commandment, and the first time she caught me talking provided her with the right opportunity for "making an example." She stood me on a chair placed in the centre of the ring of children; then she left the room for some minutes, giving the class the task of watching to see that I neither spoke nor moved while she was gone. In their relief at not being the chosen victim, they stared me up and down hungrily (I felt their eye movements making prickly trails on my skin), and went on to make faces, and then thumb their noses and finally emit small insulting noises in my direction. They had got as far as flicking rolled pellets of paper at my bare legs when Miss Goff turned the brass handle of the door. At once the hands went up.

"Miss, Miss!"

"Miss, she moved!"

"Miss, she moved her hand!"

"And she turned round her head."

"She moved her—her leg!"

"Miss! I saw it too."

"So did I, Miss."

Miss Goff expressed satisfaction. "Thank you, children. Come up to the desk, Irene."

She made a clatter in the desk drawer as she got out her ruler, and the sound was echoed by a thrilled murmur from the class.

"Hands out, please."

This routine had been set from the first day of class: one sharp rap on the back of each hand. I knew what was coming, and I knew Miss Goff's hits were judged not to be as bad as Mr. Kelsey's whacks on the older boys, or Miss Hyde's slashes with the ruler's edge on the backs of your knees. But it was a heavy ruler, and the impact of it across my skinny knuckles felt cutting enough—I grabbed them together against my stomach, and tried to rub away the hurt.

"Now, do you understand that I mean what I say?"

"Yes, Miss Goff."

"You may go back to your seat."

But the grandest ceremony of those years was the formal expulsion of Henry Clay, aged eight. Miss Challoner, the principal, called a special assembly in the middle of the morning, with no explanation in advance. Normally when we marched in to prayers at the beginning of the day it was to the accompaniment of a processional on the piano, but this time there was only the shuffle of some hundreds of pairs of feet, as the teachers got their classes out of the rooms and lined them up facing the dais. A few teachers patrolled the sides of the hall, ready to pull troublemakers to the end of the line; the luckier ones got good places at the back near the coke fire in its tiled enclosure. When I got to be in the oldest class and took my turn at the back end of the hall, I would see how the teachers hitched their arses onto the hot metal railing round the fire until there was a smell of steaming woollens; then they would stand away for a minute to cool, and repeat the cycle. And if I was lucky enough to stand near the middle of the last row, I too caught some glow of heat on the backs of my legs, for precious moments before we returned to the unheated classrooms.

Now Challoner was on the dais, with the high windows at her back; over to one side, just off the platform, stood a man in a navy coat, and next to him was Henry Clay. Challoner signalled to Henry to get up on the edge of the dais. As he did so, children craned their necks to see him. Henry was not particularly tall, just square-built, and the toughest fighter in the school. He fought for the fun of it, and in spare moments would hit the girls too, making swift raids into a game of statues, or into a skipping line. He was always outside on the street early in the morning, ready to block one or other of the school gates. His face and hands were red-chapped, and he wore no balaclava or mittens; the rest of his clothes looked like cut-down adults' gear, heavy and shapeless on him. Today he wore a dark buttoned jacket, and his black straight hair was flattened down on his head. And beside him, Miss Challoner towered at the podium, tall and thin in her draped frock with built-up shoulders. She looked at Henry, then raised her head and spoke. Last week, she informed us, some windows had been broken at the school. The culprit had been found, and that child was from today expelled permanently from the school.

She paused. Henry stood like a rock, with his arms held out a little from his body, and he continued in the same posture as Challoner announced in a louder voice that Henry Clay was the name of the child. Yet, she said, it was not because he broke windows that this boy was to be expelled today. No, it was because he did a far worse thing (and here it seemed as if Henry's feet shifted slightly—in surprise?). Breaking windows was a very serious offence, but he was not expelled for that: it was that he lied about what he did. Liars would not be tolerated in the school. All must remember that, and behave accordingly.

The official, on cue, stepped forward and took Henry down from the platform. In silence he walked him to the heavy door which led to the cloakroom and outside, opened it, and took him through. Some kind of noise began to erupt from Henry's mother, who we now saw was waiting in the gloom of the corridor, but it was cut off with the closing of the door. And they were gone.

We were marched back to class without another word spoken, and without Miss Knight's "Country Gardens" on the piano to keep us in step. The atmosphere was heavy with a new threat, for if Challoner were serious about this lying business, which of us was safe? Among the five-year-old boys passing in line, several had their hands folded unconsciously over their trouser flies: such was their terror.

It was a slow time. Year after year we said the multiplication tables from one-times-two to twelve-times-twelve at the beginning of morning class. At break we played alternate chase and statues for three years, and for the next three years skipping, and catch games with worn tennis balls. At the weekend we trudged to the shops and back, or waited for the slow bus to take us to and from one or other auntie. On our road there were girls Heather's age, but not mine, and the boys had stopped playing with the girls. I talked to Ma when she would let me, and in bed at night I talked to Heather until she fell asleep, or until I realised from the change in her breathing that she slept, since for the most part she did not answer my strings of observations, speculations, questions. Then, in the darkness, I stopped talking and sometimes my lips continued silently on, beginning a poem.

These were not the same as the birthday-card quatrains which I continued to produce as required at the dining-room table: the nighttime utterances, rather than being pitched towards the approval of others, drew me in a different direction. They celebrated storms, and raging seas, destruction and night. In the mornings at school assembly we might sing "Eternal Father, strong to save," but in my private world there was no saving father: great waves towered, ships broke apart, and death had its own way unchallenged. Idyllic scenes, if they appeared at all, were conjured up in the first stanza so that demonic natural forces might erupt and sweep them away in the second and third. No consolations were allowed, no weakening of severity.

A poem of this kind, called *Deadly Nightshade,* won first prize in a competition when I was in the first year at secondary school. The event was a two-days' wonder on Agathon Way, since reporters came down from London to knock on Ma's door, and the head at Hurst Grammar School let me out of class to be photographed by them in my bottle-green uniform and hand-knitted socks. Grainy images appeared in the evening paper showing "dainty, blue-eyed Irene, with a mop of chestnut curls," and telling in the caption story about the genesis of the poem in an incident which occurred during a family hike in the country. Ma was half-thrilled and half-embarrassed, for while it was enjoyable to get the neighbours' compliments and see their jealousy, it was less so to be written up publicly as a mother ignorant enough to let her child pick poisonous berries and bring a pound of them home before she found out what they were.

Then there was the money needed to get the two of us up to town for the presentation of the award—where was she to find *that?*

She grumbled, but she found it, and on a draughty night in February we went to a panelled hall in a building not far from London Bridge station, where an old, old man with a tremor and a very wide scar on his forehead handed me a silver trophy and a maroon-bound copy of Shakespeare. When he bent towards me the bright lights played over his ribbon of scar tissue, and it seemed to me that his brain was pulsating there, right beneath the pink membrane, ready to burst through. How dreadful! The spit gathered in my mouth as before a vomiting fit, and I was anxious to get away from him; but he grasped me with a huge hand while he uttered some words above my head into a microphone which distorted them out of all recognition. I made an effort, and swallowed.

"Thank you very much." Now he let me go; the applause died quickly, leaving only the sound of my heavy school shoes, clacking across the loud parquet floor.

My seat was in the front row of chairs, directly under a massive chandelier, and next to me sat an elongated seventeen-year-old boy who had won an award for a story. He was plainly disgusted at my being so young, and whenever I turned to look at him lifted his chin and fluttered his eyelids to signify his avoidance. From the beginning of the ceremony I had conceived a fear that the chandelier above us was coming loose—I spotted at once the spider web of cracks leading outwards from it across the ornamented ceiling—and in my anxiety, as the awards for painting now proceeded, and after them the performances by winners in vocal and instrumental music, I kept cringing in the direction of the story-writer; and he, irked by my suspicious approaches, all the more pulled in his elbows and tossed up his chin. In some dim manner I connected my fear of being struck down by the great chandelier with my possession of the prizes; I thought that if I could put them down somewhere, get rid of them, I would be safer—but that was impossible. Meanwhile, why was my neighbour so secure, holding his awards with casual arrogance on one thigh? Why was he immune from the threat under which I crouched, sweated and suffered? Perhaps, unlike me, he deserved his honours—.

At last, the ceremony over, we were released, and I was taken to meet the poets who had judged the contest: there was a tall poet, thin and brown like a leaf, with his beautiful wife dressed and painted in the manner of a dancer on his arm, and a shorter poet in a jersey and corduroys. And which of the English poets, the tall one asked me, was my favourite?

But I had scarcely begun to read the English poets; I had got only as far as the frontispieces to those dusty, gilt-edged volumes on the library shelves. "Byron," I answered faintly. On the evidence of those engraved front pages, Shakespeare didn't look like a real person at all; Wordsworth and Tennyson were old, and Shelley was pop-eyed, although I liked his shirt. Byron was the clear winner (also with a good shirt). Oh, but what about Keats? But it was too late to reconsider.

The poets gave each other a wry look, above my head: I had made a mistake, then. Should I have said someone more modern?

"And Masefield," I added uncertainly. He was the poet laureate, and ought to be all right.

"Yes, yes." The tall poet gave me a half-smile, half-sigh. "Well, go on reading," he added. Both of them signed their names in my prize book, and after a word to Ma backed politely away.

At once a woman in a brocade dress appeared in their place, and I recognized her as one of the group on the platform. She too bent over me, and with the grand air of a fairy godmother grasped my book and held it up.

"You will come to treasure this book," she announced in a distinctly posh voice. "Some day it will be very valuable, not only for the great poetry in it, but because of these signatures."

She turned and asked Ma for the loan of a pen,

and when after some rummaging in the bag one was produced, she dashed off her own illegible signature on the title page.

"There!" she said, handing me back the book and offering Ma her pen as if both objects had been magically enhanced. "You must be very, very proud on this occasion."

"Oh yes," Ma said. "Thank you."

After she left, I opened my book, but couldn't read the name at all. "Who was she, d'you know?"

"I'll be blessed if I do," said Ma.

Lemon squash and butterfly cakes were laid out on a table for the contest winners and their relatives, and once we were sure we had done our official duty Ma and I tucked into them. Nobody else spoke to us; the other winners, all much bigger and older, formed a group of their own, and the platform people were rapidly leaving the scene. After a third cake—they were very small—we caught each other's eye.

"I should think this is about it," Ma said. We put the prizes in a tartan shopping bag which she had had the foresight to bring, and went to the back of the hall to get our coats.

"How do they make butterfly cakes?" I asked her.

"Oh, nothing much to it. They're little queen cakes, really. Cut off the tops, and cut them in two pieces. Put a layer of icing on the cake, and stick the two pieces in at an angle, you see? The icing has to be soft. And then you sprinkle on the hundreds and thousands, and there you are."

Ide Hill was far away, where the deadly nightshade bush of my poem grew. A slow walker, trailing along at the end of the line, I had noticed the plant and been attracted to the resplendent array of its fruit—it was covered with round, smooth, purplish-black fruit, as big as blackberries. Within a couple of minutes I had picked a bagful, admiring meanwhile the vigour and lushness of the bush. Odd that no one had found it before me. When we got home I would look the plant up in the book Auntie Vee gave me, before we ate the berries; just one I would bite open now, and taste. And I put the smooth skin of it to my lips (it felt cool and pleasant) and tore it open a little with my teeth. The flesh inside was dull-coloured; I let my tongue just slide out and rest on it briefly, and the taste was mildly sweet—dull in flavour perhaps, but juicy and good. . . .

Come to think of it, butterfly cakes looked better than they tasted, too. There were, it seemed to me, terribly few good things to eat in this world. Red meat was one, and mushrooms when you could get them, and new potatoes, and Cox's orange pippins: it was not an extensive list.

We caught the train home from London Bridge. At ten o'clock on a weekday all the platforms were empty under scattered pools of light, and the loudspeaker voice announced its litanies of stations to nobody but ourselves. In the train, Ma rested her head back against the harsh upholstery and her tired, swollen eyelids fell closed.

She had seemed unaccountably annoyed with me on the walk back to the station, passing me the shopping bag with a sharp comment—"Here, take this, I'm blowed if I should carry it for you!" As if I wasn't ready and willing. It was a puzzle, because she had seemed so happy when it all started, when the letter about the award first came. We'd celebrated with lean bacon rashers (add those to the list) fried up with tomatoes for tea that night, and I kept her company afterwards in the kitchen. Then what happened? It was clear that the business tonight had been dismal, and a waste of good money for the train tickets; but something more than that was wrong. I had been assuming, or I had persuaded myself that I was taking her with me on a destined path towards success and happiness, and that for practical purposes we lived one life between us, Ma and I, skinless to one another, exempt from the matter of liking or not liking, approving or disapproving. My poems, and my paintings and drawings, and my good marks at school were all for her, consolations and also promises for the future. And now, at the moment of validation of the highest promise of all, she turned away from me; she was no part of me—she denied it.

"Is that how it is, then?" I put the question silently, sitting opposite to her in the rocking train, my eyes full of tears; and the reply came from her closed face and the disappointed set of her mouth: "That's how it is."

I was so sorry! The tears flowed, and then quite peacefully, of themselves, stopped. Well, then. Well. In that case, one would have to have a new idea of some kind. And perhaps it was just as well—if I were to be honest, I must admit that she didn't really like poems all that much. One or two in a year, maybe, she liked, but her responses to more frequent offerings had been rather strained. She probably liked music better, Grieg and Tschaikovsky on the radio—yes, it was at once clear to me that music was what she liked best. And music had been allotted to Heather already; there was not enough money for music lessons for both.

The next thought which followed was that perhaps I would not always have to love her—perhaps even now the end of it was coming into sight, and I would see how to get out and away. Or maybe there was still time for me to be discovered, somehow, as a musical talent and I could become the great pianist like Eileen Joyce, and she would listen to me; but no, I had deceived myself long enough and stupidly enough already. I looked out of the train window at the cold lights of New Cross appearing in the complex urban darkness, and the scene transformed into one of emblematic promise in front of my eyes: yes, it was desolate and swept by a chilly wind, but it was in the open, a clear space over which to move freely.

"What are you thinking about?" The restarting of the train after its brief stop had woken her, and she was watching my expression with interest.

"Oh, nothing. I'm afraid it wasn't worthwhile, going tonight."

She said no, it had been well worth the effort, she wouldn't have missed it; and her understanding smile laid its grip on me again as we accelerated across the junction towards the outer suburbs. There were years more to run on my contract with Ma, all willingness set aside.

The general answer in this situation was to become perfect. Once the state of perfection was reached, Ma would have no reason to withhold her love, or at least her approval (reasonableness was setting in); and even if she did withhold it, the person in the state of perfection would not care.

Next, the means, which at the age of twelve I found close to hand, beginning with the report card issued three times yearly. At Hurst Grammar, *Excellent* was a virtually unknown rating; consequently a row of *Very Goods* would be equivalent to academic perfection, and I saw no reason why I should not get it. In the autumn and winter terms I came close, but my work in science was never neat enough to rate higher than a *Good,* and when, in late spring, my homework book came back with only a *Fairly Good* underlined in the margin, my patience gave way. A long session of rubbing made the ink of *Fairly* faint enough for an adequate reshaping. But my beginner's eye did not take in the erosion of paper produced by the rubber, and the faint but unmistakable smudging around the mark. When the books were called in during the last week of term, Miss Horrocks recognized the fraud at once, and indeed, as she held the page out towards me, its obviousness was shaming.

"How do you explain this?"

Silence. She put the book on the desk, and began to pluck beads of fluff from her light-blue cardigan as she waited. I had nothing to say, and passed the time thinking how imperfect Miss Horrocks was, with her wattled chin, and low, heavy breasts stretching the buttons on her blouse: how fat, and old.

"This mark has been altered, hasn't it?"

"Yes." Perhaps the example of Henry Clay prompted my admission, or I could see no point in denying so crude an error.

The following day a note from the head arrived at home. Ma called me into the back room as soon as I came in, and shut the door behind us.

"Sit down there."

We sat on either side of the empty fireplace, before which stood a wooden firescreen decorated with my own work—two pintail ducks, as I had seen and sketched them at the Tarn in Mottingham, done in tempera against a background of bulrushes. Ma held the note in hands damp and red from the washing.

"And what's the explanation for this, then?"

The perfect response appeared to me to be silence.

"Well?"

On the other hand, the campaign for perfection had suffered an admitted loss, and would have to be begun again from the beginning, anyway. "I'm sorry. I told them I was sorry."

"And that's all you've got to say?" The room lacked any source of heat, and ever since the war its window frames had been loose so that cold draughts came in freely around them. We sat quite still, shivering, and Ma's hands became slowly bluish. "Sorry, she says. I should think so! And it's hardly enough—I'm bitterly disappointed in you, Irene."

She would require tears of me eventually—then why hold back? The longer it took, the longer we would have to sit and freeze. I began to force a snivel.

"I *am* sorry. I won't do it again." These words brought on my tears in earnest, and now that she saw them Ma folded the school note, got out her own handkerchief and wiped my eyes and her own in succession.

"As if we hadn't got enough worries," she said. "So let it be a lesson."

Avis Burden and Denise Lofts knew how to cheat. They were not easy to approach, for they were in advance of the rest of us in other, more profound ways: Avis had breasts and did her toffee-coloured hair in pincurls every night, and Denise had a boyfriend who met her at the bus stop, and although she was skinny she stuffed her bra with wads of cotton-wool—when she dashed down the court as the star of our class netball team, she was a twin-prowed image of Victory, and we envied her her nerve. To begin with, I followed them at lunchtime to the ditch at the far end of the lacrosse field, to admire them while they smoked cigarettes; and after a couple of sessions I paid Denise threepence for a cigarette to try myself, and put up with their hilarity when at their insistence I poked it between my fingers and awkwardly lit up, right there.

"But you aren't inhaling!" Avis pointed out after I had done a few puffs. "You won't get a thing out of it if you don't inhale."

"I'm trying!" The other hangers-on giggled, and pushed each other into the nettles out of pure happiness at my humiliation—so much for the weedy little swot, trying to get into the swing of things.

"Here, give it me." Avis took the cigarette and put it between her juicy lips. She could even talk around the side of it. "Breathe out, then take a puff, like this."

But I couldn't do it: I filled my mouth with smoke, but could not force it into my lungs. "I feel as if I'll die, if I inhale it."

"Oh, God."

"Bisley's coming!" The lookout at the top of the ditch jumped down to warn us of the patrolling teacher's approach.

"Here—" Denise took the cigarette and briskly pinched off the end with her fingernail. "Try again later."

Next day she asked me if I had managed it. I admitted that I hadn't, in part out of a sense of the importance of maintaining an inferior posture. It was my business to learn from them how to wring those few extra marks out of every classroom test—to pick the right seat in the first place, either beside a curtained window or in the middle or the back corner, and in the next place to devise accordion-pleated paper slips to keep in socks or sleeves, or to note brief formulas on wrists or above knees—not, in my case, to squeak by on minimal homework, but to make sure of my place at the top. And achieving their tolerance of my apprenticeship with them was a delicate matter, since they could have no sympathy with my awful greed for top marks: it was one thing to cheat out of demonstrable need, quite another to do so as a luxury. But some sense of my having an incomprehensible but nevertheless real need must have come across, because Avis and Denise put up with me as long as I hung about with them, and nobody, in spite of black looks during examinations, ever gave me away.

That year, Denise invited me to her Christmas party where they played Sardines, and then Postman's Knock, in the course of which a boy whose first name was Glenn took me out into the front hall and kissed me for perhaps three seconds on the lips. An instance of a quite unassimilable event, since nothing like it had occurred before, and nothing like it would occur again for the next five years; it remained in my mind as self-enclosed as the biology slide illustrating cell division in *Spirogyra*—first, the cold air of the unheated hallway, and the barely controllable fear when the boy took hold of my arms to hold me steady; next the inner lips pressed on mine, and the suggestion of harsh bristle around the edges (Glenn was older—perhaps sixteen); lastly the cold returning on a wetted mouth, and the relief at having held my ground.

"He did kiss you, didn't he?" Denise asked me when I got my coat to go home.

"Yes. I mean, he was supposed to, wasn't he?"

"I know, I only wondered. He's good, isn't he?"

"Oh—yeah." But that question was beyond my competence.

"I might fancy him myself," Denise speculated, as if (impossible!) I might get ideas about moving into her territory. Denise inhabited not only a different place, the new estate district on the far side of the school, but a different system of expectations also. On Saturday mornings she helped out at her aunt's dress shop, and in the afternoons worked on the sideways flip of her hair to be ready for one or other church social or dance; at fifteen she would fall in love with a married man who first saw her when his wife was trying on clothes at the shop, and at sixteen she left school and had his baby. Avis, who stayed on and planned to go to art school, told us she was idyllically happy.

But on my rare free Saturdays I took my bike and went in one of two directions—south, towards the cemetery and the Kemnal woods, or northwest towards the High Street and Woolworth's, to steal. If it were to be Woolworth's, I would park my bike on a side street and walk into the shop with an air of definite intention; I scanned each counter in turn, actually checking for items near the outside edge that were both nice to consider owning and also flat enough to sit easily in a jacket pocket. Then, in the area of my established interest, I might buy something very cheap (a hairslide, a balloon) to put off suspicion, and finally I made the actual move, fixing my eyes on another section of the counter, even advancing my left hand towards a quite different decoy object, while the right hand palmed its prey.

The stolen goods could never be shown at home: Ma knew to a penny how much money each of us ought to possess at any given time, and what that money could buy; moreover our drawers and shelves were regularly sorted and checked. I therefore gave away at school my miniature pony with a nylon tail, and buried along the side of the house behind the hollyhocks my celluloid baby doll and my poppit beads.

Once, after I had gone to a birthday party I went to dig up my treasures, figuring that I could have won them at the party. And I found the beads, but either the baby doll had been accidentally turned up and thrown away, or I had miscalculated where her grave was. I never found her.

Even while on Saturdays I was a thief, on Sundays I began to reach out as one of the impoverished in spirit towards God; for I was open to any offers, and the white Jesus standing with arms spread in acceptance just where the bus turned the corner into the High Street called to me day by day. And then I received the Sign, which changed everything. The Sign came on a rain-spotted afternoon, when I was returning from the local shops with two bags of groceries dragging at my arms, the image of martyrized labour, musing on the likelihood of my being able to spit blood one of these dismal nights. I felt like a consumptive, weak and sensitive — why couldn't I be one? As I walked I kept my eyes on the pavement in front of me. Passing the primary school Heather had once found a shilling. There was always hope. And opposite our corner I crossed the road without lifting my head to look for traffic — but it was too much to hope that a car might appear out of nowhere and knock me down. I set the bags on the kerbside for a moment, to ease my arms before going the last twenty yards to home, and then I saw a necklace of whitish beads lying by the grass triangle at the corner.

On closer inspection, it appeared to be a necklace with a difference, one of those things which were in the window of the Catholic shop: a rosary, made of pearlized beads on a silver chain, with a silver crucifix hanging at the end. It was the Sign I had looked for, meant for me; and wet and gritty as it was, it went into my pocket. Before I had even latched our front gate behind me, I had conceived a new vision of my destiny — in a word, sanctity.

The Jesus of the High Street corner was Catholic, and besides, only the Catholic Church offered sainthood as a career. So far, the direction was straightforward. At the same time it was quite clear that my parents would not tolerate the bizarreness of an announcement of conversion to the Catholic faith. We knew no Catholics; Catholicism was no part of our reality; it might be for the Irish, perhaps, but we weren't Irish. Yet sanctity must not be put off. One had an obligation to begin now, if only as a matter of private commitment and inner practice of devotion. I went to the library in search of the lives of saints to serve as my models, and at once came upon the life of St. Thérèse, the Little Flower, by Frances Parkinson Keyes. When I took the dark-blue volume down from the shelves and opened it, it cracked with disuse (there were few questers after sainthood in the district of Hurst Park); but by the time I had had it for a sequence of five two-week periods, it fell open easily. There could be no more proper patroness for me than Thérèse Martin: the banal adolescent who took a negative way to extraordinary power, and the saint of desperate girls. I adored her on first acquaintance, the larval being who nested in the fat cabbage-heart of conventional life, eating it up and dissolving herself at last in the enzymes of her own ambition—a self-transformer who flew away as a miraculous, night-haunting moth. *Incomparably beyond and above you all!*—the cry of Catherine Earnshaw rang again for me in the death scene of the saint.

Through inter-library loan I got hold of her own *Story of a Soul,* embellished with admiring testimony from her contemporaries; I studied the photographs, where she stood in her ghastly mustard-brick cloister holding an artificial lily of silk and wire, and felt at once desolate and intensely excited. Here was expressed her systematic erasure of all ordinary human preferences, for the beautiful over the ugly, for comfort over pain, warmth over cold, life over death, and the furious operations of a will that had no adequate materials to work on except itself.

And I went downstairs and looked at Ma, dragging from stove to table to sink, and wanted to throw myself on the mat in front of her shouting, "Enough of it, for God's sake! Can't we at least make up our minds to die?"

I carried the rosary with me to school in the small compartment of my plastic satchel, wrapped in a muslin pouch which I sewed myself; it was my talisman, my guarantee of a significant future. At eighteen I planned to make my formal conversion, and at twenty I would apply to the nearest convent of a strictly contemplative sort. In the meantime, I began to practice occasional meditations after school, at the side altar of the deserted parish church, under a stained-glass window of St. Margaret the Scottish queen (I nursed inarticulate suspicions about the Church of England's devotion to royalty, and knew without being told that St. Thérèse was unacceptable in these surroundings, but one must begin, mustn't one, where one stood).

It was quickly apparent that God was not eager to meet one halfway. But then, neither was Ma easy of access; with long labour I had obtained some limited acceptance there, and that gave me hope in this new case. One set about the job rationally and explored the available routes. There was comfort already in the physical attitude of meditation, and reassurance in the self-abasement it proclaimed—kneeling, I confessed my unworthiness and abandoned all claims, even to mercy. And in the absence of a blaze of inner light, the sun coming through coloured glass was itself merciful; and the odour of stale incense, and the crepitation from the dry filling in the hassock as my weight shifted on it were sensations which calmed me by their strangeness. So for several weeks I enjoyed the possession of a secret world, until one Friday at random I pushed open the church door, and when I was too far inside to turn back, heard voices. It was the vicar, and the ladies arranging flowers for weekend services, laughing and chatting together. They heard the muffled thud of the door closing and turned towards me, and the vicar left the group and came down the aisle.

"Welcome," he said. I was astonished, looking at his face which in its knobbed irregularity and with its heavy acne scars seemed an aggregate of many misfortunes: even his expression of goodwill seemed to torture him. "And what brings you to us today?"

"I come here, sometimes."

"Yes? Well, we're always open." He smiled his agonized smile. "Come whenever you wish."

"Well. Thank you." There was no question of staying today, and I backed off.

"Oh, don't let us disturb you." He put his hand to his chin, clearly thinking about ways to keep me from leaving. "You know, we'll be beginning a confirmation class next month; perhaps you would be interested."

"Thank you. Well, I'm sorry I'm in a hurry today."

On the way home, the vicar's suggestion fermented in me rapidly. God would probably see confirmation class as a step forward on my part, and that evening I announced my intention to take it. Ma was not enthusiastic—there were bound to be some hidden costs, she thought, but the aunties when they heard about the idea backed it strongly. Hadn't May got her first job, in the office of a Church of England boarding school, in part because she had been confirmed and her vicar wrote on her behalf?

"You never know," Bertha reminded us, "when it might come in handy. If it opens just one door, it'll be worth it."

And Auntie Vee agreed, volunteering to supply the necessary presentation prayer book, and she added that of course Heather must be confirmed too. In fact, she had better be confirmed first, as the eldest.

Heather was furious. But the machine was set in motion: Ma herself, who saw the inside of church only at Christmas and Easter, and then mainly for the hymns she said, approached Father Fleck and made arrangements for Heather to join the class now beginning. I would have to wait six months until the next class was formed, to save the expense of making two white frocks. It was a disappointment to me, to be delayed until Heather, the rank unbeliever, received the privilege of Communion first. Yet St. Thérèse herself had been refused when she applied for an early entry to the convent; therefore I practiced the suppression of my desires, and even limited my visits at the church to one afternoon a week for prayer and purification, in addition to the Sunday Eucharist.

Father Fleck gave Heather a red booklet of instructions for religious development when she joined the confirmation class. After the session was over, she came straight home and upstairs into our bedroom and threw it at me.

"Here—you can have this! Just your sort of thing. Shoes on the bedspread again, I see?"

My feet were up on the bed—well, on the very edge of the bed really, but this was a practice Ma had absolutely forbidden time and again. Heather found it easy to deflate my pretensions to virtue. More than that, her mere presence in all its energetic health and athletic competence (the hair lifted and blown back from the bike ride home, the long limbs and broad gestures) had the capacity to diminish mine. Meanwhile the booklet had struck me dead centre in the chest. I offered a forgiving look, but she turned her back on me to shrug off her white blouse.

"Old Father Fly-speck! Ugliest mug in the world. You'd have enjoyed all about contrition, today. And for your benefit, the sins are all listed starting on page thirty-five."

Her wide shoulders and long, lean back showed only for a moment before she dived into her Fair Isle pullover. Heather was intensely modest. And yet—how puzzling—she already had a boyfriend, and therefore must be liable to impure thoughts.

"Ta-ta, enjoy yourself."

She was gone, and I turned to the right page to find my own special sins: Lying, Theft, Envy chief among them. And what about Impurity? I was so far from actual temptation (for weeks might pass without a word exchanged with one of the local boys, so separate were our schools and our lives) that its actual application to me seemed problematic. Swearing could be counted, and the reading of *Forever Amber*. The categories listed in the book referred to Thought, Word and Deed, and I could claim guilt under the first two, but Deed? I had conveniently forgotten the game of husbands-and-wives I played with my friend Valerie on overnight stays—Valerie had moved away to Kent six months ago, and it would be a long time, years, before the memory of her dry lips and hot laughing breath on my face came back, and the recollection of her thin, downy arms and the bony pelvis digging into me as we rolled about the bed. It was perhaps that nothing whatsoever in my current experience reminded me of the self I was with Valerie: St. Thérèse had intervened and cancelled it outright. And neither did it occur to me to include among my sins these just now beginning early-morning illuminations of the body, which arose out of dreams or quiet sleep and drew the hand irresistibly towards them. They were certainly among the most real and sweet of happenings, making the heart beat faster and the skin all over kindle to heightened sensation, and fading into the most perfect stillness and warmth; but there was no name for them in my vocabulary—I could only assume that they were some kind of spontaneous natural phenomenon, sent ultimately from God in his kindness towards creatures.

I had much to repent in any case, and much pleasure in the repenting, whether at the feet of St. Margaret, kneeling on the bare wood of the church floor, or in private with my newly bought postcard of the Virgin of Lourdes held up on the edge of the bed beside which I humbled myself. To commune with my Virgin was dangerous (for Heather might come in

101

suddenly, or Ma), and I kept her most of the time between the pages of a little notebook which was tucked under the corner of my mattress (it also contained my notes on the Order of Discalced Carmelites); but the ritual was delightful too—Mary was so helpless in her attitude of mercy, spilling roses in an abandoned way out of her tiny hands. Two rosebuds had landed on her bare feet as they perched on a golden crescent moon, and a ring of tiny golden stars surrounded her head. It was a special pleasure also to see at the bottom of the picture the bizarre inscription, in gold again: *Je Suis L'Immaculée Conception.* For like my saint this Virgin spoke French, and at times I would make my confession to her in that language (with my dictionary close to hand), savouring the release from a culture with no sense of anything but the dead-level of daily existence.

St. Margaret lacked the Virgin's exoticism, her blend of exaltation and absurdity, but my penances before her were more severely cleansing, and the echoing space of the church controlled my meditations better; as I rode my bike afterwards down the hill towards home, I knew that I had suffered and worked with an end in view.

And as I opened the gate, here was Ma weeding behind our hedge in old gloves and a pinafore. She straightened up and put a hand to her back. "Where've you been? At that church again?"

She must have heard the last notes of *Holy Holy Holy* as I brought my bike swooping in to the kerb.

"Well," she went on, "since you've nothing better to do, you can give me a hand with these marigolds: they're running riot in this bed."

The first time I tried to discuss with Ma a difficulty I was having with one of the harder sayings of Jesus, she asked if I were not about to get my period.

"What's that got to do with it?" I was furious; I had not yet accepted the humiliations of those bloody towels and the perpetual embarrassment of their concealment, and objected to her reminder.

"Well, something that isn't a problem at other times can seem like a problem then."

A moment's calculation told me that she knew exactly where I was in the monthly cycle, and I left the room in disgust. But that was only the beginning of my effort to show her the possibility of a spiritual life, for I could never resist for long the mute cries her presence sent me over the washing-up, or the cloud of depression gathering to a headache on Sunday afternoons. How could anyone stand by and leave her comfortless? But Dad fell asleep under the Sunday paper, and Heather and the twins went out with their friends, and so it was that Ma and I began to take walks under the overcast sky, circling at a steady pace through the suburban maze of streets.

Depending on the temperature and the strength of the wind, we might add a mackintosh or a wool coat over our cardigans, and Ma wore a soft beret or a scarf tied under her chin. We walked arm in arm, hers locked with a tight, muscular grip on mine, drawing me down a little on that side. By the time we turned the corner at the end of the street I had adjusted the length of my step to hers, and begun to recall for her the main points of Father Fleck's sermon that morning. To talk directly about the Bible seemed even to me a bit tactless, but the Eucharist sermon fell more into the category of minor local news. And she would respond to my embroideries on the text: yes, Father Fleck was better than some vicars, he didn't harp on obedience and one's proper station as much, and perhaps she would go to hear him next week, if she found the energy. From time to time we paused and looked into one of the front gardens, to admire its arrangement of lawn and flowerbed or to assess what needed doing by way of maintenance or improvement.

So far, so good. But when we turned the next corner into Hurst Lane, her mood changed with the scene. Hurst Lane was a wider, busier street, and its houses were built in the older terraced style like the house within sight of the Thames where she had grown up. These terraces had been put up at the turn of the century for workers in market gardening and in the new chocolate factory; they were smaller and narrower than our semi-detached, and either fronted directly onto the pavement or had merely a couple of feet of token front garden. And they represented—although the subject was never plainly discussed by us—an alien way of life and a source of anxiety, of threat.

It was not possible to become friends with people from a terrace house. Ma knew some women who lived in the terraces, through the Labour Party, and she was no snob like Auntie Vee, but there was no visiting back and forth except on occasions of dire sickness or childbirth. Children on Agathon Way said there were no toilets in those houses, only sheds down the garden. Ma smacked us when we repeated this to her, and denied it hotly; then we went round the back alley behind one of the terraces, got a foot up on the wall and saw the sheds for ourselves. But that did not mean, Heather pointed out, that the sheds had toilets in them: we had our own shed, in which the lawnmower and bicycle were kept, didn't we?

"Yes, but ours isn't a *brick* shed—it's wood."

"Well, but why does that matter?"

I was embarrassed to have to explain. "Well, there are cracks between the boards. You can see through. You couldn't have a toilet in there."

"Anyway." Heather searched for a point with

which to finish off the argument, and found it. "Gran and Grandpa have their toilet outside."

And Grandpa had worked in a Works, like the terrace fathers who had local jobs in the tool factory whose siren marked the noon hour only, now the war was finished, or in the chocolate factory or its biscuit-making branch next door. But Gran and Grandpa were from another time and place, and had nothing to do with here. Our terrace families were rude, and rough: the children ate bags of chips, standing on the corner of the main road, and spat out their phlegm like their fathers in the morning outside school (we swallowed ours), and Henry Clay was still their Demon King when he was let home from reform school, ready to heave bricks at any stranger who was tempted to take a short cut through Blanmerle Road. Moreover, terrace children could read comics, which were absolutely forbidden to us; and they could roam at will after their evening tea, while we might leave the house only to go straight to the library and back.

The fathers from the semi-detached rows took the train to work and came home with the *Daily Telegraph* or *Evening Standard* tucked in a raincoat pocket, without ever calling at the Gardener's Arms on the way. Their monthly salaries were committed down to the last ten-shilling note for mortgage, rates, insurance, food, season-ticket and clothes. And their wives had stopped them at one child only, whether a boy or a girl ("I told him, I wasn't going to go through *that* again!"), or at most two—Ma had betrayed our closeness to working-class origins by having three pregnancies. The fact that she gave birth to twins the last time was regarded as a judgment on her: she should obviously have stopped at two, never mind if they were both girls. Half of the families on Agathon Way had cars, and sent their children to the private schools that were

105

housed in large Victorian villas on the hills towards Eltham and in former country houses a couple of miles farther out. But Dad's lack of progress on the bureaucratic ladder, together with Ma's fertility, kept us in the less advantaged half. How anxiously, through marginless budgeting and endless self-denial, Ma maintained our foothold in the hopeful class; and how much was at stake for her, as with uncontrollable haste she tore open the envelopes containing our reports!

Along Hurst Lane it all came back to her, how she and her sisters had set themselves against the life of the terraces, then and forever. It came back to her how the other children mocked and tormented her about the glasses she wore in order to read, at seven years old, and at school how the teachers criticized her worn-out uniforms, passed on from her older sisters, and punished her when, half-blinded and sickened by migraine attacks, she could not do her work properly.

"Sit up *straight*, Hilda. If you keep your spine good and straight, you will not suffer from headaches. Practice good posture and self-control; and to begin with, stay in at morning break and balance this dictionary on your head for fifteen minutes."

Later, there were teachers who recognized her talent for learning, and wanted her to stay on until matriculation, but then it was Grandpa who objected. One particular teacher came to the house to talk to him about it, but that was no use.

"He wouldn't have what he liked to call 'a bloody female' dictate to him. In those days, it was the father's word. And we were supposed to start paying him back for our upbringing as soon as possible; but your Gran insisted on the secretarial school for me. She wanted at least that. And he allowed it, because May and Bertha'd done well, with the certificate."

Gran helped her to sew the navy dresses with

their detachable white collars, for her first office job, and quietly allowed her to keep her first Christmas bonus to buy herself an evening outfit.

"It was a green voile—green and white, with a white slip underneath, and a little jacket over it, in emerald—no, more of a *dark* green—velvet. And I remember, I came downstairs wearing it, as I was going out with your father that evening, and Dad saw me from the kitchen. Well, and he got up and took a good look, and just laughed at me. 'All guyed up,' he said. 'Old clothes for the Guy! Little Miss Muck, aren't we?' I wished I could've sunk through the floor!"

She went out with our Dad for six years before they married; at first she was waiting until they had both saved enough to move away from the old neighbourhood, but later it was Dad who held back.

"I think now that if his Mum hadn't died he never would have got married. It was that, mainly—she had a stroke at Easter, went into the hospital and died six weeks later—and then the fact that another friend of ours was taking an interest in me. So we got married in October."

And then the story of her marriage unfolded, and I must brace myself time and again to receive the heavy mantle of this privilege—knowledge of the early quarrels over friends, then the quarrels over her working, and on and on to the catastrophe of my own beginning. But there was still more.

"I was carrying Colin and Brenda—it was wartime, of course, and he was being sent here and there, in the Army. And he came home on leave, with his laundry to do, and I was going through the pile of clothes turning out pockets, and here I find the photograph of this woman. Well, I had to ask him, of course. And he didn't deny anything. Didn't bother—anyway, there was writing on the back of the

107

photo. Imagine—there I was on a Monday morning, in the kitchen, with a pad of benzene in my hand, going over his suit for spots! I'll never forget that. And I waited till he'd had his breakfast before I tackled him about it. I offered to divorce him, you know. And d'you know what he said? Said it wasn't worth the trouble. Said he didn't think he was really cut out for marriage; might as well leave things as they were, unless I thought otherwise. So that was the end of that, me being pregnant and all you children to consider."

And now?

"If he'd only *talk* to me—if he'd only talk!"

But he was far off on the inland sea of his memories of India, waking in his mind in camp to unfamiliar birdsongs, the bulbul and the mynah, going to bed at night in the gloom of the jungle. He was gone.

"Anyway," she said, "as long as you children can get a good start in life—"

I hugged her arm, speechlessly. At the railway bridge we stopped as we had always done in the days when Ma brought the pram with the babies along here, in the hope of seeing a steam-engine go under with its dramatic white plume vanishing and then bursting forth on the other side. The wind along the cutting blew away any tears that had gathered in Ma's eyes (she was brave, and restrained herself so that they rarely fell). Then we continued up a slope which seemed to me, dragging the burden of a mind half-paralyzed by dread and pity, a summing-up of all hopeless, featureless obstacles. Not a single house in that stretch of Hurst Lane comes back in memory. And yet we invariably reached the crossroads at which we turned left, downhill towards the station and the shops; and passing the large red villas with doctors' offices on the ground floor our pace quickened and new subjects of conversation arose to distract us. There was an outbreak of measles in Blanmerle: thank heaven we were over with that particular stage; but the tobacconist's wife had gone into hospital to be operated on for a growth.

We turned left again at the traffic lights by the library, and passed the bus shelter where bored children were kicking a gong-like dissonance out of the metal uprights. As the circuit was completed, I realised each time how little could be seen from each point we had passed: except for the railway cutting, opening a narrow vista back and forth, there were no long, deep or wide views—nothing beyond the immediate row of houses, or the turn into the next row, the next thicket of small privacies. Rosedene. Glenoak. Alvera. There was no apparent way out of the sphere of personal life, replicated in all directions like an infinite mass of bubbles: there was no vantage point, nowhere else to stand, no way to *see.*

When I was fifteen I got a weekend paper route which took me a little further, up to Larch Avenue where the mock-Tudor houses were, set back among banks of rhododendrons. It was a mystery to me who lived in these places until Dad explained: "Stockbroker wallahs. And a couple of surgeons too: I've got their expense accounts on my desk this month. If they're as brilliant at the operating as they are at inventing expenses, they can cut me up any time."

It was winter when I began my route, and at first I noticed little more than my damp, chilblained hands numbly stuffing papers into the narrow letter boxes. I covered first the stockbrokers' row (they liked to get their papers early, according to the news agent who had a shrewd respect for rank), then a winding road of semi-detached houses, and a short side road of mixed semi-detached and bungalows: the full tour took an hour and a half, and I ran home from it bedraggled and red-nosed, anxious to begin the good pain of returning circulation in front of the coke grate in the kitchen. But as spring came on, and the matted clumps of perennials along the garden paths put out new shoots, it was the serial unfolding of these carefully plotted enclosures which drew my attention—not the large-scale shrubberies on Larch Avenue, but the front gardens of the semi-detached houses.

The elements making up these gardens were uniform, and included not only flowers and a lawn but a shrub or flowering tree in each front corner (ornamental broom, or cherry, or laburnum) and a row of rose bushes between them, and in addition some central feature to focus the whole—either a bird bath with aubretia at its foot, or a standard rose, or the intersection of two narrow paved paths. Yet the owners of each plot, if they gardened at all, contrived to do so with a difference. By June, it was as if each morning I entered a new set of treasure chambers, crowded like Egyptian tombs with the goods of a dozen church plant sales and a hundred swaps of cuttings over the back fence; those transactions were familiar to us from weekend afternoons.

"I hope you don't mind—brought you these little violet roots—they seed in everywhere, quite a nuisance, but a few of them'll fill up an odd corner."

"Well, that's awfully kind of you, Ruby. They *do* look healthy, don't they?"

"Oh, you can't kill 'em, no matter what you do."

"But as long as you're here, I've been dividing up my irises. Every four or five years something has to be done. And I've got several left over—mauves or yellows, can I offer you some?"

"Well now, I don't want you to think I came round begging, I mean violets are one thing."

"Well, it's a matter of what you can use, isn't it? I've got just the place for these little roots, you see."

110

For whatever Ma took, she was obliged to find room for in her planting, and so was everyone else. And the heavy soil, enriched by horse droppings from the baker's and greengrocer's carts and by compost laid down by the *avant-garde* among the growers, supported great densities of vegetation.

And one morning, there was one garden which as I approached it hung out a yellow climbing rose to me like the offering of the Communion cup: I touched it, and drank the drop it left on my finger, and then cautiously pressed the metal latch of the gate. The air was still, and grey with a dawn mist, but directly overhead the sky was turning blue, and the sun was rising in a whiter haze between the houses across the street. As soon as I got inside, I saw the orb web spun between the wrought-iron gate and the hollyhocks in the border next to the fence; it was heavy with water beads, and had sunk down with the opening of the gate into a lovely set of curves, like a blown veil. To the left of the path, thrum-eyed white and pink phlox flowered above blue pansies; further along delphinium clumps spired over an alternating border of pinks and lavender. Sprays of white rosettes arched outward from a bush under the windows of the bungalow, and along the far side of the miniature lawn, seeded with dew, was a row of glossy young dahlias, each accompanied by an inverted pot on a stake to catch earwigs; behind that was a violet-starred clematis along the fence.

To be first in this place, taking in the still scentless flowering moment, even before the owners had worked their way past the *Daily Express* headlines, was a mysterious gift, *gratis*. Not a curtain moved behind a window. For once, perfection showed itself incarnate.

I went back along the wet-frosted path, and carefully swung the gate with its dependent web closed.

That's what there was here: gardens. That was why Dad, even, who had no particular devotion to gardening, went out every summer evening, although exhausted by an eleven-hour day of account-books and travelling, to pull up a weed or two and spade the beds. The main point was to stand around in the mild, odorous drift of air from the neighbours' roses, and listen to the blackbird up on the chimney pot, singing first in one direction, then in another. It was the sanctuary between the house walls and the world outside the fence—between misery and blank necessity, a margin.

It was not possible to hold back: I asked Heather what confirmation—I meant Communion—was like, and she told me.

"Oh, nothing much to it, really. Don't get worried. The wine's all right, not the sour kind. But the bread's awful—not real bread—" she paused, and I thought *it's true, the miracle!* "more like a bit of white cardboard, only lighter. It seems to take ages to dissolve, and you aren't supposed to make a noise chewing it."

I heard the armhole seam of the white dress (which was to be passed on to me) tearing a few stitches as she pulled it impatiently over her shoulders. It was that sound, as much as her words, which made a small, penetrating wound in my heart of devotion and let in the conviction that my own Communion would be as null an event—a dry, awkward positioning of the hands, the lips, the tongue: a set of motions like any other. I could explain afterwards to myself that it was because I was not yet a Catholic, and that conversion would make all the difference. But under all the explanations I knew that Heather had the true Gospel, and her unredeemed, untransformable world the only world. And so it was.

In my turn I hung the white dress, washed and ironed, back in the wardrobe, and then went downstairs to get a dose of antacid mixture to calm the indignant burning in my stomach.

"Are you ill?" Ma asked, turning from the sink.

"Don't think so—just this awful pain, here." I pointed under my ribs, to the right.

"Is it your period?"

Not this time. And neither antacid nor aspirin had any curative effect, so that she could only put me to bed with a hot-water bottle after a while, until my body had digested its rage and utter disappointment.

I continued to take Communion however, once a month, because Father Fleck and the Deaconess and Ma and the whole family understood me to be a devout Christian, and rather than admit that I had made a mistake I would put up with my own hypocrisy and with the recurrent insurgencies of my stomach—at least until a decent interval of time had passed. And what else had I to live for, now? A pretence was better than nothing. Prayer, strangely, was still possible, in the mode of pure supplication endlessly repeated until the mind became tired and therefore calm. There are adolescents whose entire being seems focused into one message to the world, whether it is *I want to fuck!* or, *Care for me!* or, *Let me out!* And mine must have been an unutterable *Find me!*

Ma and I talked less, now: we had exhausted our respective subjects, and there was no way forward for either of us. Outside of school hours I became heavy and slow, sleepwalking about the house, taking so long over drying the dishes sometimes that she would become maddened and tear the towel out of my hand.

"Good—*God!* Was anyone ever so *slow*? You stand there like a half-wit—deaf, dumb, blind and stupid! Dreaming life away. What in the name of mercy is wrong with you?"

I couldn't say. Then a report card would come home, and she would be puzzled again.

"I give up! Heather works twice as hard as you seem to—you just dash through homework so you can stick your nose in a book for the rest of the evening—and yet you get marks like this. It doesn't seem fair. I sometimes wonder if they know what they're doing, the teachers."

Of course it wasn't fair—I could only shrug in agreement. Nor was it fair that Heather constructed a hopeless world for me to live in, and yet mysteriously evaded its conclusions herself: she who made it was not bound by it. And she had a future arranged for herself already, thanks to an alliance she had formed with the cooking teacher, Mrs. Akins. Alone among the teachers at Hurst Grammar, Mrs. Akins was married and had children; she only worked part time, but she confided to Heather that her earnings were fully three-quarters of a full-time teacher's, and any time she wanted to, she was qualified to go to work as a dietician and make twice as much again. Heather had already made out applications to the three best training colleges in the field. And now that she had grown to her full height, she even resembled Mrs. Akins to a remarkable degree—the same erect, columnar figure, the same glossy chestnut wave over the left temple, and the identical crispness of gesture which inspired unthinking respect. They knew exactly what they were doing; they were in control.

When a conference night was held at the school, Ma and I went together to discuss the problem of my future, since Heather was settled. For the occasion she put on the pearl clip earrings which hurt her earlobes, an emerald plush beret and her best coat in brown

115

flecked tweed, passed on from Auntie May. On the bus, as it cranked spasmodically up the hill to the High Street, she asked me if I had any ideas. I had none. But I knew what the girls in my class thought they would do: one was going to be a gym teacher, several were going to be nurses, and the rest would be secretaries, except for Jillian Poore, whose mother had told her she would go to college and think about a job later.

"I could take a secretarial course."

Ma's expression was pleased, but doubtful: she knew, after all, what the job entailed. "Good secretaries are always in demand. But I wonder if you'd be quick enough at it? It's all very well to be clever, but you've got to be efficient. Organized."

In the main assembly hall we came quickly face to face with Miss Bisley, who was prepared for us.

"Good evening, Irene. I was hoping you would introduce me to your mother."

They made a sad contrast, the two of them conversing: Bisley rocking back and forth in rhythm with the pronouncements issued vaguely downward from her gaunt height, just as she did in the classroom where no one had the nerve to think the mannerism odd; Ma bobbing six inches below, fingering an earring from time to time, uttering a half-sentence here and there in the pauses, helpless as an unshelled crab outside the carapace of home. The sheer awkwardness of the pair of them made it difficult to concentrate on what was being said—dronings about "opportunity" from Bisley, and small protests of "if possible" from Ma—until the interview slowed to its conclusion.

"I do appreciate your coming tonight," said Bisley, "and the sacrifices parents like you make for their children. Obviously a third year in the Sixth might be necessary for Irene, but the chance at Oxford or Cambridge is surely a worthwhile cause. Isn't it?"

116

She bent her head towards each of us with dignity and firmness, shook Ma's hand, and ended the audience. We were halfway down the drive before we dared speak to one another.

"Well, I suppose that's that," Ma said.

"I'm not staying for a third year. I'd be nineteen."

"She says you might have to."

"Well, I'm not going to."

She took my arm, and pressed it in appreciation. "We'll see, anyhow. You'll apply next year, since they're so set on it, and see what happens."

At home, she took off her hat and her earrings, and opened the kitchen door. Dad was busy resoling a shoe, with his cobbler's tools scattered over the table, and there was a radio play on in the background.

"Seems they've made up their minds about this one," she said, and picked up the kettle off the stove for refilling. "They want her to go to Oxford. Or Cambridge!"

I waited in the doorway, listening for his response, but heard only the rush of water into the kettle.

"You might say something, once in a while!" Ma faced him, after turning on the stove, and he removed a tack from between his lips.

"Well," he said. "We'll see, won't we?"

All right, but if Bisley wanted anything of me, she should have it: I had stores of devotion to offer and an infinite receptiveness to be put to her uses. Whatever she told me to learn, I would learn. I gave myself to her direction, and although I would not say I loved her—a gawky spinster with stiff hanks of grey hair welded into a bun—still I loved her.

Jill Poore and I, since we were both designated as candidates for university, became friends, and our first enterprise together was the imagining of Miss Bisley's

117

private life; she lived only a mile away from the Poores and shared a flat with Miss Halloran. Perhaps, though we did not overtly entertain the thought, Jill and I would be the next-generation Bisley and Halloran—and what would it be like?

"On Saturdays they go shopping for those hats of Halloran's. 'Darling,' she says, 'that one's you all over. The pheasant wing.' "

"Halloran makes the coffee, I know that. She was talking about it inside the staff-room door when I was waiting. The smoke in there!"

"I know. I bet Bisley's useless in the kitchen. So Halloran cooks up the coq au vin, and she does the vacuuming."

"Or just lies on the sofa in a brocade dressing-gown. 'Pat, darling, sling me another cup, would you?' Waves her hand, flings ashes all over herself as usual."

"Halloran reads detective stories: she told the History class."

"This is Bisley: 'Oh Pat, how can you stand such futile trash? Here's this marvellous article on the letters of Keats—it thrilled me to the marrow!' "

" 'I'll thrill you to the marrow, Mary darling!' Kiss kiss."

" 'Not in the daytime, dear, the neighbours might twig something,' she says."

" 'Oh, twig away, you've roused me past the point of bearation.' "

"*Bearation?* 'Oh, Patty-Pat!' "

Jill had been at a boarding school—"a sort of free-thinking one, like Dartington only not so famous"—for three years until her parents decided they couldn't afford it, and at her suggestion we wrote an underground newsletter in which Hurst Grammar was reinvented as the boarding school of pornographic

118

tradition. Teachers came by night to their favourite pupils' beds, ostensibly to place a cool hand on a fevered head, but in reality to send the fever higher. In my contribution to the final issue, Bisley came to the prefects' dorm when all were asleep except our heroine, Christabel. Bisley's hot-water bottle had, she said, sprung a leak, and there were no dry sheets—matron had locked the laundry room and gone for the weekend. Fortunate emergency! The girl trembled at the fulfilment of her secret dream: that aquiline profile outlined against the moonlight, and the full bosom swaying forward under thin muslin folds.

"You are trembling, child!"

Indeed. And with a spontaneous meeting of hands, then of lips, came fade-out. For what *did* women do together, when they weren't just playing husbands and wives?

The newsletter stopped abruptly once we recognized that we were really and profoundly in love with the French teacher, Blaustein. She had been hired by the school, young and with first-rate credentials, to ensure that we would be adequately prepared for scholarship level, and it was the perfection of her French which moved us first of all. Later, her mere appearance at the turn of a corridor could set all the classical symptoms going.

"Irene, you've gone *white!*" Jill commented enviously, the first time it happened. Then came the sense of faintness, the racing pulse, the tremors and blushes—we compared notes and found them all, even the inability to eat. Once, Blaustein to her own embarrassment was obliged to keep me in after lunch for failing to eat while she was on lunch duty; torn between shame and delirious joy, I explained to her that I had a nervous stomach which caused me difficulties, and that other teachers—seeing that I was a sixth-former—preferred to overlook the problem. With adorable seriousness she told me that she must uphold the rules, as a new teacher; but the next time she was on lunch duty she kept her dark head bent closely to the pages of the *Guardian* as the line went by.

Blaustein was a former refugee from Germany, the sole survivor of her family; brought to England during the war, she was taken in and adopted by two philanthropic women from the Lake District, and given an upbringing which I imagined as an intellectualized version of Wordsworth's Lucy's. Her skin, thick and pale and foreign, had been refined by seasons of cold northern rain showers and was tinged in the mornings with a faint lavender-rose. Her full lips, parted over almond-shaped teeth, spoke a tranquil and rational English. Winter afternoons of hockey and spring sets of tennis had developed her long legs and straight shoulders, and when she turned back the cuffs of her blue checked blouse in warm weather, smooth-muscled forearms showed only the faintest dark shadow.

She was of course Jewish, but what did that mean? Jews were so rare in our suburb that I could form no idea of the category which they might constitute. We had Mr. Hirsch the tailor, and his daughter, and they were small, meagre people with not the least resemblance to the superb Blaustein. There was no route to understanding that way. I could only come back, with an inward sob of obliterative longing, to the thought of Blaustein turning back her cuffs, or Blaustein raising her sea-grey eyes from *Britannicus* in a pause for questions which fled from my mind in the moment of contact. Like Ma, she was severely myopic, and sometimes she would lift her heavy glasses from the bridge of her nose as if the weight of them bothered her. If one could ever gain the right to do that service for her!

Mary Lou, whose father did secret work for the government and whose uniform was altered by Mr. Hirsch to fit her slim figure more precisely, looked out of the classroom window one morning at Blaustein arriving on her bicycle, and said: "Blaustein has negro hair, did you ever notice? It's in the Bible, you know—Jews and negroes are related."

I also was gazing out of the window, but her remark broke my concentration. "What's that supposed to mean?"

"Well, they're the kinky people, the wogs."

"You're disgusting. Why do people like you kink their hair up with perms, anyway?"

"It's wavy, it isn't kinky—that's the difference."

I pulled out a strand of my own hair. "Mine's kinky, if it comes to that. So I'm a wog too, aren't I?"

Mary Lou was, above all, conscious of her ladylike upbringing, and the need to avoid sinking to the level of the rougher elements at Hurst Grammar—but she couldn't resist the temptation to answer. "Well, like calls to like. There's got to be a reason why you're stuck on her."

She flushed up at her own daring, and started to back away as I moved in.

"Mary Lou—" I reached out and grabbed the shoulder of her tunic—"I'm a Communist, and I hate your guts! You'll be strung up when the revolution comes. And I'm a Lesbian woman, too, and I'll make love to you first. Think I'll start now—"

She twisted out of my hands with a loud squeak, and went scrambling across the desks in an amazing display of panic, her legs flying like a hurdler's. Jill and the others in the room fell about with laughter.

"I'm coming after you!" Another shriek from Mary Lou, who had reached her desk by the far wall, but now started for the classroom door.

"That's enough," Jill held me back, and the bell rang and Bisley appeared in the doorway.

In the spring of that year there was a total eclipse of the sun; it occurred in the late morning, and a special recess was called. The older classes milled about in the area in front of the school building to watch. As a brownish shadow overspread the scene, teachers passed among the groups hushing them so that we might all hear the sparrows and starlings stop their chirping: thus birds and children alike observed the ritual of a false dusk. The gloom deepened; many looked up through handmade devices and cellophane at the blackened spot in the sky, while we who were not in sixth-form science stood in front of the French doors to the staff room and hoped our goddesses would come past us on their way in afterwards.

And now the brown twilight began to lift, and Blaustein, wearing a shirtdress printed in pink and white stripes, came down from the tennis courts and found me in her path. People were still looking about them as if the eclipse had brought to birth a changed world. In just this way, Blaustein paused and glanced at the tree in the front courtyard, and remarked at large: "I wonder what kind of tree that is?"

It was a question I was ready to answer, *designed* to answer.

"It's a weeping ash, Miss Blaustein."

"Yet it doesn't look like the ash trees I know."

"But you can tell by the leaflets, and the leaf scars, and the buds in spring. 'As black as ash buds in March,' only as it says in *Cranford*, they aren't quite black. It's a hybrid."

She went close to the tree and lifted a small branch to look, upon which I reached out my hand, pointing to a leaf scar, and in withdrawing it, brushed against her fingers.

122

"A weeping ash," she repeated, smiling calmly as if to herself. "Thank you for that information."

The eclipse was over; the sun was high and round in the sky again, and Blaustein went indoors.

"You lucky bitch, you," said Jill. "I saw."

"Aren't I?"

In my last year at Hurst Grammar it happened to be Blaustein who put her head into the Upper-Sixth classroom after lunch one day and called my name. A few of us were lounging about the tables with our green and silver ties loosened and our feet propped at angles on chairs and ledges.

"Irene?"

I started up. The blood drained from my face, and I lurched clumsily between the scattered chairs towards the door. Blaustein retreated into the corridor.

"Calm down—heavens, it isn't an emergency!"

She pulled the door closed behind us and stood in the dim corridor so near to me that the aura of her electric hair prickled my skin. When she began to speak, looking down from an elevation of merely two inches, I trembled and burned. I met her unbearable eyes for one moment only; it was easier to look down at the floor, feeling across my face the current of warm talcum-smelling air from her body.

"Well, Irene, you've been accepted," she said, in a tone of excitement that surprised me—why did people take such an interest in this business? "Congratulations! Your mother telephoned a few minutes ago. Of course she opened the letter, since it was from Oxford, and it's an acceptance."

I leaned against the wall, blessing Oxford with all my heart for this moment of her full attention.

"I suppose it's really too hard to take the news in, all at once?"

"Yes. . . ."

123

Blaustein laughed; then she took me by the arms and gently shook me for a moment.

"Wonderful news, Irene."

Nobody ever rolled such beautiful r's through my name: a cross between the European and English varieties, inimitable. And she walked away to the stairs, and before I went into the room again I kissed the places where her hands had been, on the sleeves of my dark green pullover. The right side and the left side.

"What was it then?"

"You're blushing, you know."

I stood over them, and sighed. "Yes, well she grabbed hold of me."

"*What?*"

"It'll never happen again; it was because they heard I got in. You know, at Oxford."

In the silence around the classroom following this statement I had my first revelation of the change which Bisley had in a few words precipitated on my life: "We haven't finished with her yet." That silence had a tremor in it of mistrust, and an invisible gesture of withdrawal.

At home, Ma was in the garden; it was late November and even the sunshine was chilly, but she was slashing the last dead-heads off the chrysanthemums.

"You could've come home, y'know! I thought you'd come as soon as they let you know—they'd have let you out."

"Well they never said I could. They just told me the letter came; they didn't say I could come home."

A resentful silence. Rustling and snapping as her knife broke the stems.

"Go on in, then. Don't just stand there—the letter's on the hall stand."

124

She'd wanted that first reaction, the first celebration, and she'd given it away in her haste, to the teachers. But the truth of it was that the letter should have been for her, in the first place; for her with her lifelong hunger for insight, her endless longings. It *should* have been for her.

The Watkins parents gave a party at Christmas for the young people of Agathon Way. It was the first time such an event had been held at their house; they were quiet people in what was anyway an extremely quiet neighbourhood. They were worried, Ma said, about their son's lack of a social life; he was in his first year at Imperial College, doing chemistry, and he had never taken a girl out, ever. Heather and I both went to the party. She was back from Loughborough for a few weeks, where she was taking her dietician's course; and Marion came, who was taking something to do with fashion at Goldsmith's College. The two of them, with their Toni perms kept beautifully in shape by nightly pincurling, were confident of dominating the scene. On arrival they at once attached to themselves their only potential rival, Suzanne the rich girl, new in the neighbourhood, who rode her horse up the street every Saturday (it was stabled a mile away, in Sidcup) and rode it back again. When the horse left a pile of manure in the road, Suzanne blushed with annoyance, but gardeners on each side would run out after she had passed and quarrel over their rights to a share of the precious stuff.

They took their seats in the bay window, to survey the room. Heather and Marion wore taffeta skirts with wide belts: both had made a point of losing weight as soon as they started college, and had achieved waists of under twenty-four inches. Marion also wore a V-necked pullover with a marcasite brooch and matching earrings ("The plum colour's too old-looking for her: it was a mistake," Heather commented to me cut of her hearing). It was agreed later that Suzanne's blue draped chiffon dress was the most expensive in the room, but not quite appropriate to the occasion ("I can imagine wearing it at Covent Garden, for instance, in the circle seats," said Marion). That view had to console me for my personal catastrophe: having worked for two weeks at the post office delivering Christmas mail, I had earned myself the margin of four pounds to buy a pair of silver sandals and a pale blue nylon dress with accordion pleats in the skirt; at the time, I had thought the combination beautifully brought off, but Suzanne wore dyed-to-match slippers with her dress, and the dress itself hung softly and vertically where mine was stiff and stuck out awkwardly when I sat down. There was, in short, an inevitable and damning comparison between us, and as a result I clearly could not sit with the group. I ended up on the far side of the piano, next to Barry, a cheerful boy whom I remembered for having punched me in the stomach on the way to school years before, apparently out of sheer good humour with life. On my other side were the Brand girls, in white blouses and contrasting moiré skirts (no doubt about it, Heather and Marion had got it right), and plain court shoes with medium heels.

I sat quite still and upright with my shoulders braced, so that the pink cotton straps of my bra (a detested garment passed on by the family of a Labour Party member who died of a stroke the previous year; Ma had thought I might "grow into it") would not show. And Mrs. Watkins took the opportunity of complimenting me on my posture.

"Lovely to see, when most young girls go slouching about, *I* think!"

Now the rest of the boys arrived, in a group for safety: an assortment of David Watkins' old schoolfriends, and with them Marion's boyfriend, a handsome rugby player doing a third year in the sixth form at Mottingham and waiting to hear from Cambridge. Heather's view was that nobody else at the party would be worth bothering about; but then she was already half-engaged herself to a Midlands boy whose photograph she carried in her handbag.

David did a few conjuring tricks to start off, and demonstrated his new gramophone. Then we played charades and paper-passing games until refreshments were brought in at ten: Nescafé or cold orange squash, queen cakes and chocolate wholemeal biscuits. Valerie Brand and I talked about our French teachers at Hurst Grammar; she was going to the Institut Français after her A-level exams to do a bilingual secretarial course, and we went on to that.

"You'll be able to go and live in Paris," I told her, regretting again Bisley's disposition of my case.

"I don't know about that. I expect I'll be living at home for a few years."

I smoothed the outer edge of my eyelids where Heather had applied blue shadow: was the effect too pronounced?

Barry had now vacated the chair on my left, and a boy I had done one of the charades with came over to sit there. He had a face slightly roughened by old acne scars, and short, wavy black hair parted on the side. And as he crossed the room I saw Heather's head swivel round, which meant he was an interesting prospect. We had been introduced before, but he asked my name again, and I explained too that I was Heather's sister. He knew Heather, he said; she had gone out for a time with a friend of his—Colin.

"Yes," I said. "I remember Colin."

"They had quite a thing about each other."

I did remember. Colin had joined a Christian

group which started fervent prayer meetings in private houses. It hadn't taken with Heather. And he had told me to stop reading *Gone With the Wind*, one day while visiting.

"She's informally engaged." I told him, "to someone she met at college last term."

"So I heard. Colin's got in at London, by the way. I didn't—I may go to Bristol, though."

"Are you at Mottingham?" I asked.

"Yes—third year. Where do you go?"

"Hurst Grammar."

He asked if I was taking A-levels; he was sorry for me, doing it the first time—you didn't know what to expect really, but then every year there were some changes. What would I do afterwards?

I mumbled the name of the college where I was going, as one might hesitantly repeat an offensive word on the demand of a teacher, and could do no more then but observe its drastic effect.

"Oh?" He was already getting to his feet. "One of the clever ones."

And was gone. I sat there for a few minutes, pretending I had noticed nothing, and Heather came over to me.

"What happened?"

"He asked me what I was doing next year, and I said."

"Poor you! But there you are then—one of the disadvantages, I suppose."

The conclusion was there to be drawn: my feet had apparently been set on the track which led in the end to the life of the Vees and Phyls, the Bisleys and Hallorans of this world, the affectionate sisterhood filling teapots, cocoa mugs and hot-water bottles for each other with harmless consolations. Had they in encouraging me sought their own replication, sterile as they were? I couldn't bear that thought—I knew I had never loved them—it was only Blaustein, a real woman, whom I had loved, never those frauds, those ghosts, those pretend people.

And now poetry itself was quickly wearing out its acceptability on Agathon Way. My subjects had been going downhill, it seemed. First, the scenes of nature had become ever bleaker in tone:

Teasels hiss in the wind,
Dry heads in autumn weather—

and when I got away from nature altogether the results seemed (at least to Ma) worse yet.

"Why do you want to write about a nasty subject like that? If you don't even *like* someone, why write about them?"

But my dislikes seemed to be all I knew for certain. And I could hardly write about what I thought were my likes, about Blaustein's quiet breasts shaded by the cardigan over her shoulders, or about the mauve undertone to her pallor on winter mornings. I must therefore face in the reverse direction, towards ragged characters smelling of piss who rode on the tops of buses, and women in Kardomahs who made fruity little eructations and dabbed their mouths. I wrote about hairy moles and the vomit outside public houses—what else?

It wasn't only the "nasty" poems that were held against me. In my last two years at home I grew from a thin wisp of a child under a cloud of hair to a hulking female three inches taller than Ma herself, and bloated by a diet of Nescafé made with milk and served with biscuits at all hours. She could not mistake it: I was a woman now, and the otherworldly authority that I once possessed for her as a child-artist vanished completely.

129

She might concede my cleverness ("Oh you can argue from here to the bus stop, I've heard you do it"), but no more than that. Ma *knew* that women were beasts of burden; there was no going against destiny. Bisley and the Head could push her into keeping me on at school—yes, and they laid it on thick about "talent," but she took everything they said with a grain of salt. The end of it would be the same: marriage, the process of being ground down to a dead-level existence. Or it would be Vee all over again, nerve problems, ulcers, migraines, a spinster's misery.

Even so, in February Miss Sutcliff, the new English teacher, straight out of Cambridge and Maria Grey training, laid before us one afternoon Eliot's *Journey of the Magi.* We read it aloud, and then sat at the table, six arrogant, clever girls, reading the poem over in silence and unable to construe. It was a terrible crisis for us and notably for me with my extra pretensions: I knew French, Latin and German, and never had I been faced with so daunting a text.

Sutcliff put a straight question about the meaning, in her tactless way (tactlessness was her great charm as a teacher). We looked sideways at each other under our eyelashes. I opened my mouth slightly, poised between bad alternatives, baffled. From word to word the language worked; indeed I saw its merit; and yet between the phrases a gulf opened.

"Well, Irene?" Sutcliff wore plain dark dresses in rotation, each accompanied by its own piece of silver jewelry; on this indigo one she wore her basilisk brooch, the crowned serpent. She sat now as she often did, in silence, stroking the downy length of her cheek with two fingers. The silence became portentous of my defeat.

"No," I said, "I don't understand it."

The quick smiles directed along the table caused

my face to heat up—they had their little revenge now, didn't they? But my relief at speaking the truth was as immense as my need to find out what Eliot was doing.

"The person who speaks is of course one of the Wise Men, looking back on the experience."

"I got the first part. It's what's going on in the second."

The words she used now were not in our vocabulary: *juxtaposition, cinematic.*

"Wait a minute—please—I didn't catch that." I didn't care if they thought me humiliated; I needed a few minutes of time and adjustment in my head to get the new lens working. And then—then perhaps only those who, like my beloved Blaustein, wear glasses can easily recapture the experience of watching an opaque blur transform into meaning on a white page.

After the class I took stock of my situation, and suffered from fear and bitter resentment on realizing how far behind I was in cultural terms. The writers who had been represented to me as modern were Rupert Brooke, De La Mare and Blunden. If (as I had no doubt) Eliot was indeed the man, then I was far worse than misinformed: I was utterly disoriented.

On Saturday I took my school prizes of the past five years—excepting only a Thesaurus—off the shelf and loaded them into a shopping bag. There were two copies of the works of Longfellow, a volume called *Georgian Verse* and a Browning. I sold them all at the second-hand shop on the Sidcup road.

"Afraid I can't give you much on Longfellow," the aproned man in the shop said, giving the books a slight push as he turned them over on the counter. "Not much call for Longfellow."

"I'm not surprised."

"Two copies, eh? Forgot they'd given you the first one?"

"I s'pose they had a surplus."

"They're in good condition though. Four bob apiece?"

"All right."

"You could take 'em elsewhere now—someone might give you more. Now these two are very nice: good bindings. Six and six, let's say, and seven bob? Best I can do."

"All right."

Some of the money would go on taking Jill to an early Bergman film at the flea pit in Lewisham; some was saved for birthday presents, and the rest I laid out on new books: *The Waste Land and Other Poems*, and *Fleurs du Mal*. Walking down the Charing Cross Road with these narrow paperbacks in my hand, I began to see that I lived in a specific time and place in the world, whose nature and context could actually be thought about. But I had little idea as yet of the strangeness of my predicament. It was after all Lucretius who had converted me the year before (in *nineteen-fifty-seven*) from a sentimental Christianity to something like a rationalist position. It was not Darwin, or Whitehead or Russell, for none of these formed part of our curriculum at Hurst Grammar; rather the Penguin version of *De Rerum Natura* instructed me in the first of all subjects, *what* I was.

A child of the blitz, I would walk into college out of a lost world—fifteen miles from central London and millennia out of date.

The State sent us a cheque for twenty-five pounds in August, as an advance to defray the costs of equipping me for the coming year. And from the college came a list of necessary items to be brought; these included to our astonishment an evening dress and a stole or cape.

"What *do* they expect you to be doing down there? I'd hardly've thought it was dances in the evening."

I leaned across her to look at the list again. So many things! "Just cross it out. I've got my blue dress anyway."

"Still, if they put it on the list, there must be a reason." Ma remembered her respect for authority. "That blue dress isn't really what you'd call an evening dress. Leave that till last, I'd say, and see what's left in the kitty. Some dresses come with stoles."

A midsummer sale was advertised in the *Telegraph* at Selfridge's. We took the list with us, and the cash, and caught the nine-fifty train. Under a heat haze our suburban station looked countrified, with swags of blossoming convolvulus invading the platform, patches of wild strawberries on the steep banks of the cutting, and bees humming low behind the benches. The train approached in an almost soundless rush; after halting it began to talk in a ticking voice to the electric rail. We got in, slammed the door to and smiled to each other. This was the high point of the summer—going to town to spend twenty quid all at once (we kept five in reserve). Ma carried her handbag with the money in an empty shopping bag: we hadn't brought cheese and tomato sandwiches with us to eat in the park as we usually did, because we intended to spend some of the State's money on lunch at a Lyons. The train pulled away past the recreation ground, then past what I had for years called the "gold flinks." Golf was an unknown concept to me, and I hadn't yet learned to read when Rosanna who lived near the place told me stories about the half-crowns that were to be found in the long grass next to the fairway, so I interpreted the name of the place in Rosanna's pronunciation as indicating the treasure that was to be found there—the "gold"—and "flinks" as a way of saying that the treasure was in metal coins which made that kind of noise when handled. Strangely, while I ignored the word "golf" on the sign board for years, I read one of my first words on the asphalt drive beneath it: BUGER, inscribed in chalk.

In our vicinity people didn't even get their curses spelled right.

Just this side of Lee station a screen of poplars on the right marked the end of Blaustein's road, where she lived on the ground floor at number two. I had biked all round that area and knew it by heart; and even though she had already gone away for the summer, back to the cool Lakes, my pulse rate rose when I felt her in my mind. Perhaps after college was over I would come back and meet her again as a friend and an equal. I might even come back to teach at the same school—but no, that wouldn't happen since Bisley had forbidden me to train as a teacher.

"Teaching and writing don't mix," she had declared, with an emphatic tap of her hand on the desk. "My considered advice to you is not to take up teaching."

In any case, Blaustein would surely be married and gone by that time. Past Hither Green we were finished with trees; the railway ran along the backsides of factories, across canals, through canyons of flats, until the bridge over the Thames took us into the arched terminal. We walked from there to Oxford Street, passing on the way Auntie Vee's special shoe shop where we stopped to look in the window.

"Thirty guineas for that one pair. Who'd spend that much?"

Ma gave me a sideways look. "Your auntie says they told her it was no wonder she couldn't get regular shoes to fit her—she has unusually narrow feet with high insteps. But she always liked the best of everything."

We passed Liberty's and didn't even think of going inside to look. Ma couldn't imagine outfacing the dragon-ladies who guarded the counters in such a place. And she knew—I didn't—that we looked every inch what we were, the respectable lower orders in person. We were among those who made a little effort, put a dab of powder here and a dab of lipstick there, who mended our nylons with little pulls of thread and wore unshaped blouses that pulled unevenly out of homemade skirts: we hit that particular unsatisfactory mark dead centre.

At Selfridge's, sale stuff was piled on rank after rank of tables. We clung hand in hand and pressed through to the towels, then to the lingerie. The list had specified three nightdresses. Why three, when two had always done me all right?

135

"Better be safe than sorry," Ma said. On our second round of the displays we found a stack of cotton flannelette nighties at five and eleven: an extraordinary price! Carefully we ventured out our hands and unfolded a pale yellow one from the top of the pile, and the reason for the price was clear. These were early imports from Czechoslovakia, cut on some crude industrial pattern; they weren't gathered anywhere, but rather cut in a broad trapezoidal shape with straight seams everywhere. Untrimmed, the slit neckline was finished with segments of white tape in front, and on each side of the slit a trio of red flowers had been stamped or stencilled. The effect was of a hopeless awkwardness—the garments looked, simply, Neanderthal. Ma sighed.

"What a pity they couldn't have brightened 'em up a little. Just a bit of ric-rac, even."

"What about the material, d'you think?"

Together we felt the stiffness of it between our fingers.

"It's thick enough—I imagine it'd last." Then, to give her credit, she hesitated. "These colours though—they aren't really attractive. I don't know."

It was I who pressed on, nailing myself to the bargain. "See, I've already got one good nightie. We could get a couple of these to make up the number. I mean, they're warm, and nobody's going to see them."

"No, I suppose not," she agreed, with an automatic readiness which finished me. "And it's two for the price of one, really, at that rate."

"A pink and a yellow."

We went on to C & A with almost twelve pounds still in hand, and bought a white net dress with daisy-embroidered shoulderstraps and more daisies scattered in the folds of the skirt.

"Most suitable for a young girl." The assistant

cheered us up with her approval, shaking out the full meshes of the skirt, folding them and bundling them rapidly into the carrier bag.

"My daughter," Ma responded, "is going to college in October." One moment, there, of expansive pride. And we gathered all the bags firmly in our hands and bore them away to the Corner House and sliced ham and salad for lunch.

At the beginning of September, on a rainy Friday afternoon, I changed buses at the Hurst Grammar School stop on the way to Jillian's house. Standing under the shelter holding together the edges of a tear in my plastic mackintosh, I looked at my watch and calculated that in two and a half hours Blaustein would come out of the door to the right of the ash tree and walk along the drive to this very bus stop. But there was only an echo of resonance in that thought. I was no longer Blaustein's business; if we met we could have nothing to say to each other of any interest. It would be no less than horrible to make pointless conversation: "I've been working in my father's office, Miss Blaustein. Filing and typing." Atrocity! Better to contemplate the rainy gusts and the leaves torn prematurely from the poplars on either side of the gate, and recite silently—

Gone is the bloom, and with the bloom go I!

Jillian did not come to my house; hers was quieter for one thing, since she was an only child, and the books there were more interesting. It was also a fact that her mother saw no advantage to Jillian in visiting Agathon Way, and particularly since it had been learned where I was going to college a certain bitterness on her side had been deepening. Why, she must have thought, does the child of a wretched little bookkeeper and his former typist wife get a State scholarship while the child

137

of cultured people, professors at the Polytechnic both of them, gets repeatedly passed over?

On this Friday I had been in Jillian's room, drinking cocoa and trying which of her cardigans could be worn backwards for just over an hour, when her mother came in with the pretext of needing to fit a dress she was making.

"Sorry to interrupt—" for she was a friendly mother, a good sort—"but this material is raw silk, and I absolutely can't afford to make mistakes with it. I'm going to need Jilly's full attention for quite a while, I'm afraid."

Jillian walked me to the gate, embarrassed, twisting her eyebrow between thumb and fingertip.

"She's obsessed with getting me all the right things for college." Jillian was going to Durham. "If you'd only get a phone put in we could talk more often."

"I suppose we can't afford it."

"Come *on,*" she said, irritated. "They can't be that dear. I mean *we're* not rich."

"Well, I don't think it's manageable. So, let me know what you think of *Cold Comfort Farm.*" As a recent admirer of *Gone to Earth* and *Precious Bane,* I had been gratefully bowled over by Stella Gibbons's parodic masterpiece.

"I will if I can. But we're going down to Faversham for a week, did I tell you?"

She had not, perhaps because last year I had been invited down with her to the family cottage.

"Well, but there's the end of September still, before you go off."

"Oh yes. Well, Marx forever."

"Workers' Unity."

Her use of our old salutation had an apologetic ring, but I thought she was getting quite reconciled to the idea of letting me go for good. There was no point in blaming anyone; if you did, there would be faults on both sides. Ma, like Jillian's mother, was not at all sorry to see the friendship in decline. She disliked Jillian's "cynical remarks" and her "bohemian" background, and blamed her for introducing me to the idea of Communism (the word itself was taboo in our Labour Party circles); had she known that I first heard the word Lesbian from Jillian's lips also, she would have forbidden her the house outright.

It was Jill, Ma thought, who was the cause of lamentable changes in my poetic style and led me into obscurity and the sordid side of things. She drew this conclusion after she heard about the one and only student poetry reading ever organized at Hurst Grammar, which Jill and I put on during the lunch hour in the gym, before an audience of seven people, including the three authors and Miss Sutcliff and—thank God!—Blaustein. Jillian had typed ten programmes on her father's typewriter:

"Railway Bridge".. I. Tanner

"Silver Birches" .... J. Waldegrave

"Oppression".. J. Poore

"A Sonnet"... J. Waldegrave

"New Cross at 3 a.m."... I. Tanner

The last item was a three-page rambling pastiche of Eliot, which Jill and I read together antiphonally; up to the very moment of its reading I had taken it with the utmost seriousness and pride, and only discovered in performance how hard it was to read with a straight face. After the moment of applause, we dared to look at Sutcliff—impassive as always, weighing us tacitly—and Blaustein, with her eternal smiling kindness. How had we done? Impossible to say.

Janet Waldegrave was satisfied with her part of

the reading. One year younger than us, she was Bisley's new candidate for university entrance; plump and fair and in excellent mental health apparently, she was happy in the knowledge that her poems were recognizably the real thing.

"About that last one," she asked, "was it supposed to be serious?"

"Well, yes actually," I admitted. "To begin with."

Jill picked up the cue. "Then again, something about the situation sort of—" And we broke down in laughter.

I should have had the decency to keep such things away from Ma, but I did not.

"But where's the *sense* in it?" she asked. "What's the point when people don't understand it?"

"Well I mean, *we* understand what we meant."

"And is that enough for you?"

I opened my mouth to reply, but the pain of exclusion that registered in her tone of voice silenced me. We said no more about it.

A few weeks before my departure Ma began to go to church regularly, and asked me to go with her, although it had been clear to everyone for the past year (I thought) that I had lost interest in God. To my dismay it appeared as if she was taking up the religious solution where I had so carelessly abandoned it.

"I'm surprised," she said when I expressed reluctance at getting up in time for the Communion service. "There was a time when you couldn't be kept away."

"I suppose my mind's been taken off it by other things."

"It's understandable, considering what a busy year you had." Suddenly Ma was forgiving everything, from plain laziness, as in this case, to the obvious inconsiderateness of going to bed late with my Nescafé

140

cup unwashed, or not getting the washing in when it rained.

Indeed I was terribly, blindly preoccupied with my hopes for the future to which the State had undertaken to raise me. I was to go through an unknown set of transformations and become, I believed, at the end of them a poet. And what was a poet? A tall man in brown corduroy; a smaller man in a fisherman's jersey; a man with an open shirt, walking in the hills or standing on the shore of Italy.

Ma's remark, often repeated, was entirely to the point: "For a clever child, you can be awfully stupid!"

III

13 Carlisle Avenue

Here is the turn. It's a street of red-brick houses with white porches, quite clean: that's a good sign. Am I positively to go down it, or does Singleton's face, if I call it to mind, mean anything to me—is there anything in it which would make a difference?

I stop and look back along the road to Kensington High Street; nobody is in sight. Here, then, is the face, which immediately thrusts forward with wide-open eyes, and I feel a jump, a slight recoil. It is a face made for public, not private exchanges—its strong musculature has been defined by the practice of strenuous argument—and vividly human and intelligent as it is, its tone is helplessly overbearing. And to my surprise there flickers through this face the face of the cripple whom he made put out that cigarette: I see one and then the other, the tanned full face and then the candle-wax profile alternating.

"Which would you rather have—a cigarette, or some recognition that you're a person, like anyone else?" That *was* a good point. Yes, but.

Anyway, he's probably pacing the floor at home this very minute, cursing himself: "God, why did I do it?

145

What if she takes me up on it—how will I get out of it?" No—sod him. Sod them all.

I walk rapidly down to number twenty-six and ring the doorbell. A small grey-haired woman with a fluffy cardigan over her dress opens the door. I ask for Nanda.

"Who?" It is soon clear she has no idea what's up. "I'm afraid I don't know anybody round here of that name. But what were you wanting exactly?"

That, I can't say. Back on the street I look in my pocket diary again. It is *impossible* that I should have made a mistake in copying the number. Linda must have got it wrong. But I have the telephone number still; I can go back to the High Street and find a box to call from.

I cross the road.

I am absolutely sure that Linda used this address. It's difficult to understand how she could put it down wrong, unless perhaps she wanted to keep it secret, and used a cover number instead of the real one. In that case, what would the real number be? Sixty-two would be the reverse of twenty-six. But this road doesn't look long enough for the numbers to go that high. Twenty-six is also twice thirteen. And thirteen is the bad-luck number; possibly that gave her another motive to avoid its use.

Thirteen is only a few yards further on: why not try it? Although the bad signs are piling up, I go in and ring the top doorbell at random. After a full minute's pause the door is opened by a women whom Heather would label right away as "bohemian": she wears a kerchief over long hair, a smock printed in tropical pink and turquoise, and Indian leggings underneath.

"Hallo. I'm looking for Nanda?"

"Right," she says happily, as if I'd just won a "Name This Woman" competition. I do feel rather proud. "Come upstairs and make yourself comfortable;

'Nurse' is going to be a bit late, I'm afraid."

She pronounces that title with a little space around it, leaving as it were room for doubts of its legitimacy—another bad sign. Of course she herself is not the abortionist; I see, once we go into the large room at the front of the house that she is a painter, for the walls are stacked with canvases and there is a great mess of paint rags, jars, spatulas and old brushes in the fireplace hearth. Near the window stands an easel holding the unfinished portrait of a nude woman. Nanda goes over to it.

"D'you want some tea, before I get back to this?"

"Oh thank you, no really."

"Absolutely sure?"

"Absolutely, thank you all the same."

I watch from the large broken-gutted sofa as Nanda takes up her brush and an encrusted palette. The nude figure, curiously, echoes the colours in her smock with its hectically flushed limbs outlined and shadowed in blue-green. Its thick legs are planted a little apart with a dash of bluish pubic hair between, and it sits on a chair beside a deep-green potted plant. The face is done in simplified planes, with smudges for eyes. Roger has a Modigliani print a bit like this; I suppose Nanda may be quite good. She is working on the floor section, doing it in a strong magenta colour; and now that I look past her and see the potted plants in the bay window and the brown floorboards under them, I guess that the picture's setting is actually this room. It is a moment of embarrassment, when the mismatch between the reality—clear sunlight playing through the maze of dracaena and philodendron leaves onto velvet-dusted boards—and its brutal death on the painted canvas must be faced and swallowed. One ought not to have to face the subject and the work of art at the same time: there is too much pain in the encounter.

But Nanda is brave. After twenty minutes of careful dabbing she steps back, considers, and lights up a cigarette while she considers some more. And then she turns to me and smiles.

"Getting on! D'you smoke, by the way?"

"No, thanks."

"I do like that shirt you've got on," she continues. "It goes well against that yellow. One doesn't often find a good blue, in clothes."

There I'd agree. "Yes—I don't know why it is. This one improved with washing."

"Sometimes on china you get a good blue."

The doorbell rings, and I'm up in an instant. Nanda goes down; there's a musical exchange of greetings, quickly lowered to a murmur, and she comes back with company.

"This is a friend of mine. Ardis, meet—what did you say your name was?"

"Irene. How d'you do?"

"Hallo dear! Poor thing, Nanda was explaining—"

"Hope you don't mind," Nanda breaks in quickly. "Ardis has been through it—well, we all have in our time."

"*God,* have I?" Ardis fluffs up her wild dark bubble curls with both hands, and turns her heavy, black-rimmed eyes on me. "My latest count is seventeen. But I still remember the first; that's the only one I cried over. Couldn't stop for days. And I kept it in a jar for ages—couldn't part with it. My boyfriend objected, but I wanted it in a jar. I expect this is your first, isn't it, by the look of you."

She sits down in the other corner of the sofa, angling her black-stockinged legs towards me, and I sit down too.

"Yes," I say, avoiding her stare. "And my last."

"Oh, we all say that. Next thing you know, a

148

good-looking fellow comes along, and reason flies out of the window. Mark my words. I'll give you a little tip, though."

"What's that?"

"Use a little sponge soaked in Dettol. A nurse told me about this. Cut off a piece of a regular sponge, see, and run a needle through it with some strong cotton. Tie the ends of the cotton so you've got a long loop to get hold of. Then you soak the sponge in Dettol, as I said, and tuck it up inside, right up in there. Next morning you can just pull it out by the cotton, rinse off, and there you are. Works like a charm, it really does."

"Really?"

"Absolutely! Except that the sponge is never there when you happen to meet the good-looking fellow, eh? Such is life."

Nanda has been putting away her brushes; now she sits down and looks at her watch. "Nurse is terribly late. Shall we have a glass of sherry—what do you think? It's after five."

"Oh yes, I think so." Ardis looks at me in a considering way.

"Thanks awfully," I say, "but I'm not sure I ought to."

However, Ardis is sure. "It doesn't matter. Take the edge off, if anything."

Nanda goes behind a curtained alcove at the back of the room and comes back with three little tumblers and a bottle of Dry Sack.

"Cheers to all." We drink to one another. Ardis takes a second swallow, and rests her glass on the sofa arm.

"I remember," she says, "in the war there was this woman. She used to do it by massage—she could *draw* it out of you. Amazing. I went to her twice. When her husband was demobbed he made her give it up, so that

149

was the end of that, or I'd still be having it that way."

"But how did she do it?" Nanda asks.

"She'd put you on a table—" Ardis's rough contralto voice quietens to a hoarse whisper—"and move her fingers in circles, not even terribly hard. And you'd feel this electricity in her fingers as she went on, and she'd press a bit more, and you'd get this strange feeling, and after about half an hour it would come out all by itself."

"Extraordinary."

"It was."

Nanda and Ardis are well into their second glass when the doorbell rings. Up the stairs comes a round little woman in a round felt hat; "Nurse" is carrying a substantial leather bag and is in a hurry for business.

"You'll be all right, you know—" Nanda sees me off kindly, with her head tilted on one side, as I follow the navy hat down the back corridor to the bathroom.

Nurse is so tiny that I tower over her in the narrow space of the bathroom. She takes off her hat and belted navy coat and hangs them on the hook, revealing a grey cotton uniform—so she really is a nurse. With her pure white hair springing from a pure pink scalp, and her round face with puffy pink lips and eyelids, she looks like some fairy-tale magic godmother, or like an old stuffed doll.

"Let's have those panties off." She speaks briskly, with a Scottish accent, rummaging in her bag on the floor. "Now. Get yourself sitting on the toilet—*well* forward, more, so I can examine."

The room is dark; dirty frosted glass fills the one narrow window; but Nurse does not seem to need the light on—with her rubber-gloved hand she proceeds by feel, crouching at the fork of my legs.

"The womb's gone right back. Must be over four months, surely—couldn't you come before?"

150

"I did try other things, before this."

"Never mind. Can't be helped now, can it?"

She turns on the hot tap in the basin, runs it for a while then puts in a red bar of soap and a good shake from a plain bottle. With one hand she froths the hot liquid, while with the other she fills a red rubber douche bag with an extra-long tube attached to it.

"Now, dearie, pull yourself forward again. I'm going to pass this up inside, and you let me know when it starts to hurt with a strong pain. Not before, though—you've to have a strong pain."

Of course there must be pain—I expected that, and then whatever it is will drop into the toilet bowl and be flushed away. Three, four minutes pass, while the hot stream floods into my belly and out again over my anus to cascade into the bowl; I pant with the strain and ache of the position, gripping the edges of the seat.

"It hurts!"

But Nurse is not satisfied. "A bit more, yet." She refills the bag and starts again, and this time there is pain from the start, intensifying until I cry out and squirm away from her hands—but I can't get away, and she goes on until I push in desperation at the bag.

"That'll do."

She lifts the apparatus into the basin, rinses it, shakes it and wraps it in a white cloth, while I still sit dripping and waiting for whatever else is to happen.

"Now." She turns to me at last. "Here's a sanitary towel to put in your panties. You go along home, and in about eight to twelve hours the pains will start; then nature will take its course."

"But—how long will that take?"

"It depends, at your stage. A few hours, then everything will come away. Nature takes its course."

I get up, dripping into the pad; and pull down the skirt of my dress which is luminous in the shadows.

Nurse is waiting for her money: I get it out for her.

"Thank you, dearie." And without a word more, she puts on her coat and hat and is off on her little trotters, tapping down the stairs.

I follow her, with a quick wave to Nanda, and walk out of the house with my head down. I feel sick and abused. So it is not over, this thing I dreaded. What I have just been through is merely the overture, and now the event itself is coming towards me with accumulated terror. I haven't understood anything. Eight hours!

Waiting on the Underground platform I feel renewed pains in my belly, and become dizzy so that I have to lean against the curved wall while one train comes and goes. I catch the next, and get to Paddington where I buy some orange squash and another sandwich. Perhaps I am faint from hunger. But although I can drink, the sandwich stays uneaten in my hand; I put it to my mouth, but my lips feel stunned, unable to function. Better to rewrap it in cellophane, and make sure of catching the Oxford train—I mustn't collapse here.

Almost nobody is on the platform for the seven-ten train. I walk to the mid-point and get into an empty compartment, but as I reach to shut the door I feel a sudden rush of liquid from me.

"Damn, damn!" I fall onto the seat: is this it, now? But nothing more follows. The train starts while I am still waiting; the jerk of it pushes me back, and I lie half propped in the corner of the seat, faint again and drifting out of consciousness.

The next thing I see is an apparition in the seat opposite—it is Auden, the Professor of Poetry himself, wearing thick tweeds and speaking in German.

"Ach, was ist's?" The voice echoes round in my head, sadly.

"Nothing," I say.

"Aber auf Deutsch!"

"Nein, ich versteh' nicht gut," I complain. I realise that I am lying sideways with my head on the armrest, but I simply cannot bring it upright. Things must be as they are.

"Aber doch," Auden continues, "mach' ein Bisschen Effort! Hölderlin is necessary, Rilke is necessary. These you must know."

"Must, must. *Wolle die Wandlung!*" I am trying.

"Not enough," he insists. "You must work by days, by years, *twice* as hard as we did. That's the rule."

"Und darüber, must one be queer to be a poet?" I surprise myself with the question: where does it come from? Yet he seems to take it evenly: there is no change in the corrugated landscape of his face.

"Wahrscheinlich it's of considerable help."

"Yes. But why?"

"Fidelity," he says. "Fidelity."

Then a different voice sounds from outside, calling: *Pangbourn.* I sit up, alone in the compartment. *Pangbourn.* It's more than three years since I first made this journey; then it was December, for the interview, and the fields by the river were flooded, I remember that. And the next time, I felt I was off on a wonderful skive, with State money in my pocket. Of course I didn't understand anything then, either.

IV

The College

That first term, at table or beside the mailboxes it was as if I carried about with me a barrier of distance across which no one could hope to speak. Or rather, recognized as a stray from the benthic social levels, I was myself a walking chasm to be avoided. But how did they know this about me? My clothes? Hardly: in such a stringently chosen group of intellectual women there were more eccentrics than myself—people dressed like railway porters except for their heavy German sandals, and people who wore the same checked shirt for ten days in a row. If I wore somewhat clumsy, home-knitted jumpers, and old school shoes, as I did, that could have been merely a statement of inattention. It was perhaps my voice, during some very early exchange unnoticed by me, that condemned me to future silence. That, yes, and also what I said.

"And where did you go to school?" This question comes back to me, always the second to be asked.

"Hurst Grammar. It's in South London."

The voice, carrying this information as well as its own message, must have been enough to place me outside the network which had St. Paul's, Cheltenham,

Perse and Westminster Tutors as its central core. I know I did not say " 'Urst Grammar"; I had had four months of elocution lessons with Miss Kershaw, after Ma caught me slipping into vulgarities when I was fourteen. But I did not use the fiercely aspirated "h," or the intonation which turned all utterances into commands; nor could I force an imitation.

After failing the first test, it would be up to me to recognize and claim any appropriate cues in order to enter a conversation. I listened, and listened more, but could never hear my cue. Only at the seminar table, where the task of translating from Latin or from Anglo-Saxon rotated through the class, did I find myself legitimate; and there, in a voice shaky from disuse, I read out my over-polished versions. And these were no better calculated to make me friends: the scholars observed me with a deprecating expression—these appalling grammar-school drudges!—and the weak students, dim daughters of well-known professors or admitted for their Bloomsbury lineage, looked hurt as though by some new revelation of the world's injustice.

At dinner I persisted in sitting with the group reading English. They had to understand that I had nowhere else to go—that I was driven to this business of hanging about in the downstairs hall and following them up the stairs in order to be sure of a seat at the right moment, not too early (to avoid being avoided) and not so late that I would be shut out. At least I had the decency to sit at the corner of the table, disrupting life as little as possible. And it was here that Caroline, one evening when she was late to dinner, found the last free seat at the table opposite me.

First she went up to the dais in her long gown and bowed to the principal, who acknowledged her with a smile; then she sat down, and sliding her eyes past me spoke to Henrietta.

"Lady Stiles kept me there *so long!* We got off onto Greek poetry—it was wonderful." She allowed the maid to put a bowl of soup in front of her, and continued: "I was almost tempted to change my mind and go over to classics."

"I knew you'd be the favourite," Henrietta said. "I could tell on the first day."

Caroline shrugged. "It isn't my fault, is it?"

I had already finished my soup—we ate fast, at home—and I watched her. Clearly it annoyed her, but I couldn't help watching. There had been no such Pre-Raphaelite faces in Hurst Grammar, with the massy fair hair growing low on the broad forehead, or with the generous orbital arches and extraordinary length of jaw.

"It's a shame, don't you think?" she said at large, "that they make us read Virgil instead of Homer. Latin as a language is so clumsy compared with Greek. And Homer is simply *better.*"

I realised that she had actually given me an opening. "But I suppose there wouldn't be time for people who hadn't had Greek before to catch up."

"Oh well. Those people could have a different class, then."

"I agree," said Henrietta. "Those of us who have learned Greek ought to have a chance to go on with it. It's certainly *the* most beautiful language."

"Isn't it? *Much* harder than Latin, of course."

"In what way," I heard myself asking, and couldn't stop in time, "is it harder?"

Caroline's eyes, in their majestic sockets, were oddly narrow; now they crinkled up even smaller. "Well, one can't really explain to someone who hasn't had the actual experience."

I helped myself from the bowl of floury potatoes, passed it on to her and began on my plate of braised beef: food came first. My left hand, indeed, suffered a

159

tremor; at some level I felt thrown back into the savage country of childhood, faced again with the rule of Heather the merciless. All that I had learned in the middle years, the tight code of politeness which was to be the basis for all advancement, and the daily practice of small avoidances and concessions in a small house run by quietly desperate parents, was now put into question. Unlearn, and defend yourself! Only, when I took an inventory of the weapons I had used before—my patience, self-concealment, and gift for intimacy to practice on Ma—I knew their inadequacy.

There was for instance absolutely no chance of my getting close to the tutors we were assigned. One was the daughter of a viscount, a second the daughter of a bishop (who was the second son in a ducal family): they might at most have a grain of compassion to offer me, but I had already taken in their instinctive pulling-back withdrawal from the raw odours of my social displacement. No intimacy, then—besides, Caroline was ahead of all of us there. And patience? That could be a temporary expedient only, for one Heather was enough. There remained work, and poetry.

In work, it would take me two of the three years to catch up with the competition. It was not the aristocrats in the group, or the very rich who were the threat to me there—for them a seven-day working week, nine hours a day at the books, was an impossibility, given the stream of invitations and the cars waiting outside on Saturday morning to take them to house parties—but the products of the professional upper-middle class, intellectuals by inheritance and superbly educated. They had Greek; I would never have Greek; the eleventh edition of the *Encyclopedia Britannica* was encoded in their lives, not in mine. Above all, they had company, whereas the four scholarship women in the English group were perfectly unable to come together for mutual aid of any kind.

It was as if we had been sent here from our widely scattered grammar schools—from Crawley New Town, from Luton, from Bexley—like advance scouts from armies quite unknown to each other, and then abandoned in foreign territory. The idea that we came from solid, close-knit communities was terribly false: every one of us took the train out of an accidental sowing of escapees from the true working class. Our parents were the generation in the wilderness, huddling to themselves in frustration and disappointment. Perhaps, when a son of such a family left as we did, the mother's blessing went with the move; but when a daughter broke the ties of shared hopelessness, it was a capital violation, and all loyalty was forfeited. We were gone—they were done with us.

I met Shirley as a result of the only invitation we received during the first term: it was from the Puseyite Christian group, to a cocoa and prayer evening. The prayers came first; Jennifer, the leader of the group, wanted to become a missionary in Africa, so the main appeal to God was to exert his influence on both races in Kenya to bring an end to Mau Mau violence and the answering repressions. I observed the bent heads, and recognized Shirley's as that of a resident in my building: I thought, as I had thought before, that she must be peroxiding her hair. Afterwards we were encouraged to attend services in Pusey House, then we had cocoa and signed petitions. Shirley and I walked back together.

"What is this Pusey House?" I asked.

"You must have passed it," she said. "It's on St. Giles, on the right. I think it's supposed to be very High Church."

"Lots of incense? I might go."

"I think I might try it too."

There was a great deal of incense, clouding the

high Victorian gothic vault of the chapel, and the service with its meticulous ritualism reminded me sweetly of old fantasies. My Virgin of Lourdes would not be so out of place here. On the way back, I hummed the tune of the Athanasian creed under my breath.

"Are you a Christian?" Shirley asked.

"Oh, well. I suppose not in the full sense." I looked sideways at her; her darkly pencilled eyebrows rose under the blonde fringe, and we broke into laughter.

"Shut up," she said, "Jennifer's behind us."

"Are you?"

"I take an aesthetic interest."

"That seems reasonable," I agreed.

"I almost went to art college, but my school wouldn't let me turn this down. Pusey House is a nice example of its own architectural style."

Should I admit that I took it for the real medieval thing before I read the dated plaque on the outside wall? No: better play the game as it was played.

"Where did you go to school?"

"Bognor. Did you know that the dying words of King George the Fifth were on the subject of Bognor?"

"No—what did he say?"

"He said: 'Bugger Bognor.' *Very* appropriate."

"That's marvellous. We had an annual Labour Party charabanc outing to Bognor."

"Did you? Awful, I bet."

"Well, it did rain, more than the usual shower here and there which you expect. We sat under the pier. It was just dripping, there."

"Did you sing the *Red Flag* to keep your spirits up?"

"No—we aren't political on the annual outing. As a matter of fact, we generally aren't, probably because we haven't had a ghost of a chance at the elections since I can remember."

"Same here."

"Still, I remember one good thing about Bognor. My mother got completely fed up by about three in the afternoon, and we went to a fish and chip café on the front. Plaice, chips and peas—it was a bang-up tea. Then it was still pouring outside, so we went back under the pier till the bus went."

"I should say you got a representative view."

Shirley was reading French. As she explained it, this was because her father left his wife and small child early in the war and never came back; later, her mother acquired a boyfriend who was with the Free French, and even after the war was over he would come back from time to time and refresh their acquaintance with the French language and culture. Her mother worked in the local library, and rented rooms mostly in the summer. After some years, the boyfriend stopped visiting, but he sent over occasional French renters for the rooms; one of these was his eighteen-year-old nephew, who during Shirley's next-to-last summer at home taught her how to make love and took her to the films twice a week.

"The turning point in my life," she called it—not so much the sexual side of the experience, precisely, but something else. "The French have an idea of *style*; I think that's the only word for it. He got me to have my hair cut short, and blond it. And he told me how the girls dressed in France—tight belts over their jumpers, and very full skirts. Mum was dreadfully upset. She got him out of the house with two days' notice. Then I went back to school, and the headmistress said I was immoral; but they had to back me up for the scholarship because there wasn't anybody else ready for it in my year."

She wore deep red lipstick, pancake make-up and

mascara, and over and above that, eye shadow and rouge even in the daytime. The names on the containers, which she left strewn casually along the mantelpiece in her room, were Max Factor, Helena Rubenstein, Lancôme; as far as I knew, even Heather had only progressed from Woolworth's best as far as Max Factor, and our local chemist's didn't even stock these other kinds.

By the end of the term I was fully equipped, although bright lipsticks made my lips peel so that I had been forced to go back to Woolworth's "Natural"; and when I arrived home, turned the corner of the path by the coal bins and found Ma in the very act of scooping up kitchen dirt in the dustpan, my cheeks were "Rose Glow" and my eyelids layered "Sea-Green" over "Azure."

I saw the shape of her face change, before she found the words she was looking for.

"You—Jezebel!" That was a new word, on her lips; I thought by this time I knew her repertoire entirely—*you look like the wreck of the Hesperus, a dying duck in a thunderstorm, a drowned rat.* Grandpa must be the source.

She pushed past me in the doorway to go and empty the dustpan in the bin. I looked in the mirror over the sink while she was gone: what was she on about? It seemed to me that I had been discreet with the stuff. Think of Shirley.

Here she came again, dropping the dustpan noisily in its place beside the dresser. "Is that what you spent your grant money on? You'd better get upstairs and wash it off before Dad comes in—you look like a slut."

I made a movement towards her.

"No—don't kiss me until you've got some of it off. I don't want it on me."

I took my suitcase upstairs, and unpacked the

164

Pond's cold cream. Didn't she know you weren't supposed to *wash* it off? That was what the prefects at Hurst Grammar did with girls who came to school wearing obvious make-up: it was a punishment, not a technique. You would see them sticking the offenders' faces in the wash basins. I studied myself again, in the dressing-table mirror, and thought it must be the cheeks she was objecting to: all right, but I was going to keep the eyes. Toned down if necessary, but I wasn't going to disappear completely just to please her. Heather would understand. And as for Dad noticing anything, it seemed to me that she had another think coming, there.

That vacation I read Elizabethan sonnet sequences, and thought about changing my name to Renée with an accent. I practiced signatures on scraps of paper: Renée Tanner. It was an important decision, because as soon as next term began I intended to send some poems in to the undergraduate magazines. Meanwhile, at night I found myself walking in my sleep; I would wake up at the edge of the stairs, trying to remember the compelling purpose which brought me there and contacting only a vague sense of urgency; or I would find myself at a window with my hand on the cold iron catch, ready to open it, caught and held in a liminal moment.

Although the bishop's daughter was keeping us away from Donne (we would not be offered the Metaphysical poets until our third year), I came back for the second term convinced, as a poet, of the necessity of initiation into love. One way or another I must have it. Shirley, on a drab sofa in drab Bognor, had received it, and she was not even a poet (but talented in drawing, I granted). And the matter was urgent—on Boxing Day I had gone to see Auntie Vee, and been welcomed as a recruit already halfway inducted into the profession of teacher-celibate; something must be done to break from the track.

What was to be done? Scholarship women had no social network to explore, and the men at Oxford were said to prefer Radcliffe nurses and secretarial-school students—they felt threatened, we heard, by the college women. But after a Pusey House coffee, a theology student invited me to see *On the Waterfront* with him. Here was a beginning, then, and I had no need to take a closer look: I accepted. In the gloom, as soon as the white image of Eva Marie Saint appeared on the screen, he took hold of my hand and drew it to his side

166

of the arm rest where he began to press and knead it. Then by degrees he moved up to my wrist, my forearm, kneading and squeezing each segment with increasing force. I had glanced at his fingers earlier—of even length and spatulate in shape, and the oddest part of an otherwise palely conventional appearance. The intensity of their clenching massage troubled me even before it reached the point of causing pain. But when to say something, to interrupt? For Brando on the screen was the image of the precious beast who must be allowed, must be loved generously, in order that he might become human. It was worth *some* suffering.

Yet it was pain, now, enough to make me grit my teeth in the effort to keep still. How much pain could be properly demanded of a woman?—that was the difficult question. In the end, I said faintly: "Ouch."

He dropped the arm at once, and made no further movement, staring straight ahead at the screen. Well, that clearly was that.

Shirley looked at my bared arm under the light in the kitchenette, when the reddish prints were turning purple.

"Christ! What's the matter with him?"

"I don't know. He didn't talk, really. But he comes from Wales, said he was lonely here."

"Not much of an excuse. I mean, we're all from somewhere else."

"Unless Wales is worse than other places. Or better? Well. I'm not sure I'll go to Pusey next Sunday—perhaps not for a week or two."

"I'll tell you if I see him there, shall I? But when you think about it, one wouldn't trust a theology student anyway, would one? They've got to be odd. Look at vicars."

"Yes. Quite so, now you mention it."

I went back to rinsing out my four-day supply of

cocoa mugs; decorated with blackberry sprays, they had been a going-away present from Auntie May. Shirley continued to stir her pan of cream-of-chicken soup on the stove.

"Did they," I asked, drying a mug with Auntie Phyl's presentation tea towel, "say 'one' in Bognor? As in 'would one,' I mean?"

"Christ, no." Shirley blew on the first spoonful of soup, eating it straight from the saucepan. "And did they say 'quite so' in south London? I suppose not."

"There it is—we're being dragged down. Soon we won't even notice it."

"No. But it's hardly our fault, is it?"

"When we go home, it's like that line in Eliot—'We have lingered in the chambers of the sea'—you probably know it, I suppose, and the way it ends—'Till human voices wake us, and we drown.'"

"Rather like that; but I've pretty well given up talking to them at home."

"Still—"

The bruises had faded to a greenish blur on the morning when I reached into my mailbox and took out a letter of acceptance for two of my poems. It was signed by Sean Tiernan, whom I knew by sight from poetry society meetings where he introduced visiting poets. And who did *not* know Tiernan, with the Dylan Thomas curls and the fisherman's pullover hung on a gaunt frame? The letter ended with an invitation to drop in at the poets' coffee hour in the Cadena, on a Thursday morning.

Here it was, then, the opening of the next door. If I went, I would have to cut Bowra's lecture; but that was all right—I had never understood why such crowds went to hear him; whatever he said was not addressed to me, certainly. Five minutes later, walking along the path beside the cedar tree, I remembered what I had written in the accepted poems and thought: *my God!* They had been composed in imitation of some *fin-de-siècle* translations from Sappho which I had got—by request—as my last school prize; and they addressed a version of Blaustein, under a Greek pseudonym, as my imagined lost lover. Only now did it strike me that I had never considered an audience of male readers. I had never had a male reader: Dad did not, on principle, read anything written by a woman, and he had informed me so.

"But what," I had asked him, "if you read a book and liked it, and then found out that it was written by a woman—like something by George Eliot?"

"I would just have made a mistake," he said. "But in any case it wouldn't happen: I think I can tell."

And Colin had always been too young; I never thought of showing him things of mine. But when I thought of undergraduate men reading those poems, it was some recent conversations with Colin (now thirteen) which came to mind.

"D'you know what *cunt* means?"

"Of course." Having an immediate intuition of the word's obscenity and its connection with myself, I lied.

"Well, what's it mean?"

Ordinarily I liked feeding Colin information, especially of the kind neglected by our contemptible school system; for instance, I had been happy to explain the terms *capitalist* and *proletariat.*

"I don't feel like explaining it."

"D'you really know what it means?"

"Of course."

It took a couple of days' searching, at that, to get the definition, even though I was sure I had not misheard. And I had to absorb the humiliation, then, of knowing that Colin had a five-years' start on me in the area of sexual realities.

"They put me in the back row, this term," he told me. "They did it by last names. So there's this big bloke in the next row, always wanking away behind his desk. 'S a bit much."

This time, I was willing to ask. "All right, what's wanking?"

"Don't you *know?*"

"Gimme a hint, I'll guess after that."

"You know, with his *thing*. He even pulled it out once—we could all see, in the back."

"That *is* a bit much."

"We sing this song, too: 'Robin Hood, Robin Hood, wanking up the glen—'"

"I see."

"So do girls do the same?" he asked.

"They can't exactly wank, obviously, not in the same sense," I said, thinking it over and noticing how certain things fell conceptually into place. "But there's sort of an equivalent. Not in school, though, as far as I know."

Now what had I done, in these poems written in dreaming evocation of a world of wholly feminine enlacements? An innocent mind might construe them as expressions of affectionate friendship, but Colin's older equivalents would undoubtedly see the schoolgirl Lesbian, the pervert, the freak. I got out my carbon copies and looked: these were pretty vague phrases, but I couldn't mistake the double meanings, having put them in myself. No—I couldn't go to the Cadena, to be stared at, nudged about.

But I went: *do this, or give it up once and for all.*

The reigning circle at the Cadena was made up of Sean, Jeremy, Peter and Trevor, and such friends or junior adherents as they chose to invite; but not once in the next two and a half years did I find another woman present. The four of them were all six feet tall, at least, willowy and stilt-legged, and cloaked when they walked outdoors in dark raincoats thrown over the shoulders. They were above all severe and judicious: they attended only the lectures of dons whom they knew to be critically aware (who acknowledged, that is, the work of Leavis at Cambridge); at poetry readings they often stared grimly at the floor, and applauded faintly and briefly. But over coffee, on that first morning, they were exchanging wisdom on the proper tending of a poet's hair.

"The fatal thing," Jeremy said, after the briefest of introductions by Sean, "is to wash it too often. Six weeks is about right."

This was something new. At home we washed our hair every week, each person having a regular night. One would expect it to become smelly and grease-laden, like the hair of gypsies who came round selling clothes pegs, if it was left longer; but Jeremy's hair, combed sideways with a slight wave in front, was magnificent—thick, and a rich brown with a lustre to it.

"Some people," Peter said, "are intrinsically clean. I'm suspicious of that. It's all a part of your scrupulous tendencies: you'll end up a scholar and critic. I can see it coming."

Peter talked with a slight accent which I couldn't place until Jeremy made some cracks about his American connections. It seemed he liked to hang out at White's Bar, to commune with the G.I.s from the air bases; and in poetry Poundian modernism was his creed. But he did not go so far as to sacrifice his springy, dark brown hair for a crewcut—it was combed back in a sweep from his broad, knotted forehead and down behind his ears, and this together with his heavier build made him look older than the others. Trevor, who had given me the briefest introductory nod, was (apart from Sean) the best-looking of the group; his narrow face was acne scarred, but he had precisely the style of sombre intellectual ambition.

"And what does Trevor think?" Peter asked.

Trevor sat back, and tapped his fingers on the edge of his chair.

"I can tell you," Sean said, "that he agrees with me—once every two weeks, *very* gently. Gets it clean, but doesn't disturb the precious fibres themselves."

"Hold it," Peter said. "I think he's had it cut again. Short back and sides, by God! This is a betrayal, Trevor—you're letting us down."

"It's in a good cause," Sean said. "His novel. He goes to dances in Cowley now on Saturdays, getting in touch with the workers, like. Getting material—"

"Women."

"—and women, of course. He'd be duffed up if he walked in with long hair."

"Bloody right," Trevor said. From under his tangled forelocks I caught a resentful look: this one, at least, did not want me here.

"I wouldn't call a *novel* a good cause," Peter pushed on. "That's joining the system. Selling out."

"Wait a moment—what about *A Girl in Winter?*" Jeremy objected.

Sean raised his coffee cup. "Nothing against the system here, please! It's seeing me right. And here's to the State, my noble patron."

"And mine too," I said, joining him. "To the State."

"Right! That's the new blood, the future."

When we left, Jeremy caught me at the door for a moment. "The other poem you sent in, by the way, the one Sean didn't take."

"Yes?"

172

"It was on the right track, I thought. If Larkin had written the last four lines at the age of eighteen, he needn't have been ashamed of them."

"Thank you." I had not yet read Larkin, but recognized from the tone of voice his status here as Master.

"Sean's more a Barker man, at heart, I'm afraid."

But I had not read Barker, whoever he was, either, nor had the term *neo-Romantic* been uttered yet in my hearing. "I see."

"You'll go to the Abse reading, I suppose?"

"Yes, of course."

They dismissed one another, these poets, with a kind of curt nod; the one Jeremy now offered me carried just a shade of complicity in addition to registering the bleakness of the age, but I could find in it only the promise of a stylistic alliance. I thought I would take that anyway.

Sean Tiernan, I saw, was not for me—if only because his grand abundance of copper-tinged curls made my own darker fleece look muddy and thin: it was too clear that we did not belong together in one frame. Still, at the Abse reading where he sat beside the visiting poet, his magnificence took my breath for a moment—the light breaking over his cheekbones, defining the hollows underneath, and then the bold coral of his fisherman's knit pullover set against that hair. He certainly drew in audiences, that year, providing the major part of the spectacle, and the poets beside him—at least until Empson came and showed us his white mandarin's beard—looked more like a set of bank assistants.

Nor was his appeal limited to women; on dull weekends he accepted invitations from certain homosexual dons, and the poets at the Cadena did not let these occasions go uncommented.

173

"Be honest," Peter teased him. "What do you *do* when Ramsay pulls it out and starts waving it at you?"

"The occasion doesn't arise, I assure you."

"*What* doesn't arise?" The question came from Roger, Sean's friend and old grammar-school companion, grinning broadly.

"Holy Mother, blast these unbelievers, will you, with a squirt from your sanctified left tit! Look—it's one thing when Ramsay goes trolling round the lavs in the Woodstock Road. This is quite another. He respects my mind."

Roger winked at me; the rest had given way to laughter, helplessly.

"Ho yus! Ho yus!"

"The most that has ever happened—the *most*—was a spot of nude swimming, last October. And I mean, that's what's done, on a private beach in Wales. Everybody does it. So I let him have an eyeful while I was nipping down the rocks: a minute coming and going (bloody freezing it was). And quite enough for the old man too, at his age."

"Christ, Sean," Jeremy said. "Why do you do it?"

"Well, for a start, the old boy's food is superb. He takes down a nice terrine of hare from the College chef. A couple of large steaks. Excellent claret. Besides which, Ramsay's an extremely bright man, whatever else you may say about him. Also very useful. The thing is, you see, to dismiss all foolish ideas about *obligation.* The fact is you're doing them a favour, and why not?"

Sean's women were kept away from the Cadena, but they were seen at the readings in fur-lined jackets and high heels, and he was eloquent about their generosity, as if they were fountains of gifts and good things of other kinds beyond our poor imaginations. He was a born taker, he admitted, but then some people were born givers. And he himself was nothing by

174

comparison to someone like George Barker, whom he had once seen in action at a party in London.

"The man could go up to a woman he'd never met before—I've seen this—look her in the eye and absolutely *master* her, like a snake with a rabbit. He'd take her right off to bed, like that. And she'd go. Amazing. There's an extraordinary power in the man."

"Loose metaphors, though," Peter grumbled. "Hollow language—no tough thinking."

I walked back along St. Giles with Peter and Jeremy, and their complaints continued until we reached the Eagle and Child, where they turned in for lunch: Sean was too much the opportunist these days; his poems also were woolly—too many lonely figures in vaguely natural surroundings, and too frequent use of the enjambed pentameter line.

"I'm afraid," Jeremy said, with judicial slowness as if the case were capital, "he's stopped developing. He plays directly into the worst romantic patterns. And he won't see that you *can't* do that any more. Fatal."

Together they contemplated a time when Sean would be eased out of his editor's position on the magazine, and off the poetry society board. But Sean would never be eased out of anything: in his last year it would be he who dropped poetry, and retained the poets only as drinking acquaintances. He had seen that poetry would do nothing for him after college was over, and what was important was a high score on the Civil Service examination. He had his eyes on the Treasury.

After each of these sessions I had a new name to learn—Larkin's the first, then Empson, Pound, *early* Auden—and had to scramble over to Blackwell's in guilty haste to buy *The Less Deceived, Poems,* and *Personae* on account. It was immediately clear to me that these narrow-bound pages held the real thing, the poetry of this century, and that Eliot's way was not the

175

only one; so, after all, it would not be necessary to work on and on at synthesizing the heavy perfume of his metres. In fact, when I hesitantly brought up Eliot's name, it met with a deprecating response: the man was ga-ga these days, and religion had ruined him.

And all this, and heaven knew what more, had been kept from me up to now! I sat at the table in my room in a tremor of rage. It was unforgiveable of Miss Sutcliff to have left me in such blank ignorance. A betrayal. Hopeless bloody school—I hadn't even the words to curse it adequately. Just add this to the growing list of major realities which were carefully excluded from consciousness at Hurst Grammar: the class system, the political system, all history after 1945 when the Socialists got into power, all literature after 1918. Well, now my education could start.

Yet another point of which I had no knowledge (Roger told me later) was the fact that I was becoming a question that required resolution, in the poets' group. Since I did not appear to belong to any man, to which man ought I to belong? A woman couldn't be left lying about, like an armed grenade: she required defusing, and quickly.

But Jeremy was as good as engaged to a woman in London. And Trevor put himself out of the running: University women, he maintained, weren't real women at all—he'd stick with his factory girls, thank you, and the occasional *au pair.* Peter, with his mother's aid, was busy working through his own roster of acceptable women at the moment; besides, a poet would be crazy to get mixed up with another poet. Notoriously unstable, especially the women, if they had any talent. And there were nurses available still for the odd uncommitted weekend.

What about Sean? they asked. It was pretty clear that someone had to take me on, and Sean took

176

everyone on, in time. But Sean refused. He had this *need* nowadays, he confessed, for rich girls—for the special things about them like their silk blouses which transmitted their body heat instantly at a touch, and their extraordinary stretch pants, and the smell of good cosmetics, along with their musical speech, all vowels and restful vagueness. He had studied me, certainly, and thought there were possibilities—the hair was nice—but those clothes! Marks and Spencer's and British Home Stores at best. No, he'd reached a point where he just could not get it up for that sort, poetry or not. And Peter was right, too, if women were any good at the business they were probably batty.

On the other hand, he could think of a friend or two who might serve the purpose here.

Roger was happy enough to receive a crumb from the poets' table. It was not that he lacked all resources of his own; he had always ranked higher than Sean at school, and in soccer games was as good a fullback as Sean was a centre forward; but he wanted a firmer connection with the world of little magazines and the parties which went on in it, and the girls who came to those parties. I might prove the means to that end.

Something of this I guessed at when he came up to me with two tickets to a student production of *The Changeling;* but I saw the opportunity for a fair trade—he might exorcise for me the dreaded spell of the Aunties, once and for all. And if he wasn't Sean Tiernan, still he wasn't so bad: his shape was bearlike, thick, with long arms and bushy brown hair, but his eyes were quick and bright, and his neat fingers flicked the ash off a Gauloise with promising dexterity.

He made no effort to hold my hand at the play. In the interval we walked along the vaulted cloister which was penetrated by the smell of rain-wakened grass.

"D'you smoke?" He held out a packet.

177

"Not really."

"What d'you think of De Flores?"

"He's terrific."

"I know him slightly," he said. "Charles Levy, I mean. Good actor. Wasn't he superb with that last gesture, picking up her glove and thrusting his hand into it?"

"Yes—absolutely. Only—perhaps he isn't quite disgusting enough. I mean, he's so far ahead of the game, so much *brighter* than Alsemero, it seems as if Beatrice-Joanna ought to prefer him. Don't you think?"

That pleased him immensely. "I see your point. But most women go by good looks, after all."

"Do they?"

Mid-week he sent me a letter inviting me to tea the following Sunday, and telling me that he had not slept the night after the play. Thoughts of me had obsessed him: he could scarcely believe his luck, that I had agreed to go out with him, and now he felt scared by my innocence, yet he couldn't help wanting to see me again.

A love letter, then—impossible, but here it was in my hand. But I couldn't go next Sunday. I would be getting my period on Friday, and what if things were to come to a crisis with him over tea? It would have to be a week later, and I would make some excuse—work, say, an important essay to be finished, and that was never untrue.

Roger lived on the top floor of a house on St. John's Street, at the back overlooking a garden with trees. He had cleared a space to sit in front of the gas fire; outside it every possible surface was covered with papers and stacks of books with slips protruding from their ends, and shoeboxes full of filing cards were stacked on the dusty carpet.

"You're really, really serious!" Indeed, the scene

178

took me by surprise. I knew what it was to work hard doing what one was told, going from one task to the next, keeping the bosses satisfied. An investment of these dimensions, however, was qualitatively different: clearly Roger thought in terms of the systematic acquisition of a body of knowledge and its maintenance as a permanent resource, for himself.

"Of course," he answered directly. "What's the point of being anything else?"

These were new thoughts.

"It isn't that I don't work hard—" I said.

"I know. Women dons are known as slave drivers. But you people reading English have a *comparatively* easy time—it's a woolly little subject, after all."

"Is it?"

"Oh yes. English, and modern languages, those are the easy ones. P.P.E. and history—much tougher. I'm grinding through bloody Stubbs Charters this term—you'd have no possible idea what it's like."

"How many hours a day d'you put in?"

"Between eleven and twelve, six days a week."

"I see." This was a different league: I had been taking nine or ten as a reasonable average.

I sat in the broken-down armchair while Roger made tea and toasted two crumpets at the fire; we used one upright chair as a table, and he sat across from me on the other. He did not look well; his eyes were reddened and sunken.

"I'm sorry," he said, "if I'm rather poor company. Partly the sheer amount of work. And I'm a bit depressed. One sees these Winchester-and-New-College types sailing through as if they've known the stuff all their lives, and it makes you realise what you're up against, coming from a tin-pot State school."

"Yes, I know."

"Right."

He got up, and went over to his gramophone beside the desk. "Which would you like—Beethoven or jazz?"

"Whatever you like." I didn't know then that the men operated on a theory developed by a Brasenose don, that classical music was for seduction, jazz for relationships to be kept pure.

"Let's have the violin concerto," he said.

Four soft drum beats sounded in the room; it was the first time I ever heard them, or the theme which followed, rising with unearthly confidence in its power through the air.

After a time Roger came and sat on the floor next to my legs. "D'you mind?"

"No."

When the cadenza began, he put his arm round my knees. "You have glorious legs, Irene."

It was a wholly new torment, to be pulled between this amazing sound and the imperative of the sexual moment.

"Wait," I said, and heard immediately the sigh of his hopelessness. He thought I was refusing him! "No—I didn't mean that."

The rest of the movement would be lost anyway.

"Let's go to bed," he said. "Shall we?"

Roger was covered with a warm fleece of light brown hair, so that although naked he seemed still clothed as in fur, and unfrightening. Gently he searched me with his fingers, and gently put my hand on the bareness of his prick. As the clock ticked past five-thirty, he fetched a condom from the chest of drawers at the end of the bed, and walking back, took for an instant a wrestler's straddling pose.

"Don't you think I look like Henry the Eighth?" It was true—the massive head, the deep-chested torso and short, thick legs. And instead of a codpiece, it was the prick itself jutting forward.

Leaning on one elbow, he rolled the rubber onto himself with a brisk little crackling sound. Now he moved over me, paused there between my raised knees, and after a moment during which I felt the air of imminence chilly across my genitals, moved back and laid his head down on my shoulder.

"No," he said. "I can't do it."

"Why not?"

"You're so—*absolutely innocent.* This hasn't ever happened to me before. God!" He groaned heavily.

"Oh, well—never mind."

"I *do* mind, letting you down so to speak. Damn it!" And he hit himself audibly on the forehead with his fist.

"Don't."

"If only," he said at length, "you weren't so incredibly young and pure."

"I am doing my best not to be."

We lay and stroked each other for a while longer, then dressed and drank some Landrost sherry in front of the fire. I promised to come back again on Tuesday.

"We'll be more used to each other," he said.

Was that true? The next time I prepared myself by taking two codeine (in case I would mind the pain of defloration), and by burning a lock of my hair in an ashtray with an invocation to make sure of the success of this enterprise. When I arrived at the house, Roger opened the door and took me by the hand; on the landings as we went up we kissed long and deep, and when we got to his room we did not bother to have tea. Quickly, quickly, we were on the bed, were undressed, were in bed, and Roger arranged a pillow under my hips.

181

"Is it all right?" I asked.

"Perfect," he said. "Feel." Under the thin rubber he felt hard as bone; then I took my hand away and kept very still, and with only slight resistance he entered me.

I heard his voice, sounding as strange as everything else: "There. All right?" And in the same breath, as I held on tighter, he began to thrust.

It took a long time, even after he had become still except for the heartbeat resonating through my own rib cage, for me to open my eyes again. Outside, past his shoulder and the window beyond, it was still daylight; branches were tossing about with their new leaves in a rain shower. What kind of tree was that? I couldn't say; I didn't recognize it at all.

The question for the next day was, what would he do now? He had promised to meet me outside my building as I came back from the Vergil seminar; but my long experience of the world of English love from Clarissa to Tess made me expect the worst. I would wait before telling Shirley anything, because if the affair were not to continue—if I were to be exploited and abandoned—I would need an explanation consistent with my true self.

"I thought I'd see what it was like. Interesting, yes. But I've decided to wait, now, till I'm in love with somebody."

But when I turned the angle of the path I saw him already there, walking up and down and taking quick puffs from his cigarette. I came closer, and he dropped the cigarette and put out his hand. We ran inside to my room.

"Lock the door," he said as we began unbuttoning, "I'm worried."

I turned the key, then punched him lightly on the bare chest: "Are you frightened of the women, then?"

"Does *this* look as if I'm frightened?"

"Just wondered—"

We wasted no more time, but reclaimed the territory first explored the day before. It would remain strange for some time, but had in it some mysterious heart of familiarity, a quality of return, perhaps to farthest-back infancy. In it we bathed and played, and meditated.

Before getting up, this second day, Roger raised himself on his elbow with the look of a lecturer summing up. "I said I loved you, didn't I, yesterday?"

"Yes. I thought that was a bit soon, you know?"

"Well. I may not have then, in fact. But the point is, it's true now. I'm crazy about you: I do love you."

"O.K. I love you." So that we could do more of the same, whatever it was called.

Afterwards I cooled my red cheeks, abraded by his shaved beard, and my swollen lips in cold water and witch-hazel, and went over to dinner. Shirley caught me afterwards.

"You've been up to something, haven't you?"

"Yes. Got my first fine, too—I didn't sign out last night, thought I'd be back."

"Ah. Ruined, then?"

"Seriously ruined."

"That's nice."

"Well it is, rather."

This dialect by which all of us seemed to be bound was clearly no use in getting anywhere near the truth of the matter. In the effort to find a language, Roger showed me Donne and Lawrence; I translated for him Baudelaire (Blaustein's last gift to me was the mention of his name), and we made our recognitions by degrees.

Meanwhile, we took our place in the short list of canonized lovers in the college. Two of the women in my year had arrived wearing engagement rings, and

184

their fiancés, both older men, came devotedly most weekends to take them out to dinner. But their version of love was ceremonial and restrained; they did not burst dishevelled from their rooms at odd hours, running to the bathroom. A handful more were cautiously approaching engagement by way of long walks and conversations in the parks; and a third group went constantly to parties, to flirt and scan the field. It was in this year that the Playtex panty and girdle in one gained popularity as a means for women to enforce above-the-waist limits.

"They can't get it off, and they can't get inside!" Helen the mathematician announced at a weekend coffee session to which Henrietta brought me. Henrietta was writing her second novel; it was to be about love, and she thought I might make a minor character but so far was not sure how it would fit in.

And where *did* Roger and I fit in? It puzzled me now, since passion was so easy and so absolutely delightful, why everyone else was not in our situation. They had only to let go of the branch of conventional *pudeur* to which they seemed to be clinging, and drop into happiness. Why didn't they?

But this was not a question which, sitting here on the floor of Helen's sunlit corner room (the scholars were set apart also by being allotted the best rooms) among the coloured circles of cotton skirts, I could simply put.

"Helen, I'm not a prude," Linda said forthrightly, "but I don't think most of us are interested in your messy details."

"Yet attention to detail is *essential,*" put in Shirley, imitating the dean's voice.

"A drunken man," someone else picked up the mimicry, "is occasionally funny: a drunken woman, *never!*"

185

"But unfortunately that's still true." Caroline's high, chanting tone had kept its authority, and the sequence was broken. And next to her there was a movement from Anne, whose status as the ranking scholar in politics was equal to her own, and we waited for the pronouncement.

"The problem," she said slowly and intensely, "is finding the most intelligent men. I think one ought to aim for the brightest man of one's generation in one's field. I mean, that's the sensible thing: one is *not* going to be happy with anyone who's not up to one's own level."

"Exactly," Caroline said.

"I would make an exception," Henrietta said, speaking I imagined from the artist's viewpoint, "for the sexual genius: a novelist ought to marry someone who's good at life. Not someone necessarily with the same interests."

"Of course there are exceptions—I'm talking about the reasonable thing for most of us here." Anne's look travelled round the room, skipping me, I thought.

"Yes," I said, "all very well, but how can you be sure about who's the brightest at this stage?"

"Well," Anne said, and paused to tuck a strand of her heavy blond hair behind her ear while others answered in her support.

"One gets to know these things."

"It isn't difficult—"

"I'll give you one example," Anne continued. "I've met quite a few of the people doing P.P.E. here, and just by talking to them I know who the exceptional minds are likely to be. One of them, David Grant, I happen to know quite well already. And I mean, it's quite clear. He mainly corresponds with this professor in London, and he does what he likes as far as tutors here

186

are concerned. And he's got a paper coming out already, next autumn."

A nominee from another corner of the room had already been given the most prestigious postgraduate scholarship. "He'll be a Fellow before he's twenty-five." Another had taken first place in last year's Civil Service examination.

"All right," Shirley said, "but what if you find him—the perfect candidate—and he's queer?" There was a silence. "Doesn't like women, *you* know."

"Of course we know," Henrietta answered. "But it all depends—for some men it's that they were at some school or other where it was part of the tradition, so to speak. But now they're away from it, they can put it behind them."

A quick look from Shirley, but nobody smiled.

"Yes, quite," Anne said. "And then there are those few who'll stay that way."

"Quite," Henrietta said.

Helen sighed in an irritated way and we waited for her comment, looking meanwhile at the perfect match between her lipstick and the red belt on her polished white dress: she was immaculately turned out always, a pleasure to see, and at the same time disheartening.

"People talk too much about homosexuality here. I get about a lot, and I don't see it. And really, I *don't* believe it's something that goes deep. Schoolboys—that's what it amounts to."

"I disagree," said Henrietta, "but I don't think it's fair to give specific cases."

One other nominee for the title of brightest man of the current generation was a postgraduate in philosophy whom I had met; it was a a party given by a friend of Sean's (Sean himself never gave a party), and the man had been trying to stuff sandwiches into people's drinks.

"He *is* remarkable," Caroline hummed. "Most extraordinary mind. I suppose almost too sensitive: he was in the Warneford last summer, wasn't he?"

"I believe so," Anne said.

"That's another thing," I put in. "Suppose your person is really odd, or unpleasant."

"Oh—*odd*, well who *isn't* odd? Anyway, I think bright people tend to get on with each other. The alternatives, after all, are worse."

Some weeks later, Roger asked me about the women in my year: "Are they virgins?"

"We don't talk about it. Probably most of them are."

"I think you ought to invite them over and introduce Sean. He'll be happy to offer them a good lay."

"I believe they would only go to bed with their fiancé, when they get one. I don't think Sean would be much use."

"What they need is a good lay."

"Is that all?"

"Well, if they can't be like us, I mean."

That spring I was reading first *Sons and Lovers*, then *The Red and the Black*, and was astonished by the evident vocation for love which appeared in these scholarship heroes. The coincidence could not be accidental. And it could not only be referred to lower-class freedom from sexual repression, as Lawrence thought; the capacity and gift for love went back to those mothers (Stendhal left out Julien's mother, but she must have been there, in the space behind) who were all of culture, all art, science, holidays, journeys and presents to the child without other privileges. The Juliens of this world carry out of childhood with them an exorbitant gift and need for intimacy; they tumble about the social void with sensitive hooks outstretched, and once they find attachment the quality of attention they bring to it is close to perfect. I recognized, I *knew* that, seeing in them my own obsessive focus on the details of response, my own ecstatic compulsion to please. Whatever else they had in mind, whatever else I myself had in mind, love was central to the business.

Roger could not have imagined for himself a more patient and devoted apprentice.

"Lightly now, lightly. The penis is a very delicate instrument: don't drag the skin.

"Not so fast!

"Faster! Keep it up, yes!

"Now, for this we'll need Vaseline."

In the interests of my fuller education, Roger sometimes compared my performance with that of his former girlfriend, Dilys. She was his girl back in Thame where he came from; he had started sleeping with her the year before he came up to University, and they had been unofficially engaged for the next eighteen months. Just before he first met me, he said, he had told her that they were drifting apart, and broken it off. But he kept a framed photograph of her in his desk, which he showed me. Dilys was standing beside a stile set in a hedgerow, holding a book in her left hand and a white handbag under her arm.

"What's the book she's holding?"

"Let me see. Oh yes—Plumb, the Pelican volume on the eighteenth century. I bought it for her. That was last summer, we were hiking for a weekend in the Cotswolds. She wanted to get an idea of what I was doing."

The face in the photograph looked up hopefully, with sun-dazzled eyes under a wavy slant of hair; she looked kind, and soft, and wore a white pullover which outlined her heavy breasts.

"She doesn't like her legs," Roger explained the trimming of her image at the knees. "She thinks they're fat."

"What did she say when you broke it off?"

"Not much: I think she'd been expecting it for some time. Oxford, and so on—she didn't think she could compete on that level. She works in an estate agent's; actually, she's quite happy doing that."

Yet here she was, reading what he told her to, trying not to be left behind completely. "But it's so sad!"

Roger twitched the photograph out of my hand, and put it back in the drawer. "Don't waste pity on Dil. She's got her own life; you have no idea. She's very strong."

He was sure she would be happily married within a year or two. She was so good-tempered—never any scenes, perhaps a few quiet tears at most—and she made love very well. "No fuss—she just likes to fuck, you know. And a velvety cunt: like sinking into a plush sort of cushion it was."

"I see."

"Is my Piglet jealous?"

"I certainly ought to be."

"Piglet has a *much* better cunt—a beautiful, athletic cunt—Pooh's favourite cunt in the world."

Yet if I was jealous, it was only to the extent that he wanted me to be, to spice that next encounter; even under provocation I felt no rage, no hatred, only curiosity and the sting of a challenge I was sure of winning. And by the time he told me—a year later, after he caught me out with that love letter from Willy—the rest of the Dilys story, jealousy was the smallest part of what I felt. He would tell me then that he had been deceiving me from the very start. Did I remember how he had been impotent, the first time we went to bed? That was because Dil had come up to stay with him the

190

day before: "I'd no idea *you'd* come to the point so quickly, so we were screwing away until eleven o'clock that morning. I was shagged out, to be honest. Shagged to the eyeballs."

After that, every vacation he went back to her, but kept her away from Oxford on the plea of too much work.

"And didn't she suspect?"

"Eventually. Last Christmas we had it out. But she thought I might come back to her, you know, afterwards. Then this chap from Reading started taking her out and getting serious about her. So at Easter she wouldn't see me any more."

He had never, in fact, broken it off with her. She had done the job herself at last.

"It wasn't that I still loved her, Piglet. It was more of a habit. See, I was still fond of her, as an old friend."

"Yes, quite." The main thing here was not to suffer: suffering was the pure obscenity to be avoided. Fortunately I had enough guilt on my side to deter any indulgence in it.

That same spring, Henrietta took too much aspirin and was put in the Warneford. When she was able to have visitors Shirley and I went over; she was on insulin, and getting fat, and she looked at the space between the two of us when she spoke.

"I've realised," she said, "that you can't feel sorry for anything you've done. You've *done* it, therefore how can you be sorry? It's simply a fact."

Exactly so. This was what Roger the historian was teaching me now: never mind the irrelevancies of preference, just see clearly and accept *what was the case.*

On the bus going back across Magdalen bridge, Shirley reviewed with me the progress of her current affair with a Fellow of Queen's. "The food's gone downhill really fast. No more nice dinners at Woodstock—but by the way, did I tell you about the restaurant at Minster Lovell? Terrific scampi, and then veal chops *and* asparagus. Anyway, now he pretends he'd really rather go to the Cellar—spaghetti and coffee."

"Is he a good lay—does that make up for it?"

"He's all right. Quite amusing, actually."

"But rather a shit, evidently."

"Yes—I mean, it's a bit insulting, an eight-bob meal."

"Rather a glaring case of taking for granted," I said.

"Yes, rather."

"I suppose you could put it: no steak Diane, no fucks."

"I could," she agreed, "if I had someone else in the offing. And then, he's been talking about getting me an invitation from a friend of his to the Commem Ball. He has this sort-of fiancée he has to invite; we'd make up a group party."

"Interesting."

"On the other hand, I don't know. He has this re-usable thing, not like the usual Durex. He washes it out and hangs it up afterwards—rather awful."

"I think you ought to start looking round a bit more. That's disgusting—stingy to the last degree. And what if it developed a crack?"

"I know. It's worrying."

At the end of Trinity term, in June, Roger and I spent a week together out at Abingdon in his aunt's house; she was on holiday, and Roger was to look after the place and feed the cat. For us two at any rate there would be this perfectly happy time.

We arrived very late at night, so that the neighbours would not see me, and slept for the first time

192

in the luxury of a double bed. In the morning the grey cat watched us coolly from a chair as we made love; tinted by the pink gloom of drawn curtains against the light, we saw ourselves in the triple mirror on the dressing table as a phantasmagoria of parts—arms sprouting between buttocks, breasts rising above knees, and all a luminous silver-rose, all in harmony. When we got hungry we fried up sausages and bacon and tomatoes for breakfast; afterwards Roger hosed down the garden and went to buy bread while I read through the pile of old *Woman's Own* magazines in the living room.

In the afternoon when the weather was hot and still, and the neighbours rested before tea, I slipped out of the front door while Roger left by the back, and we met past the bend in the road to go for a walk in the fields. There were places to make love away from the footpaths in high grass, and when the sun began to go behind the hedgerow trees we took a longer way round to the fish and chip café in town, for supper.

We could not go back to the house, now, until dark, for the neighbours would be exercising their dogs, and weeding their gardens as long as the light allowed them. So we walked a mile to a pub on the upper road where Roger was unlikely to be recognized, to spend the evening playing table skittles or darts, and drinking beer. That walk, up a long, slow rise, stays with me as a memory of complete ease and pleasure. Where we turned onto the main road you could see for miles across the country; lines of hedges beaded with may trees and oaks at the corners ran between the fields, and the fields themselves were deep in grain that was beginning to change from green to ash-blonde. Near at hand there was a barley field moving gently with a shining moiré pattern under the low sunshine and evening breeze; the same light made the shapes of the

193

trees full and heavy with detail. All week the weather would hold in a charmed stability, fine and warm.

What could we have talked about? I had no previous history of love affairs to draw out and out, in that unavoidably interesting operation by which later intimacies are spun. There was very little altogether of myself which was interesting to disclose—besides, I was so busy forgetting what seemed no longer to the point. I must have listened, for Roger was just discovering his powerful gifts as a lecturer, and now I remember that rolling movement of his as he walked along, picking up speed as he clarified the chain structures of political influence in Restoration England and adduced examples for every nodal point. And any woman who knows him well (I give up the question of number) knows how deep the passion for exposition goes—how he will get up refreshed within minutes of climax, light a cigarette and pace (naked or clothed, it doesn't matter) up and down in a sudden access of thought which cannot wait to be elaborated. I thought all that enchanting.

On our last evening at the Radley Arms, a Saturday night, we got into conversation with another couple at a table in the crowded saloon bar. They were newly married, and thought we should be too—there was nothing like it. For an hour we bought rounds of drinks in alternation, two pints, a half-pint and a lager with lime for the young bride; then, as the dart board was free, we began a game. Roger kept score for us, since I had barely learned the rules. The other pair were better players, but the beer had taken its toll on all of us, and at the last double they stuck, while we caught up with them. At fifteen on the board, it was my turn to throw; all the others needed was a double three.

"Throw a one," Roger shouted over the noise of the bar. "One, then a double seven to finish!"

The three of them laughed at the confidence of his directions.

I weighed the darts in my hand, and threw one; it missed the board altogether.

"Watch it!" said a man turning from the bar.

"Never mind him," the bride said.

"You wanter mind that wall, lass."

"Come on," Roger said. "Give us a one."

I threw a one. Roger was ecstatic. "All right! Now the double seven."

Without hesitation I raised my arm, looked for the right segment on the board, and threw the dart straight into it.

"She's done it!" Roger said, shaking his head. "That's the game."

The moment was hilarious; all four of us looked at each other and burst out with laughter, clapping one another on the back, and the bartender gave us a complimentary liqueur.

At closing time we shook hands, and set off by ourselves on the dark road.

"I felt like Svengali," Roger said. "It really was extraordinary. Well, now you can play skittles and darts, you can be one of the boys; we'll get you on to pints next. And I bet you've never heard the rugby songs, have you?"

"No—what songs?"

"Oh—we learned them when we went with the team, Sean and me. I'll teach you. Let's see, the one about the gay old tinker, the Ball at Kirriemuir of course, Eskimo Nell—well, what shall we start with?"

"The Ball at whatsit."

"All right, we'll start with the chorus—this is very important—"

And we continued down the long incline, singing:

Balls tae your partner
Arse'les tae the wa'
If ye dinna get fucked on a Saturday night
Ye'll niver get fucked at a'.

It was Saturday night and we were all right; *we* were going to get fucked.

"And shall I tell you the real difference between the Cavaliers and the Roundheads?"

I had stopped going to the poets' coffees; even before Roger told me the details I suspected them of pandering our affair, and was embarrassed—besides, I was writing nothing, I had no poems to show. Like Dilys before me I was being introduced to the work of Napier and Plumb, masters of discourse who were as essential to the mind as Larkin and Leavis, Roger argued. And beyond them were the authorities on discourse as such: the linguistic analysts, the philosophers.

"At some point," Roger stated, "you'll have to read Ayer's *Language, Truth and Logic.* It seems a bit crude nowadays, but it broke a lot of new ground. Later, there's J. L. Austin, and Strawson—those are the names to conjure with, now."

For my birthday, he gave me a slim manual with the flyleaf inscription: "To teach her how to think." It offered a concise taxonomy of statements, from the metaphysical (those which mentioned God, for instance, which by definition were non-factual) to the analytical (propositions in logic) to the empirical. My own field of English was virtually disqualified from intellectual seriousness, Roger explained, by its heavy

197

dependence on value judgments—a category of proposition for which no reliable grounding could be established.

"Strictly speaking," Roger said, "value judgments, which include moral dicta such as 'fornication is a bad thing,' are merely pseudo-statements. To what, we may ask, does 'fornication is a bad thing' refer?"

"Factually speaking? Well, to fornication. . . ."

"Ah, but 'bad' is the problem, you see."

"You mean 'bad' isn't *out there,* in the same way as 'fornication.' "

"Quite. It's unverifiable—purely subjective."

"I see."

"We no longer believe like G. E. Moore that 'good' and 'bad' are real in the same sense as this point of bitter. It's questionable whether they're describable as real in any *ordinarily used* sense of the word."

"I see."

At home for the summer on Agathon Way I practiced the classification of statements.

Heather: "All these black clothes you're wearing—I think you're getting awfully *peculiar* since Oxford." Value judgment.

Ma: "You weren't very nice to Mrs. Watkins, sitting there silent as the grave." Value judgment again: a pseudo-statement.

Indeed, it had become hard to speak with any degree of spontaneity, when the criteria for valid utterance were so tightly drawn. As for writing, that came down mainly to a twice-weekly letter to Roger (expressions of love were an allowable variance from the rule of tough-mindedness), and some tinkering with translations from Baudelaire and Rilke's sonnets. I had a job filing in the B.B.C. archives all week, which mercifully kept opportunities for discourse at a minimum. There, in the ballroom of the old Langham

Hotel, crammed from floor to ceiling with manila folders stacked along endless shelves, I filed letters from actors.

"Just a note, my dear Andrew, to fill you in on what I've been doing. . . ."

"I don't know if you caught my latest show, at the Lyric. . . ."

"Should the opportunity arise. . . ."

The lighting in the stacks was dim, unless you happened to be in one of the rows under the original chandeliers of the ballroom, and the filing went on without beginning or end. In the morning I received a batch of letters for one segment of the alphabet, checked the names and the order, and began to file. One grew sleepy within half an hour in the stagnant air and the gloom; after a while the whole task seemed a matter of maintaining that level of half-consciousness which represented efficiency.

Out of this Tartarus of failed communication I emerged blinking, with just enough money to pay Ma for my keep and to buy some more black clothes: a tiered poplin skirt, a V-necked pullover and a pair of pointy, strapped shoes. It would soon be time to go back on stage—to nerve myself, and to meet Roger's new demands.

He wrote to me in September to say that I had made progress, and that he thought he could soon risk introducing me to his intellectual friends. "Last year they would have destroyed you, Piglet. I've seen them deal with nice fuzzy people. And to be honest, I didn't want you to make me look like a fool." As it was, he even thought I had better start aiming at a First. "You may not be a first-rate mind—too much of a magpie style perhaps—but I think you might do it, with luck. The main thing is to think like a man. Keep your distance a bit from the women tutors; they don't (from what I hear) really grasp the way the game is played. I can probably help you there."

Jeremy was now editing an issue of *Boreas,* and as soon as the term began he met Roger in the street and asked him what had happened to me.

" 'What have you done with her?' he asked. I said, the usual things, and he was apparently very pissed off. 'She's a poet,' he said. 'We've got to have those poems.' So you'd better get on with it, Piglet."

"I've had too much to do. Anyway, you can't think like a philosopher and do poetry at the same time. Keats knew that—it's in *Lamia.*"

"That's balls. What literature's *supposed* to do is to bring together the mind and the emotions."

"Why don't you do it, if it's so simple?"

"I can't," he said earnestly. "I need you to do that—no use at it by myself. You haven't an idea of what it was like before I knew you. Dilys was all physical and emotional. It was always a split."

"The trouble is, I can't write about you."

"That's all right—perhaps I wouldn't like it anyway. Write about something else."

But what? What? Unable to produce more than half a dozen new lines, in which I found myself imagining a woman drowning, I went back to an old packet of material from the time I left Hurst Grammar: poems to Jill, to Blaustein, which had never quite worked out. There was no choice, love had to be my subject one way or another—everything else, including work (which I now controlled on Roger's principles), was done as it were with my left hand. But like all the other poets whom I read I could only *write* out love for a woman. And now, knowing more about the body of love, these earlier phrases seemed dull and vague; and as I crossed out, over-wrote, took a new sheet and expanded, it became clearer how these poems should

200

go—I knew what it was that more than a year ago I was trying and failing to understand.

Then I looked at them finished, and said: "Damn!" He was not going to like them; so I sent four translations to Jeremy instead, and a week later went over to the Cadena at coffee time. It was a changed scene from the previous year: Sean was not there—he came only rarely now—and along with Jeremy, Peter and Trevor there was a golden-blond boy from Wadham (watch out for him, the murmur went round afterwards, he's going to rise in the world, wings and all), and a cheerful freshman who carried about with him a thick and growing manuscript of poems in a brown leather portfolio.

"I got your stuff," Jeremy said quietly.

"Well?"

"We tend not to do translations, you know."

"I see."

"They're *very* good. I think we might make an exception for one of the Rilke pieces. I think we could about do that. Baudelaire—a bit fruity, I feel."

"All right."

"But you've got to do your own stuff too—where are the new poems? You must have something, surely."

"I have, but I'm not sure—"

"Let me see them."

I picked out two, and showed them first to Roger, explaining carefully that these were revisions of poems from well before his time.

"Jesus!" he said, looking up after a quick scanning of the pages. "I'm not sure how these will strike people."

A useful idea came to me. "Look—why don't you show them to Sean? Take the carbons. I won't do anything with them meanwhile."

Roger came back the next day with good news. "He likes them a lot—thinks they ought to be published. And I agree, on second thoughts."

Sean had pointed out to Roger that he could take the credit for converting me from Lesbianism to a more proper way of behaviour: there was no doubt, after all, that I was Roger's property now, so where was the harm? Everybody knew about the two of us, surely.

So Jeremy ran the poems in his next issue, which sold better than any in the last five years, and kept the Rilke sonnet for the following Spring. I could fall silent again for the duration.

This was Roger's final year, and as the winter came on his obsession with preparation for Schools intensified. Gradually my world was contracting along with his, down to the gloomy bed-sitting room which was the staging place in his drive for a First. All morning he worked among his shoebox files which multiplied every month; in the afternoons he collected library materials and came back to work on them through the rest of the day until late in the evening, with one break for dinner. And, suspicious before the need arose, he demanded that unless I had a tutorial I come and spend each afternoon and evening with him. There was no second desk in the room (he had moved from St. John's Street to a narrower attic on Walton Crescent); I worked sitting cross-legged on the bed, or on the floor beside the gas fire. Even in daytime the inner recesses of the room were poorly lit; Roger sat at his papers directly in front of the one window, and in whatever place I chose to settle, I found myself in his shadow, looking up at his silhouette against the narrow rectangle of light.

Once a week, on Saturdays, we might go out to the Indian restaurant for dinner, followed by a couple of hours at a party or spent drinking with the boys. On these occasions I bought my share of the rounds, kept up with the drinking pint for pint and composed my share of the obscene limericks that were in fashion. Sunday afternoons, after a walk on Port Meadow, were

202

still reserved for love-making; but for the rest of the week I must make do with what Roger called "quickies," when he joined me on the floor of his room for fifteen minutes of masturbation.

"Put the kettle on, Piglet!" I would hear at four o'clock, and I would fill the electric kettle from the bathroom, and plug it in.

He now put aside the book he was reading, and while the kettle heated he kissed me; I felt him up while he played with my breasts under the loose pullover; I worked his fly open while he fluttered his hand inside my briefs; I worked on him harder and faster, and he took out his handkerchief in readiness. Then the kettle boiled, and he came. And we had tea, before going back to work.

According to Roger, he enjoyed this routine just as much as fucking. "After all, we have the *Hauptsache,* don't we? The proverbial *Endpunkt?*"

It annoyed him when I disagreed. "Some women can *only* come this way—by hand." Surely I could make the effort. But his impatience itself discouraged me, and so I learned to imitate gratified desire.

In the next phase of this downward spiral, I must give an accounting of each afternoon and evening spent away from him.

"What did you do after the tutorial?"

"Walked back to Carfax with Sally. We went into Culpeper's on the way; I bought a honeycomb. Got the bus up St. Giles."

"You must have been back by five, or half-past."

"I had a bath before dinner."

Or again, if there was a poetry society meeting: "Who did you meet there?"

"Just the usual: Simon of the golden hair of course, Jeremy and so on. Sean was there, he can tell you."

203

"What about afterwards?"

"They went over to the Turl; I came back."

"Who with?"

"Nobody."

"Mm."

He began to be preoccupied with my character—with signs of weak will that I had shown in the past, for example, the easy way I had given in to him. Perhaps I might be tempted to do the same with some other bastard; and God knew Oxford was full of men who thought of nothing but getting into cunts. There was nobody you could trust, not even your friends. Sean himself couldn't be trusted.

One night, after a meeting of the Writers' Club to which Roger was not invited to belong, I came out at eleven o'clock and found him pacing the street under the melancholy Clarendon Press bell, in a rage. Without a word he gripped my arm and marched me away.

"You said," he finally burst out, "you'd be round at a quarter to!"

"It was a story—it kept going on."

"What story?"

"Stuart's—actually it was quite funny, we were drinking wine, and people were wanting a piss, and the door handle fell off, and there was Sean banging on the door to get the landlady to come and push the handle through from the other side so we could open it, and all the time Stuart kept on reading in spite of the noise. We just broke up; and it was such a serious story—"

"All that time?"

"Yes!"

"With those lechers? What's really going on? Is it Sean?"

"For Christ's sake—*nothing* was going on!"

"Liar. Call themselves writers—just shits, I know

204

them. Who did you let feel you up in there? Did Sean feel you up?"

"Oh fuck off, Roger!"

In an instant he had me slammed against the window of a launderette, and shook me back and forth.

"Bitch! Whore! Pretentious bitch!"

"Stop it! Nothing was going on—ask Trevor, he doesn't like me even. Ask anyone." But I must break down in tears before he was satisfied, and even then, letting myself into the back door of the college by a borrowed key, I was followed by the last of his tirade: "I know them better than you do, the shits, so watch out!"

The day after this scene he appeared greatly refreshed and infinitely affectionate, full of apologies; but in a couple of weeks it began again.

"Trevor saw you in the Welsh Pony at lunchtime yesterday."

"Yes. I went over with Shirley; we thought we'd vary the routine. Juliet was with us."

"Who else was there?"

"Well, Trevor just gave us the usual nod. We talked to some people Shirley knew."

"Who were they?"

"Well, one of them was from Queen's." I thought it best to suppress that name. "Then there were a couple of Australians; one was a Rhodes Scholar."

Roger's reaction was violent. "Australians! Randiest buggers on the face of the earth! Screw anything that moves, sheep included. Disgusting turds. Where did you go with them afterwards?"

"Nowhere. Shirley knows them; I just met them in passing, then we came back."

"They made a pass at you, didn't they? Asked you out?"

"Look, I stayed out of it. The one they were really interested in was Juliet."

"I find that hard to believe, considering that she strongly resembles a fucking *horse!*"

"According to you, that shouldn't matter."

"Fuck you! When are you seeing them again?"

"I'm not."

"Liar!"

"I am not!"

"Just remember, I'll be watching you."

The month's vacation in March was a respite from tears and confusion. I stayed at home, working, and got weekly letters from Roger, loving enough except for the regular postscript: "Just keep away from your little Sapphic friends, darling."

One Friday I took the train in, and walked up Charing Cross Road to Foyle's to get a copy of Mallarmé: it seemed one must know more than simply Baudelaire. I met there one of the other poets—those who wore denim rather than raincoats, and having heard of Kerouac and Ginsberg called the Cadena group "the Establishment." He offered me a couple of small pills.

"Bennies," he said. "They perk you up."

I took them. Then he suggested we walk round to a pub where someone he knew would buy us a beer.

"Why would a stranger buy me a beer?"

"People do," he said, "if they've got lots of money. I'll introduce you as a fellow poet—unlike some people we won't mention, I think you *are* a poet. And there's this painter, we'll probably meet him there too. Willy something—Polish—very interesting guy."

Roger found the letter from Willy when he came on a rare visit to my room after lunch, in the second week of term. I had made coffee for the two of us in the scullery down the hall, and was bringing the tray in when I saw him turn towards me with the tissue-thin sheet of paper in his hand.

"What's this?"

"Just a sec, let me put this down."

I recognized perfectly well what he had found. Willy's letter was all too clearly a love letter, and it had been the enjoyment of that fact which prevented me from hiding it away safely: I kept it accessible for re-reading under a book on my desk.

Since I thought Roger might very well hit me in the next few seconds, I quickly defended myself by taking my coffee cup, sitting down and lifting it to my lips.

"All right!" He stood facing me, breathing like a runner about to begin a race. "Who is he, this clown?"

"Just somebody I happened to meet a couple of weeks ago in London."

"What's this then—'an unforgettable night'? 'Your

incredible sweetness to me'? You laid him, didn't you?"

"Actually no, I didn't."

"Look here, woman, it's in plain black and white!"
That was true: Willy typed his letters, keeping a carbon
for posterity's benefit. "You spent the night with him!"

"It was an evening, a party. Let me see the bit
you're talking about." I put my hand out for the letter;
astonishingly, he gave it to me to look over. "All right, it
was a long party, then we went to this all-night place for
coffee. We were talking."

"Talking my arse. You laid him, it's obvious."

"He doesn't say that. And in fact I didn't."

The important thing was to keep up the tone, the
coolness, and to close off any opening. We argued one
point after another, handing the letter back and forth as
if we had a knotty problem in textual interpretation to
deal with. This was something we were both good at.

"Look. Allowing for the fact that this is a
sentimental *git* who's writing, the implication is crystal
clear that he *fucked* you. Admit it."

"I'm not admitting it because he didn't."

"And moreover, he's in love with you, isn't he?"

"Well, perhaps, but I can't help it if he is."

"The stupid bastard can't even spell!" Roger
waved the letter in front of me. "Look at this: 'I still can't
believe it'—e before i. He's uneducated."

"He's Polish; he wasn't born in England. And
anyway he's a painter."

"Polish? God! Bloody peasant twits, the *thickest*
frigging clods in the whole of Europe. How in hell could
could you *do* it?"

He lashed himself visibly into a fury, pacing up
and down, then sitting on the end of my bed and
slamming his head repeatedly against the wall until a
smear of blood appeared. When I went over and put out

my hand to stop this, he knocked me clear into the centre of the room, and pounded the wall with his fists until my neighbour came round.

"What on *earth* is going on? I can't hear myself think!"

"Sorry." I went over to Roger again, not too close. "I think you'll have to leave; they'll be getting the Dean down here."

And he left, after exacting my promise to come over to his digs at eight o'clock; and then I sat down and began shaking.

But I had held up, hadn't I? Hadn't given an inch, not an inch. It had helped that there was some truth in my story: Willy and I hadn't actually gone to bed, because he was married and his wife was at home in theirs, and we hadn't the money to get a room in a hotel. While still at the party we had begun to make love standing up in a bathroom, but we were unpracticed in the technique, and perhaps somehow ill-fitted to one another, and it didn't go well. He had come at last into my hand, just as the knocking of full-bladdered guests at the door became peremptory. And if Roger wanted to call that a fuck, he might, but I called it a fucking disappointment; and when I thought of Willy, the pathos of his hard life and bad teeth, and the faintly chemical smell about him, I didn't think I would try it again. Yet it was nice to get the appreciative letters. It reminded me of last year.

At one minute past eight I was at Roger's door, tired out and wanting only peace.

"Well, have you decided?" he asked. "You want this man, I suppose."

We stood on the doorstep—he was not going to let me inside.

"No, I don't. I've told you already, he was just

209

somebody to talk to. Look, for this entire year I've not been supposed to say a word to you, hour after hour, so you could concentrate!"

"But it was just for this year," he objected, "because of Schools. I thought you understood. God, it's unbelievable—it only meant waiting for three more months!"

"Well. I'm sorry about it, I really am."

"Sorry! First you absolutely wreck everything, my chances for a First—you *destroy* me, then you come back and say sorry."

"Well, I *am* sorry."

"Well, what happens now? Is this the end, or do you want to go on?"

I looked down at my hands. "I'd rather go on. It's up to you, though, of course."

"You're so bloody *cold* about this! I can't make it out: you obviously don't care much about this other bloke, but you seem not to have any feelings either way. What's happened to you? You were such a sweet kid, and now you're like a different person."

"I wouldn't know."

Soon after that Roger sent me away, and kept me waiting for two days before announcing that he would take me back. Meanwhile I found the story of my defection spread abroad, and there were cool looks not only from the men in Roger's circle but from women too, even Shirley. I had disgraced myself, apparently; and if Roger had decided to split up, I would have been stuck with the reputation of a whore.

Once we were re-established together, he broke to me the full story of his relationship with Dilys. I admired his sense of timing there—the way he grasped a double advantage, and left me with nothing at all to say, speechless with amazement.

The date of Roger's examinations was closing in,

so that I was banished as a distraction except for the hour before dinner, when we met at the Bird and Baby for a pint. Sean often joined us, to compare tutors' advice on the handling of certain subjects and to rate the chances of contenders for a First. Afterwards we went separate ways—I, heavy with beer and webbed about with uncompletable strands of thought, passed under the plane trees along St. Giles and on to dinner and the slow study of *Paradise Lost.* Everything was so tiring these days: it was all I could do to stay awake until ten, and in the mornings to drag myself to breakfast by eight-thirty. Day by day the sadness at the back of my throat became a more distinct ache, and then a strong pain. At the infirmary they diagnosed glandular fever, and I was put to bed there for a fortnight.

"It's just as well," Roger commented. "Nobody else can try and steal you while you're in there."

At the year's end, Roger got his First ("but as my tutor remarked, *not* quite at the high level he expected") and a post-graduate studentship besides, which would take him to Balliol and then the following January to Berlin. He decided to buy me an engagement ring. So we went to the Oxfam shop and looked through the old jewelery, and there were some lovely earrings with peridot drops in the case.

"Couldn't I have engagement earrings?" I asked. "They don't cost any more, and they're awfully nice."

"Keep your mind on the subject, Piglet: rings."

So we bought a broad gold band, inset with pearls and garnets—rotated inwards it could pass for a wedding ring, to be worn on our weekends hiking on the North Downs.

And I have lost it already, a year later: when Roger arrives next Tuesday that's another thing I must tell him. It was lost while I was drunk and blacked out somewhere, so for my weekends with Stuart I've had to get a replacement, made of gold wires in an endless knot, which I prefer since it's mine. I have also lost the green silk scarf Stuart gave me so recently, and my bicycle which Ma and Dad gave me when I was thirteen and which I loved so much, then. Everything seems to blow away from me, as if in some fierce existential wind. I just cannot keep hold.

I suppose I went on with Roger so as not to drop out of social existence altogether—so as not to be utterly lost; I don't know of any fear to be compared with the fear of that happening. But in the past six months, since he left, the scene has looked otherwise—

De Bailhache, Fresca, Mrs. Cammel, whirled Beyond the circuit of the shuddering Bear—like that.

The first big party in October was a reception at the Royal Oak to welcome W. H. Auden as Professor of Poetry. By six o'clock when I arrived the crowd had spilled all the way through the saloon bar and out onto the street; Mr. Clark the famous surgeon from the Radcliffe Infirmary had been driven from the pleasures of his usual solitary drink—I saw him sloping away, his long dark jowls flushed with annoyance, and at the sight of the crush I almost turned back myself. But Jeremy was sipping a half-pint, by the doorway.

"Have you been inside?" I asked.

"I had a look-see. Craned over a few heads."

"Was it worth it?"

"Oh yes." He then paused, reconsidering. "If you haven't already seen the famous face, that is."

"Well I haven't. But look at this sodding crowd!"

Roger had been teaching me to swear, and it embarrassed Jeremy: he took a sip of beer to recover. "Oh, I think you ought to do it. There's a sort of line, but the thing to do is just push through, purposefully."

"I'm not sure."

"Go on—there's free sherry when you get to the

213

private bar. And why give up now—surely you didn't put those stockings on for nothing?"

We both looked down at my stockings: they had large diamond patterns in yellow, blue and green on a black ground, rather like a snake's back. They were a new find, and I was proud of them.

"Yes—right, I'll see you later."

I pushed inside the door and edged along a passageway past rows of people who could not possibly be poets: where were the dark raincoats, the broad-striped or purple shirts? Or the pullovers, the corduroys? Finally, at the entrance to the private bar I spotted Peter in his brown fisherman's knit, and Henry the new American arrival in a striped shirt and dotted bow tie, black on pink.

"There *was* some sherry," Peter said, showing an empty glass.

"It's all right. I'm just looking."

"We're waiting until the crowd thins out. Henry's met Auden in New York, before, so we thought we might get a little talk."

Both of them were smoking in rapid puffs, and the foul air made my eyes water. "I don't think I can stay long," I said. "Too much noise, too crowded. I'm going to squeeze in for just a minute."

The inner room was equally crammed with people—a mixture of older men in drab suits, pouchy and arrogantly careless of their warts, with a sprinkling of very beautiful young men, like technicolor versions of the plaster casts at the Ashmolean museum. There was that perfect Indian (Alexander's descendant, surely) from New College, attending to the conversation of two donnish persons with inexplicable deference; and here too were Sean and Simon, posed in as much isolation as they could imagine against the bar, with Trevor to set off their radiance. At a guess, Sean had washed his hair one

214

week before, to bring it to its peak of springiness and gloss today.

And at the far end of the room in a haze of smoke floated the monochrome desert landscape of Auden's face. Sean nodded to me when I came within range.

"A remarkable sight," I said.

"Isn't he?" Simon answered excitedly. "No question about it—there *has* to be something there, still."

"Perhaps," Sean conceded.

Trevor looked back over his shoulder for a moment, as if checking whether he'd missed something; evidently he thought he hadn't.

"Did you get introduced?" I asked.

"No point, at the moment," Sean said. "Not until that little prick Henchcliffe and his friend shove off."

Auden's head was inclined in an attitude of compassion towards a young man standing beside him with hands clutching the air spasmodically.

"Next Monday," Simon said, "I'm going to his session in Christchurch; I hear he's started it up already."

I had heard something about that too. "You'll bring stuff to read?"

"Yes. I hear it's quite extraordinary: he's tremendously helpful."

"Well, but what's it like, when you go there?"

"Apparently there's this very pronounced atmosphere, just as there was when he was an undergraduate. The shades are pulled down because he can't stand much light. And there are cushions strewn about, and people sit on the floor a lot. Rather *intime*. And you read things aloud, or give them to him to read, and I hear he's terribly nice and kind, but at the same time he makes very shrewd judgements, very genuine.

215

People realise afterwards that he was very tough on the poems."

"But if you were me," I said, "would you go?"

Simon looked to Sean for guidance; Sean raised his eyebrows and said nothing; Trevor tapped his lips in an amused way.

"Well, that's sort of a difficult question. In principle, surely: you're a poet after all. I really don't know—in practice perhaps you might find it a little awkward. Awfully hard to say."

If he had offered to go *with* me, I would have gone; but he didn't.

Then I should have gone anyway—it puzzles me now that I couldn't even think of forcing the issue, that I took one more look round that room, seeing nothing, and left; that I went to no more gatherings at the Cadena. After all, I had set myself previous exercises designed to toughen my sensibility, and succeeded: for instance the task of buying Durex contraceptives at the chemist's. These were always kept behind the counter, so there was no use hoping to put down the money and pocket them. One must say it right out:

"A packet of Durex Gossamer, please."

The first time I attempted this, I couldn't bring out the words right away, standing at the counter.

"What can I do for you?" It *would* be the cheerful male assistant, not the pale and silent girl I preferred.

"A bottle of White Rain shampoo, please." Roger had told me—that's what you say if you lose your nerve.

"Right. Anything else?"

"And a packet of Durex please. Gossamer."

He slapped one on the counter and waited impassively.

"That's all, thanks."

And he took the ten-shilling note I held out with the very tips of his fingers—the only sign perhaps of his distaste.

On later errands for the same purpose, I went further and caught the assistant's eye while making my request, to acknowledge squarely what I was doing. Subsequently I reported my progress to Roger, who complimented me: "Dil would never've done it. Now, shall we see if you can roll it on properly?"

Perhaps it depended on a specific teacher, this matter of occupying new territory: certainly I had learned Roger's way of swearing ("Piss off!" "You frigging idiot!"), his Thames valley jokes (including the famous one about the horse and cart and the giant cunt), even his precise length of stride when walking and his way of standing, shoulders squared and one hand in a pocket. But he was not a poet; he could teach me nothing about that line of business. And besides, there was the point that anyone was entitled to buy condoms—anyone was entitled to a few fucks once in a while, and to swear as they pleased in private, and to walk or stand as they wished; but not everyone was entitled to belong to the company of poets. There was no forcing of that issue. My Romantic training made me adamant on that: either the call came of itself, or not, and one could only serve and wait; practical ambition in poetry was an obscenity.

The waiting continued. In November, heavy rains came followed by a raw wind down the Woodstock Road. The sky stayed overcast for days at a time. And twice, near the Little Clarendon shops, a dark young woman in straight black trousers passed me and I wanted to ask her where she got her clothes, and her face? Was it South America? The Hindu Kush? But I didn't speak.

However, the marks on my essays had gone up

during the past year from beta-plus to alpha-minus; the odours of State-school gaucherie and narrow mindedness were evaporating, and now when I offended Miss Hibbert's ear it was with phrases from the analytical vocabulary: *hence not meaningful,* and *thus a questionable assumption.* Each Friday, thanks to Miss Hibbert's recommendation, I had a tutorial on Chaucer with the famous Miss Gardner at St. Hilda's. My companions were the famous Caroline, and Joan from Crawley Grammar. We arrived separately, but assembled in the corridor at Miss Gardner's door to make a joint entrance. Once inside, our separateness reaffirmed itself under our tutor's smiling but indifferent gaze. In turn we read our pieces: today Caroline brought her considerable learning to bear on the issue of moral incoherence in the *Troilus,* Joan pursued C. S. Lewis's line on the medievalness of it all, and I examined stylistic formulas in the lyric passages. Miss Gardner sat in her low armchair, knees placed well apart in a gesture of raw dominance (none of us dared look straight at her), keeping track of our familiar moves and making sure that our efforts were confined within the prescribed time frame. When an essay ran over twenty minutes, she got up and tidied papers on her table, wound up her clock, and if all else failed, interrupted.

"Let me break in for a moment there. If I understand you correctly—" and she would give a brisk summary not only of the approach already taken but of the conclusions yet to come, winding up with a set of questions on the secondary readings, pursued until at least one gap was found. "Ah. Well, I think you would find a look at that work very much to the point." Upon which, we took pen and paper and wrote every reference and comment down, and precisely at six-fifteen were sent away.

There was no point in splitting up now, if we

218

were all taking the bus to North Oxford. We must try at least to be civil, and it was my turn to make the effort.

"She doesn't like Chaucer very much, at bottom," I observed to Caroline. "I noticed that she rather took to your attacking *Troilus.*"

"D'you think so?" I let pass this reminder of my alienness. "Anyway, I wasn't really attacking it, just pointing out some contradictions—confusions. I suppose, though, I do feel Chaucer didn't quite *rise* to the highest opportunities of his time."

"But what would that *mean?*" If it meant anything, I added to myself. With a bit of luck she might bring up religion now; I heard she had been seen going into St. Aloysius. But Joan answered first, blushing as she spoke.

"Well, if you wanted to make comparisons, *Gawain,* or *Pearl,* are really more profound poems. I think there's a more serious sort of feeling involved."

Caroline accepted the help, with caution. "Well, yes. And there are passages in *Piers Plowman* which are quite on another level. And in Chaucer there are lots of passages which really might've been written by other people, Gower and so on, whereas Langland has this integrity which is unmistakable."

The bus arrived; Caroline and Joan took the last two seats near the front, and I stood over them.

"Actually, I've been reading Gower," I said, "and I'm pretty sure I can tell the difference."

"I think I could too," Joan said.

"One other point: granted some of what you're saying about *Troilus* is true, I think he solved the problem in the *Canterbury Tales.* Let's say you've got an established religion which denies certain aspects of life, and you want to include those aspects in your writing: a safe way is to split up the responsibility for them among different characters."

Caroline shook her head slightly, and pulled straying hairs back behind her ear. "I don't see religion in that biased sort of way."

"I see. You prefer the T. S. Eliot line. Cultural unity."

"No, I'm not saying that at all. However, I certainly don't take the Leavis line either."

I left it there. But Leavis? Curious that she seemed to believe one could follow a line of thinking without acknowledging a Master. It was all very well for her to deny Leavis, or more to the point Empson, but each of the alternative paths of interpretation led back to some shrine or other—to Eliot's, or if not Eliot's then to Arnold's, or in another direction only vaguely known, to Freud's. There was, the more you grasped the situation, only a choice of Masters: I could see no place of freedom beyond the available set. Then there was Marx, of course, to be reckoned with. And even if Caroline had chosen God (as appeared possible), she had merely picked the metaphysical Master of masters.

Perhaps what drew me towards Chaucer, yes, was the mind that manoeuvred *between* great authorities, picking their locks one by one over a lifetime, and getting access, piecemeal, to the truth about things. This was not, however, the way of these women who taught us. They were the elder daughters, loyally refraining from interpretation altogether, and preserving a grain of independence by working in neutral territory; they edited texts, elucidated sources in detail, and at their most ambitious traced universal themes. They stood back from particular meanings. It was a joke commonly told about our senior tutor, that she had published a chapter on *Measure for Measure* without any reference to any of the events of the play. On the other hand, who could bear what really happened in that play? Well, I could see Ann editing a

220

text in five years, and Caroline doing universal themes; but the questions of the Masters had their hooks in me too fast already—what are we actually to say, how must we actually live?

After dinner it was time to go to the end-of-the-month drinking conference, held at the large house in Charlbury Road where Roger now rented digs. Sean was coming down from London for it, and when he finally arrived towards eleven o'clock, so drunk that he held onto the doorpost and then the furniture for support, he had a story to tell.

"Had to have dinner with Scofield, y'know, then stopped at the Randolph on the way up. This woman, there! American! Brightest woman ever met, drank me under the table. Eleven Scotches, I gave up. No wonder they killed Dylan Thomas. Heads like iron pots."

"Well, who is she?"

"Coming to that."

"Why didn't you invite her up here?"

"Did. She couldn't come, come to the next one though."

"Think she's layable?" Roger asked.

Sean drew himself up. "My business. Leave that to me."

"What about Sarah, then?" I asked. Sarah was the most classically beautiful and best-tempered of his rich girls, and although Sean still kept her away from the drinking weekends, they were to be formally engaged at Christmas. After that, he had said, he could be more bloody sure his friends would keep their paws off her.

"Keep Sarah out of it!"

"Has this woman got a man around?"

Sean thought for a moment. "No. I'd have known if she had: the nose never lies."

"Then she needs a good lay," Roger said.

"One might well conclude that."

"All right," Trevor said. "You're engaged, Roger's engaged, leave her to me. What's her name?"

Sean turned on him. "Wait a sec! It was me that found her. I'm not asking for a line on the right, y'know. Anyway, I don't think you're in her league, Trev."

"Give us a chance, that's all I'm saying."

"Come on, Sean!" Roger held out a mug of beer to him. "We're all friends here, so what's her name? Let's have a little verification—you can keep the address to yourself for the moment."

He took a long swallow of beer. "Christ, I'm pissed!"

"Yes, all right, but the *name*."

"Coming to that. Calls herself Sontag."

"*What* Sontag? Or Sontag what?"

"That's all; that's it."

"German," Roger decoded. "My best language, as it happens. *Die Fahne hoch, die Reihen*—"

"No, Nazi pig!" Sean raised a hand in protest, and toppled back into an armchair. "Screwed yourself on the spot, you did. It's—Jewish, like."

"Damn—how was I to know?"

"I think we should invite Bernie next time," Sean said. "Bernie's extremely bright."

"What does she look like?"

"Tall. Taller than you, Rog. Dark. Darker than Sarah. Very dark. Dresses like a guerrilla, only all these thick scarves." He made a vague, looping gesture, put down his beer to avoid spilling it, and gave the whole thing up. "Christ, I'm tired."

I went to refill my glass from the keg in the hall; Roger followed me, muttering "Interesting, eh?"

"What's the point, though?" I said. "I mean, apart from other commitments, you're going to Berlin in a month."

"Come on, Piglet. There has to be something

222

special, to get Sean like this. Anyway I'd like to meet his idea of the brightest woman in existence—compare, if you like. And a little practice helps to keep up the old interest."

"Does it?"

"Oh yes. A little light practice. You wouldn't want me to lose my—powers, as it were, would you?"

"That idea never occurred to me."

Clearly I must have been encouraging him in my role as naive child, eager for fresh instruction in the grandeurs and miseries of the male. I used to do that. Neither could he ever resist the opportunity to expand, to fill the imaginary space offered with the cultic lore of the adolescent prick. We had played this game often, to pass the time before going to bed, or the late-night time between one fuck and the next, when especially he had entrusted to me the histories and descriptions of his friends' organs, and those of their acquaintances along the widening circle of the sacred grove.

But here a shout came from the kitchen: they were about to begin *Red Fly the Banners-O,* introducing the musical phase of the conference.

Next morning a low sun poured in on us under the broken blind, and by eleven o'clock I was tired of pretending to sleep. To avoid disturbing Roger I crawled over the end of the bed, and stood for a dazed moment naked on the floor until a wet trickle down the inside of my knee focused my mind. The crooked thread now dividing over my calf was blood, not semen alone. Damn. I reached for my briefs in the pile of clothes to wipe it. In this houseful of men there wouldn't be a tampon to be found: I should have to stuff in a wad of Kleenex and go back to college. Actually, given the way I felt, the ache of dehydration in my bones and the painful weight in my head when I bent down to disentangle my bra, that seemed quite a good idea. I

223

shook out my black pullover and skirt, releasing a soft dazzle of motes along the ray of sunlight, and put them on; hooked up my suspender-belt underneath, pulled up my stockings and stuffed the briefs into a pocket. Before leaving, I put a note on Roger's desk: *Got curse, had to leave: no fucks today.*

The mild warmth in the footpath through the Parks felt like a blessing; the day felt like a Sunday, with someone practising in the distance on one of the Oxford carillons. Sontag. Like Blaustein, a Jewish name. What if they were ever to meet Blaustein? "Needs a good lay." "Dying for it, probably." But that was not true of Blaustein: if ever there was a person in balance and harmony with herself, she was the one. It was so long since I had even imagined her face; now that I permitted myself to do so once more, I noticed for the first time consciously the Egyptian modelling of her lips, the symmetrically incised line. Her image formed itself with such extreme clarity that I stopped for a moment on the path. I *saw* her—but this image had after all nothing to do with this suffering body, trudging along a gravel walk; Blaustein had joined the company of past things, safe beyond her screen of poplars in a different life.

And what about this new one, then? If I met her, should I mention to her quietly about Sean and company, how anxious they were to find out if the brightest woman was good in bed? Impossible. Sean and Roger and the rest were my friends, and I had honorary membership in the peer group: one did not, above all, betray that. *Enfin,* if she was all that bright, she would figure them out herself.

"You won't go to any drinking conferences when I'm away, will you, darling Piglet?"

"Course not. I'll be working for Schools."

"Yes, and you'll get a First, and I'll be proud of you."

We were at the New Year's Eve conference, which was being held somewhere in Islington in a house which backed onto an Underground cutting. The occasion had brought together not only the recent lineage of poets, leftist critics and sympathizers who knew one another at Oxford, but some fresh acquaintances made by members who had gone down and joined the B.B.C. or the Civil Service, or who were serving apprenticeships on newspapers. Peter, who was writing radio news reports, brought a new girlfriend and some Cambridge friends of hers, and seeing us walk in came over for a quick briefing.

"You will come and meet Thea in a minute, won't you?"

"The new bird? Course we will."

"You mustn't be put off by the friends—they're actually very interesting—art magazines, galleries. Thea paints. Not very political, but after all—"

We drew ourselves a beer from the keg, and went to the doorway of the room which had been cleared for dancing. A few couples were jiving in a restrained way to a Miles Davis record which the Cambridge group had found and put on, in preference to our old Armstrong and Bechet whom Philip Larkin had sanctioned. They stood together by the gramophone passing a bottle of white wine among themselves. Thea—it must be she since Peter's massive hand rested across her narrow buttocks—was wearing black, naturally, but in the form of a jersey dress cut to a smart V at the back, and with it she wore (astonishingly!) a string of pearls fastened with a diamanté clasp, and on her feet were black patent-leather evening sandals. Her friends were smoking long cigarettes in holders, and their narrow-cut jackets seemed to have an unusual number of pockets and button tabs.

Roger edged me back into the passage. "Well, we can say good-bye to Peter. He's met his doom."

"She's very sexy."

"Yes. No tits, though. What was that he said—they aren't political? On the contrary, they're bloody Fascists, it stands out a mile."

"So. Shall we fuck off to another part of the forest, then?"

The crowd in the back room had thickened to a good consistency. Here was Trevor, steering a beehive blonde towards the corner sofa, and here was Bernie, the infinitely well-read ("and his First was a couple of notches above mine") postgraduate of Roger's year, discussing the James Gould Cozzens book with that young don whose field was the Dark Ages, Evan Price.

"—successor to Henry James," I heard Evan say. "I think it'll be seen as part of the tradition fifty years from now."

"Well, that's high praise indeed." Bernie smiled down from his pink-and-white eminence ("I am that rare thing," he'd told Roger, "a Prussian Jew"). "One sees that ambition in the book: it does *intend* to be the adequate account of life, the classic in other words. Still, I shouldn't like to swear that the trick is *brought off* entirely. A certain narrowness of vision—of moral scale? What does Roger think?"

"As it happens," Roger said, "I bought the book in view of having to take the train to Berlin on the sixth. So obviously I haven't started it; but Irene's looked at it."

Bernie raised his eyebrows at me.

"I'm a little surprised that you take it so seriously."

"Why not take it seriously?" Bernie smiled broadly; but what was the joke? I caught Roger's worried expression.

"Well for a start, I wouldn't place *By Love Possessed* together with James. The characters in James go to extremes; that's how you get the full moral scale, isn't it? And even when James is silly, there's a sort of camped-up wit about it. The pettiness in Cozzens is *drenched* in this humourless, scented prose."

"Women don't like the book, in general," Evan said. "Maureen couldn't finish it." He nodded towards a woman who was refilling her glass from the bottle of Scotch he had stashed on the windowsill behind him; her dramatic make-up, fuchsia, violet and black outlines on a thickly powdered base, emphasized her look of being ten or fifteen years older than the rest of us.

"Did somebody take my name in vain?" She turned towards us.

"The Cozzens book," Evan said.

"Oh God—unreadable!"

"Well, I did finish it," I said. "But that doesn't mean much—when I was at school, the local library

227

used to get the Stalin Prize novels every year, in translation. I must have ploughed through five or six of those. And if you can read Socialist Realism you can read anything."

"Oh, quite," Bernie said.

"Still," Evan insisted, "still, it has to be said that this book is one of the few convincing accounts of a *thinking* man's life. For that reason alone, I'd have to rate it highly."

"It covers a certain amount of new ground. Yes," Bernie said, "I agree with that."

Here Evan offered round his bottle of Johnnie Walker, and I took a couple of inches in the bottom of my empty beer glass.

"Cheers."

"Cheers."

With a quick touch on my arm, Roger ducked out of the circle and threaded his way towards the door.

"Who's that?" Evan asked.

The woman in the doorway, scanning the room for any familiar face, reminded me of Shirley with her thick bob of hair and her round cheeks, but Shirley was waitressing tonight at the Fairview residential hotel in Bognor. Then, as Roger came up to her and a vivid smile refocussed the way she looked, I was reminded obscurely of myself.

"I think it's Jean Ashworth. Roger's mentioned her; she's doing a B. Litt. in English." And my thought went on: *that's my successor with Roger, she'll suit him very well, bright but not too bright, a bit more earthy than me, and a really large bust.* How much had happened so far? They wouldn't have gone to bed—probably, that is—and his six months in Berlin would delay things. After that, though, he would move fast. He had told me that she was "fixated on John Jones" after going to his lectures, and hence not available. But that meant nothing. Ah, but what if Evan Price took advantage of Roger's absence there? He couldn't be really serious about this Maureen; people said he lived in her house during vacations, but if he were going to marry her he'd have done so, for surely Maureen must have realised there was no time to be lost.

Actually, for a man in his twenties, Evan was in some disrepair himself: the shadows under his eyes were evident despite the swarthy skin, and just as clearly he was a heavy drinker—two large Scotches in the short time we had been talking. A man of sorrows (my heart jumped slightly at the recognition), and acquainted with grief. And he wore good clothes: a yellow tie, dark indigo-brown shirt.

Some time after midnight, Jean and I were standing in the hallway over Roger's fallen body. He lay quite relaxed on his side with one hand under his cheek.

"Did you see it?" I asked her, having just come from the kitchen.

"Yes, actually. We were talking, and suddenly he said 'Christ, I think I've had too much whisky, I think I'll take a nap.' And he sort of slid down the wall."

"That's what it is, then. Pissed as a bloody coot, I expect."

"Shouldn't we see if he's breathing properly?"

I knelt down and put my ear to his chest: it moved up and down regularly, and I could hear the slow thud of his heart.

"O.K. The only problem is, putting him in the bedroom. I don't think he'll get up."

We shook him and tugged him but still he fell back, deeply unconscious.

"We'll need help," I said. "He's about sixteen stone."

"Really?"

I thought she blushed a little.

229

Sean had still not arrived at the party; Bernie had left, and Peter was dancing with Thea: who else was of a suitable size to help carry him? Then we heard the toilet flush in the adjacent bathroom, and Evan came out. He might be no more than five foot seven, but he would do. Jean and I took a shoulder each, and Evan the legs, and we got him into a bedroom and laid him down among the coats, shifting a few to make space. I covered him with his own duffle-coat, with my blue coat over the knees.

"There."

"Isn't there any more we could do?" Jean asked sympathetically. She will be perfect for him.

"He'll sleep it off," Evan said.

"It's the difference between Oxford parties and London ones," I explained. "People are making more money here, so they put out these bottles of Scotch all over the place. One isn't used to it."

Jean took her own coat from the pile, and got ready to leave; we checked Roger once more, went to the door and turned out the light in the room.

"Good night, then."

"Good night."

As I was pulling the bedroom door closed, Evan stopped me.

"Wait." With a gentle movement he lifted my hand from the door knob, and brought it to his lips, palm upward.

"What's that for?"

"For nothing. I wanted to kiss you."

He stood quite still in front of me so that I could see the charming patience with which he suffered desire, along with those other, unknown sorrows. We went back inside the darkened room, and standing against the wall, kissed. It was very good; then I began to tremble, and knew that he could feel it.

230

"Enough!"

"I know," he said, moving back and holding me by the shoulders. "Sorry. We're both preempted, at the moment."

"Where's Maureen?"

"She was dancing . . . I'd better go back."

"Yes."

He left, and I sat down on the end of the bed and wiped my mouth slowly with the back of my hand. What a strange softness his face had, and delicacy of touch. He wouldn't fuck for victory, screw me into the springs in the way Roger did, if we ever got to bed. It would be different, perhaps—or perhaps not, because Roger considered himself one of the more skilful and considerate of lovers, and that could be true. I put my hand up under my skirt, tentatively: yes, sadly, we could have had a good fuck of some kind.

Eventually I got up and turned on the light; Roger did not move. I found my handbag, took out the creme puff and lipstick, and improved my face before returning to the party.

The back-room crowd had thinned out—it was after one in the morning now—and Sean and Sarah were there, leaning on the sideboard and sipping orange juice. I remembered then that Sean had a bout of alcoholic poisoning over Christmas, and was no longer drinking.

"Hallo hallo," he said. "Happy New Year, and what have you been up to; all this time?"

"Had to look after Roger—he wasn't feeling well; finally he passed out."

Sean shook his head. "Gets us all in the end: he'd better watch it. And you know, orange juice compares very well, after all."

"I know I'm not being tactless," I said, "because anyone can see the two of you are madly in love, but

231

what happened to Sontag? You promised she'd come."

"Ah yes. Well, it didn't as they say work out. She seems to have got browned off with Oxford—last time I saw her she was planning to go off to Paris."

"What for, the art and so on?"

"No—according to her, the philosophy."

"In *France?*"

"Well, that was my reaction. If you went anywhere in Europe, it'd probably be Germany. What is there in Paris? So far as I know, only the French. And they haven't had an idea since Sartre."

Sarah leaned forward to me. "Did you know there was a husband *and* a child, in the States?"

"No, I didn't. Interesting—I wish I'd met her—I'm furious."

"Not so much interesting as appalling, I should say. You don't just *leave*, in those circumstances."

"How do we know?"

"Well, we wouldn't *imagine* doing something like that."

I said nothing: it occurred to me that we weren't very strong in imagination, round here.

"No," Sean concluded. "They're rather cold fish, the Yanks. Distinctly cold fish."

So she had turned him down—turned them all down, no doubt, and it was not unpleasing to know that.

The next day, after a few hours wrapped in a blanket and dozing on the floor of the bedroom (Roger lay next to me, the owner having reclaimed his bed), I got up and made a large pot of tea among the thicket of green and brown bottles in the kitchen. At regular intervals a train passing below rattled the window; otherwise everything was quiet, and snow was falling out of an evenly grey sky into the blackened brick ravine. The tea had a soapy taste; perhaps it was the London water. But wet and warm, Ma would have said. I

232

ran through the string of lies which I would have to tell on getting back to Agathon Way later: meeting the college friend, missing the last tube, losing the Copelands' phone number. No difficulty there.

I heard the toilet flush, and a moment later Roger came down the hall looking for tea and aspirin.

"Look at that coming down," he said, standing at the window cup in hand. "Have to get a move on before the trains stop running. Ten minutes."

"Right you are."

He poured a second cup and sat down across from me.

"I passed out last night, didn't I?"

"Yeah, about half past twelve. It was after Auld Lang Syne. Jean was there, remember?"

"Yeah. I kissed her. And you, too. Who did you kiss?"

"Let's see, Evan Price was it?" I juggled the times: what if he'd heard something, in the bedroom?

"Peculiar sort of sod. You saw the woman he came with."

"The older one?"

"The decomposing one: monster-film stuff. Odd tastes he must have. A severe mother-complex."

"Suppose so."

"Bernie knows him quite well. I'm not all that impressed: I'd say a lightweight, intellectually."

I shrugged.

"You liked it, didn't you?" He was like a mole, or a ferret in the dark, nosing through a maze of tunnels.

"I can't really remember—I was almost as pissed as you were. Anyway, I don't know him. How did you like Jean, while we're on the subject?"

"I've told you about Jean a number of times."

"But not this time."

He looked pleased, and annoyed. "She's a nice

233

kid. But you know nothing happened. I passed out."

On the road to the Tube station Roger pulled my hand into his duffle-coat pocket.

"Be a faithful Piglet when I'm away, won't you? I do need you. See, after all this time we've got to such a deep level with each other. I don't think I could start all over again with anyone else."

"I know. You don't have to worry about it."

"And in a couple of years I'll have a proper job—we'll get married."

I caught my breath in dread at the word, at the threat of these conversations being prolonged to infinity.

"Yes."

"You are an odd person, Piglet. Dil was always dying to get married. You don't seem to care."

"Well, it's just that it's a long way off, two years."

"True enough."

He gave me a hard kiss at the station where we said good-bye, thrusting a cold tongue far into my mouth as if nailing me to something; but of course it was just a kiss.

I was only a week back at college when a
telegram from home was delivered to my box: DAD
ARRIVING SATURDAY 11 A.M. MEET TRAIN PLEASE.
That was odd; if some emergency had arisen at home,
surely they would have summoned me. And in two and a
half years neither Dad nor Ma had cared to visit me here;
I couldn't think why they would do so now.

At the station, Dad got down from the train and
handed me without comment several pages of lined
paper, folded over. I opened them and recognized my
own handwriting at once—"something reassuring about
having a lover. Now I cannot imagine not having one,
whether or not Roger. . . ." It was enough. They were
pages from a loose-leaf notebook in which I had kept
occasional diary entries last summer. Further down the
page I caught sight of the phrase "going to bed with" and
quickly stopped reading. When I looked at Dad again
(we had begun walking down the ramp together), he
avoided my eyes.

"Your Ma found it in the bottom of the wardrobe.
Stupid of you to leave it there, wasn't it? Well, the
upshot is we think you'd better come home right away.

It's obvious that you can't be trusted to behave yourself, so you'd better be at home where we can keep an eye on you. My instructions are to wait while you do your packing, and take you back tonight."

"Oh dear." I kept my voice toneless enough, but the ironic edge was there for him to cut himself on if he could. In the silence which followed, I folded the incriminating pages smaller and smaller, until the wad could be dropped unobtrusively down a drain in the gutter. There—it was gone.

"Your Ma's worried herself sick, these past two days."

"I'm sorry."

"You'll have to realise that you can't get away with just—anything you please. There's a name for girls who behave like this, and it isn't a nice one: slut."

A moment later a coughing fit overtook him, so violent that he had to take hold of the Worcester College railings for support, and spit again and again on the ground.

"Dad, you're ill!" I didn't dare put out a hand to him; but he *was* ill—his face and neck were a terrible purplish red, and he kept his fist pressing over the left upper side of his chest as if holding in a pain there.

"Just a touch—" he caught his breath, coughed and tried again—"of bronchitis."

"Ma ought to've come herself if she was so bothered!" My hatred for her went to my head like alcohol: dreadful woman! "Let's stop for coffee on the way, I've got money on me."

"No," he said. "You've got to get started on the packing. What did you do with those pages?"

"Threw them away, Dad."

"Where?"

"In a drain. Quite a way back."

He rubbed his jaw, worried. "More trouble."

"Well, what use were they? The damage was done."

And we kept on walking. See, if she'd really wanted to pull this off she *should* have come herself. Just a coward, like all women—didn't want the row. She was probably lying on her bed with a thundering migraine this minute. Too bad. And with the state Dad was in, a nice cup of tea back at the room and a couple of hours' persuasion would do the trick. I sorted over my arguments: first, the State grant, two and a half years of it, which we might have to pay back (I didn't know, and he wouldn't know if it was refundable, but it was a fine threat). Second, I only had six more months here, and Roger would be away the whole time, so I wouldn't have the chance to misbehave. Then, I would promise to come home straight away in June and get some job locally (she deserved that lie—actually, I'd sooner rot on a dungheap than live under the same roof with her).

In the event, Dad took much less time than I had predicted to realise the hopelessness of the mission he'd been sent on. The college itself awed him—the lawns and the buildings, unimpressive though they were to anyone who'd seen Christchurch or Magdalen, as he hadn't. And then I represented my points to him not as contradictions of his purpose but as matters needing Ma's consideration too, before any action was taken. We needed more time, I said.

Finally, I took him out for a curry at the State's expense, and walked him down to the train.

"Well," he said, "I said what I had to say."

"Yes, Dad. Tell her I'm sorry, and things are different now."

"Well, it has been an awful blow to her."

"I'll write to her tonight, anyway. Look after yourself, Dad."

"We'll just have to see, Irene. I mean, what your

237

Ma's going to think about this."

"All right."

" 'Bye then." He kissed me very quickly, on the cheek.

I wanted to call out "Help me, Dad!" as the train pulled forward, but it was an impulse rightly controlled. Even though I had never had so clear a sense of his loving me (the fact that he didn't kiss me on the lips as usual I put down to his knowing about Roger), he was not capable of supporting me against Ma at the best of times, let alone as ill as he was.

He was not just ill, but dying. It was as if he hurried into death, this spring—he couldn't wait to get away from us. Within a month after I saw him, he was in hospital (that put an end to the contentious exchange of letters between Ma and myself: she had something else to think of); inflammation of the lungs was diagnosed, and treated with not much effect. Probably the doctors knew quite well what was wrong, for they sent him home without comment, "to rest." Ma nursed him, rather puzzled by the fact that he seemed not to be getting any better, and utterly unaware of the process by which metastases were forming in his brain. One day she noticed that his speech was slow and disjointed; two days later he couldn't speak at all, and she called in the family doctor who sent him back into hospital for the finish.

"I think," she said to me afterwards, without distress, "he had something to say to me that day before he went in. He looked at me, but he couldn't get any words out. I do think he would've said something, if he could."

Her letters to me at the time were brief and not informative: we were in a state of uneasy truce, and even as Dad slipped into his terminal coma I did not pick up from her any hint of his desperate condition. So, when

238

Roger came back for a few days at Easter and persuaded me to join him for a night in London on my way home at the end of term, I easily agreed.

On my way out of the college that Saturday morning, I picked up a telephone message from my box: "A Mrs. Copeland phoned you. Advises you come home immediately; father seriously ill." On the journey to Paddington I weighed this message against the fact of Roger's arrival at Victoria two hours hence, and of his expectations. And it seemed to me that a compromise was reasonable—I could have one night with Roger and catch a morning train home; a mere eighteen-hour delay in getting there could hardly make much difference. They were expecting me on the Sunday, too. If necessary I could say I got the message too late on Saturday to catch a train.

Roger and I got a room in a side-street hotel near Victoria, and set to making love immediately. His clothes smelled of the distant places he had been, and his body of the foreign food he had been eating; that alone excited me to enthusiasm, and we had fucked twice by dinnertime. After the first bout we fell asleep for an hour, and on waking drank a glass of schnapps from the bottle Roger had brought in duty-free.

"They haven't exploited you yet, then, the Germans," I said, feeling his erection renew itself as we sat naked against the pillows.

"No, *liebes Pigletchen*. Nor will they. And you've been a good *Pigletchen,* haven't you? I can tell: your cunt feels so tight. Closed up from lack of practice. It almost hurts, you know, getting it in: I'd really like to try doing it without the Durex."

"Oh no—no risks!"

"It's all right," he said. "I got something you can use, over there. It's a little thing you put in your cunt; it dissolves, and kills all the little sperm."

239

"Let me see it."

He showed me a packet, and together we worked out the meaning of the instructions. I unwrapped one of the small, waxy pellets.

"*This?* How d'you know it works?"

"People have told me. There's an English bloke I know over there, Gordie Ferguson; he says the girls use it all the time."

"It doesn't look as if it'd do anything."

"Well, I hear it's quite reliable. Just once, eh?"

Early next morning with cheeks raw from Roger's beard, and an aching cunt, I took the train home. When I walked in, Heather and the twins were sitting round in the front room with their Nescafé; the smell of roasting mutton came in from the kitchen.

"There you are, at last. You look like hell," Heather said. "I left milk in the pan for you to heat up. Mr. Copeland's going to take you over to the hospital after church; he'll pick up Ma at the same time."

"Thanks. How's Dad?"

Colin and Brenda looked down into their Nescafe.

"We've been trying to get through to you on the phone," Heather said. "For *days*. He's failing all the time. There hasn't really been any hope for weeks now."

"Well, nobody told me. Ma never wrote, in her letters."

"So where were you yesterday, then, or the day before?"

"I was just out. I didn't get the message in time to come yesterday. Took the earliest train this morning."

Heather was smoking; she tapped the end of her cigarette on the ashtray in an irritated way. "Well, there you are."

I put the milk on to heat, drawing the film of skin over to the side out of the way, and waited. Heather had set the kitchen in perfect order: breakfast things all put away, the table wiped, dishcloth airing over the edge of the drainer, a pan of carrots scraped and covered with water ready to cook, and the oven ticking softly away at three-thirty degrees. The one place in the world, this was, which required no thinking, only the succession of established things to do, in a round from Sunday to Sunday.

Make the Nescafe; soak the pan in cold water; take the cup through into the lounge. Colin got up as I entered, took a comb out of his back pocket and combed his wavy hair, reflected in the glass over a print of Lamorna Cove. He was sixteen now, and taller than Heather.

"Oh Colin, *really.*" Heather recrossed her legs with that small whizz of nylon pulled over nylon. When I looked at her, it seemed to me that she might be any age from twenty-two to forty; her hair was short, permed and fluffed out, she had made her face up with powder and coral lipstick even on a Sunday, and she wore a twinset and gored wool skirt. She never wore slacks, now.

"I can understand," she had told me before this, "why you'd wear them. You aren't contending with these upholstered hips. Still, you might at least get the kind with the side opening. That front zip is perfectly obscene."

Colin straightened up, and let his mouth fall open in our direction. This household of women had already begun to irritate him.

"Colin's getting really good-looking," I said. He had turned out darker than Brenda, who was still all pink cheeks and auburn curls, and he carried himself with the pleasant assurance of a favourite child.

"*He* thinks." Heather blew a cloud of smoke at him, but he was already halfway to the door. "Mr. C. will

241

be round in a minute. They've been awfully decent to Ma."

"Don't worry—I'll remember to be properly grateful."

Brenda was absorbed in reading *Gone with the Wind* all this time; Heather caught me peering to see the name on the book jacket and commented: "She's reading it for the second time. Imagine!"

"I suppose we all have to go through it."

"Oh, shut up," Brenda said.

At the hospital Dad lay under a transparent plastic cover with tubes running out from it, and his right hand was pressed over his left collar bone, just as I had seen it in January. His eyes were closed, his mouth open a little. Ma got up from her chair by the window and stuffed some knitting in a bag.

"Is he asleep?" I whispered.

"No dear. Not really—he's always like this now."

Then the nurse came hurrying in past Mr. Copeland—I must have made some kind of noise as I stood holding on to Ma with the tears hopping down my face.

"She'll have to go outside—we can't have this!"

I was sure I wasn't making any more noise, but still the tears kept running and I could feel the heavy shake of my breathing.

"Just a moment—" Ma stuffed a handkerchief into my hand. "She'll be all right, really."

"I'm sorry, but she'll have to go outside."

Ma took me to a bench in the corridor, and I sat down with the handkerchief pressed to my face; through it I could feel the convulsed shape of my mouth and cheeks, but could do nothing about that.

"I'm afraid she'll have to go *completely* outside. This sort of thing disturbs our patients."

"She'll be better in just a moment, Sister."

"No. We just cannot *have* this!"

The force of her annoyance and distaste came through to me—here we were, Ma and I, being pushed about again and told what to do as usual. No more of this. I pulled my feet together and stood up, wiping my nose.

"I'm all right now—you can let us alone."

"We can't have disturbance!"

"I've told you already. My mother's going home for a rest, I'm staying here. Excuse me."

Back in the room, Ma put her warm, dry cheek against my sticky one, and patted me on the back. She seemed astoundingly sane, maternal.

"Don't get Sister's back up, will you? She's a good sort, when she feels like it."

"All right." We went on exchanging the ritual family tokens—*really all right?—oh yes—what about you?—oh don't worry about me*—for a couple of minutes. Then she left, under the eye of the nurse on guard at the door. I took her chair by the window, and still drying my nose with the folded handkerchief watched until she came out into the parking area below with Mr. Copeland. She walked to the car with quick, neat steps. That green coat she had on was quite new, I remembered. But we'd have to get her a black one for the funeral: you couldn't dye a coat. And shoes—she had no black shoes.

The car pulled out and away. It was Mr. Copeland who said the word *cancer,* on the way here (the family had scrupulously avoided it—or did they still not know?).

"Cancer of the lungs, it is," he said. "They can tell from the X-rays, nowadays."

"Why were they saying *inflammation* of the lungs, then, a month ago? If I'd known—"

"Well, you know doctors. Lung cancer's

incurable, you see, and they wanted to give your Ma some hope to go on with."

They would, wouldn't they? She couldn't have any hope now though, with him unconscious for the past week; yet she had looked quite at peace when I walked in on her sitting here. (Here was her *Woman's Own,* too, left on the windowsill for me to read.) She had got used to the idea, possibly, because she had seen him slowly fade out; it might even be a relief to her that she could do nothing more for him. Whatever was left was the nurses' job, and the point of anyone's sitting here was only to keep watch for the moment of death itself.

I went up to the bed to see if Dad was still breathing, and he was: his lower lip quivered very slightly once in a while.

"Careful, now." A different nurse put her head round the door, instructed no doubt to keep a watch on me. "You've got to mind the tubes—don't disturb anything."

"I'll mind them." When she had gone, I said: "Dad." He seemed to be far out of reach; he must still feel a measure of the pain, though, with his hand pressed over the ache of the tumour high up in his lung. I reached under the plastic tent where his other hand lay curled, and held it—cold, it was, as if all the vital heat had been drawn away into the cancer, but flexible and therefore alive; I warmed it in both my hands.

Soon the nurse began again, looking in and out every two minutes to make sure of my behaviour, and after her third or fourth pass I retreated to the chair, to think about Dad and in some way pay him his devotions.

It wasn't easy to think about him, for the same reason surely that Heather and the others had barely mentioned him back at home: he'd effaced himself so thoroughly that his current absence made little

244

difference to the life of the household. He had been leaving us by small degrees for the past ten, twelve years. Think, but think what? The vicar was going to have a bloody hard time making a speech at the cremation, serve him right the Christian twit. "He did what he was supposed to do"—well, the minimum, anyway.

But that wasn't fair of me. Why did I cry, if Dad hadn't done more than that? Well, clearly because I made his life more miserable than it had already become, for those last three months, and I'd missed the chance to make it up to him; then, because of all the rest of the missed chances. But no more tears, now. As far as he was concerned, he wanted to die—I was sure of it. So here he was.

I got up and stretched, and took off my warm jacket to make a pillow on the low windowsill. Nobody here would mind if I took a nap. I thought of the plate of Sunday dinner Ma would be saving to heat up for me: mutton, cut in thin curling slices, and three veg, with apple crumble and custard to follow. And wished it were here in front of me.

When I knew I was pregnant, a week after the cremation, the thought came to me at once that Dad was trying to get another turn at life. I imagined his spirit abandoning its comatose body in the hospital that Saturday night and flying to the shabby hotel room where Roger was at his labours, to slip in at the right moment. Or had it happened early on the next Tuesday morning when we were summoned to the hospital, and found the tent removed and Dad's face given back to our full recognition—handsome, with its high forehead, straight nose and even-lipped mouth? Perhaps the spirit was hovering in that room, alert for its opportunity.

It did not speak well for the quality of the after-life, that he should want to come back so fast. Never mind about that, though—he was not going to get his next existence through me if I could help it. True, nothing could be done about the problem immediately: I was still at home for the Easter vacation, and each morning the rising gorge must be controlled and the full breakfast dealt with; then the letters must be sorted and replies written (for Ma had been put on tranquillizers at a high dosage, and Heather's job as a hospital dietician out at Orpington took all her time). And once the shopping was done and the casserole put on to cook at low heat, I had the *Prelude* to read and annotate—the final work in a syllabus which closed at 1830, before the first Reform Act.

However, by mid-April I was back in Oxford, and began by assessing my situation. A woman doctor in the Banbury Road examined me.

"You're at least six weeks pregnant; and that means your baby will be born in late November—approximately."

"I see." An echo murmured in my mind: *What is the late November doing . . . Late roses filled with early snow?* Oh yes.

"You aren't married, then." The doctor had bobbed grey hair from another age, and puffed mannishly on a cigarette like Auntie Ray.

"No, but I'm engaged; my fiancé's abroad."

"I think you ought to let him know."

"Oh yes, I will."

Next I talked to Shirley. "What do the bad girls in Bognor do when they get knocked up?"

"Well, there's a Church of England Home," she said.

"No no—if they want to get rid of it."

"Oh. Somebody told me a quart of gin and a hot bath, godawful thought. Oh, and taking quinine, too. Why?"

"Why d'you think, I've got a bun in the oven. Thanks to Roger. I'd like to see his balls fried on toast for breakfast, if I didn't have morning sickness."

"Oh God—and with Schools in June."

"Quite."

I collected my supplies—bottles of gin and some bitters to take off the oily taste, as well as quinine—and the next Friday and Saturday nights dosed myself to the

247

limit of my stomach's endurance. There was no sign of a relevant result, only a persistent ringing in the ears and an appalling hangover for hours afterwards, and by Monday I had given up.

Shirley had a new suggestion to offer: a friend of her friend's at Queen's was screwing a nurse at the Radcliffe, and *she* might be able to pass on something stronger than quinine.

"Philip says she adores Jim and does absolutely anything he wants. He made her take off her clothes and do it in the trees up at Park Town—and this was in *March,* you can imagine how freezing."

The message came back later that week: two tablets of ergot would be supplied by way of Philip and Shirley, but no name identifying the source must be passed on to me.

"That's fine. Tell Philip to tell her I'm absolutely reliable: I would never give anything away."

It was already the first Friday in May when Shirley handed me the envelope with a small bulge at its end; there was no time to be lost, and at ten o'clock the same night I took the pills—one, and then an hour later the second. Shirley stayed with me, sitting by the electric fire while I walked about to get the maximum effect of the drug. I had bought a plastic sheet and two cheap towels to deal with the mess, and these were laid on the bed.

"I can feel it, definitely!" The muscles in my belly were pulling themselves tight, then letting go, independent of all volition: this surely was the effect looked for.

"I'd better boil up some water," she said.

"Why?"

"You remember—they do that in novels. Makes things sterile, or something. Or for swabbing off."

She went out to the kitchen, and I held the

round, tight fruit that was my belly—still small, like a grapefruit in there. Twenty minutes later when she came back with the steaming kettle, I realised that nothing very striking was happening inside me. The contractions went on, slowly and mildly, but did not gather any momentum. An hour passed, and they had subsided; another hour, and we had given up.

"It's my body—too strong, that's the trouble. It won't give in; it would need a much larger dose."

The word came back later the next week that no stronger dose could be supplied: the risk was too great.

"I'm not going to stand for it, though—I'll kill myself before having a baby," I told Shirley.

"I suppose we'll have to discover more contacts, then."

"Thing is, the right contacts mean people who get laid. I don't know any women reading English who are in that category. Being engaged doesn't in itself count. History—no. They get engaged, but oh the purity of it."

"What about Molly Urquhart, the one who goes out with Americans? Classicists tend to be broad-minded."

"Yes, because their stuff is so *rude*. We don't know her at all, though—I mean, I don't."

"Put her down on the list anyway," Shirley said.

I wrote the name down on a small piece of paper. "A list with one name on it."

"You could ask Sean."

"If absolutely desperate. I don't know, he's so respectable now. And used to be Catholic, of course."

"Yes. But it's the Catholics who have to have the most abortions, because of not using contraceptives."

"That's very true; I'll put him down. Actually, Trevor would be the most likely source. Or that girl he was on with for a time, last year. There was a rumour

249

they'd broken up over something like this. You must know her—she reads Italian and something. Arty type, long hair, obviously pots of money."

"Linda Webber."

I wrote that name down also. This weekend I was going to get drunk—there was a big party at Balliol on Saturday night—before throwing myself on the mercies of the abortionist, whoever he was.

At the party, the first group inside the door were some unfamiliar Australians drinking bottled beer.

"Allo-allo," one of them greeted me, with a direct look up and down. "Are you with anybody, then?"

A hard question, because some of Roger's friends were sure to be here. "Sort of."

"Well, that settles that. No point in bothering, is there?" And he turned his back.

Further along I met Jeremy, who asked me how I was.

"A bit stunned. Who are those Aussies with the short haircuts?"

"Ah, you've met an outpost of the Sydney Push, have you? There is one round here. Followers of a philosopher called John Anderson, I think. He seems to have a very loyal and far-flung *Kreis* (as Roger would call it). Libertarian principles."

"Bloody savage manners."

"Well, they have these odd social rules; I don't know enough about them to explain."

"Never mind. I'm surprised to see *you* here." Jeremy had announced earlier in the year his abandonment of not merely poetry but also criticism for a life of scholarship, and this along with the loss of Sean and Peter from the scene had caused the withering away of the old poets' group; Simon and other younger writers had become a new establishment with Auden as their mentor, and the public schoolboys were back on top. "I thought you'd given up this type of scene."

"Actually, I'm in training for the don's life: I shall be wine steward of the S.C.R. at thirty. No, didn't you notice, my room's right below this one, so I might as well be here. And the work's going all right: how about you?"

"Getting through it. If I can borrow a good set of notes on *Beowulf* from someone, I'll be O.K."

"I'm letting those early periods go, more or less. I'm not going to get alphas there anyway—might as well concentrate on my best stuff—Restoration onwards."

"Isn't that risky?"

"Not really," he said. "Between you and me, it's a virtual certainty that I'll be doing a B.Litt. here. The issue of a First or a Second's immaterial; Beckworth wants me to work with him next year anyway. What will you be doing?"

"Not absolutely sure. I've put in a couple of applications for things."

There was no Beckworth for me. My relations with tutors were markedly cold, and they had refused to recommend me for any postgraduate grant. So I had been round to the careers office in St. Giles, and from their sparse files—the place was strangely quiet and empty—they presented me with the names of two companies: J. Walter Thompson and Shell Oil. It seemed to me too soon to face the harsh truths of advertising, so I wrote to Shell, and got back almost by return a letter of firm discouragement. Never mind. I could still get my old summer job filing for the B.B.C., and pass my time there in memorizing sections of the *Four Quartets.* Given Ma's situation too, I had better go back on my vow not to live at home, at least for the two months it would take to find a more profitable way to live. I would *not,* despite Shirley's advice, follow her into the training college course; and I would not stay in Oxford, with or

251

without Roger. Nobody wanted me in this place for anything but fucking.

Ian Beckworth came in later, after the prolonged dons' dinner, bringing as his guest a philosopher from Cambridge.

"*Ancient* philosophy," he added after Jeremy introduced us, "a rather different branch, you understand, from the Strawson-and-company one. As a matter of fact, Stuart almost persuaded me to stay in classics: he still occasionally makes me wish I had."

Stuart smiled vividly at the tribute, and I felt a touch of surprise—it just wasn't the Oxford style to demonstrate this sort of open warmth in friendship. Where was the irony? The open blades, testing? "But I *admire* Strawson," he objected. "There's superb work being done here, and we all know it."

"Perhaps the message was that we weren't going to have to check our remarks constantly for basic errors," I said. "Or suppress our metaphysical tendencies."

"I hope I'm as stringent as the next philosopher; however there's such a thing as variation in context."

Beckworth was evidently quite pleased with us, for he produced a two-thirds-full bottle of Glenlivet and poured drinks all round.

"Shall I get you some water with that?" he asked me.

"No no, thanks."

A couple of hours after this beginning, I woke from a blank in memory to find myself walking with Stuart in a private quadrangle among barely visible trees. It must have been the movement of open air which restored consciousness, though I still reeled very slightly in the dark. I had not, I was sure, done anything to make myself ridiculous—fainted or fallen down, yet nothing specific came back to me. On the other hand, from the ease with which I accepted this hand over my shoulder I knew that some kind of significant ground had been prepared between us. Had he kissed me? I licked my lips and thought not.

"Well," he said now. "You hold it extremely well, but you *do* drink quite desperately."

"It's just temporary—Schools, that kind of thing."

He hesitated before speaking again. "One senses an impulse of—carelessness, for want of a better word. As if you might throw yourself away somehow, for nothing."

"No, really—"

"I mean to say, don't do that."

How lovely, how irresistible: I turned towards him, grasping the lapel of his jacket in one hand, and when he kissed me once, pulled him back for more.

"Now I'll walk you home," he said.

"All right." I told him the way, and let him lead me docile as a lamb along most of it. Then, in a darkness between streetlights I slowed my steps, until he took the suggestion and put me against a convenient tree to kiss again. Under the fine, loosely cut material of his trousers, his grooved buttocks were wonderfully distinct to my spread fingers.

"My God," he gasped quietly, when at the next cue I thrust my hand down between us; and he caught it away and held it tight. "Not so fast!"

"I suppose there isn't anywhere we could go tonight," I said.

"Absolutely not—besides, you're drunk. You don't really mean this."

"O.K. What about tomorrow: can you meet me at two?"

"Only as long as you understand you're perfectly free to forget the whole thing. I'm married: I'm not in a position to make any claims on you."

253

When I stood waiting for him on the corner by the launderette, shading my eyes against the sun, I wasn't sure I would recognize him. What I had retained from the night before was an approximate impression of a voice with some resonance to it, and of a longish face in the Caesarian style, and a certain scent (later to be revealed as belonging to his anti-baldness lotion). Eventually, a grey Rover crept along the kerb towards me and stopped, and I knew—of course it had to be a grey Rover, the intelligent bourgeois choice.

We drove out to the Cumnor hills, parked where a rough track led in towards the woods, and walked for a while. We were both wearing raincoats, since the morning had been showery and clouds and blue sky alternated overhead. In the thick of the woods, cold drops spattered our faces when the breeze gusted; after the first track gave out we climbed a gate and took a grassy footpath which wandered into a copse grown up with ferns and creepers, and here and there white campion as the only flower.

"Here," I said, impatient to be sure that I was making no mistake. "This'll do."

He kissed me—no, there was no mistake so far—but not for long; obviously he was troubled.

"You realise it's Sunday, don't you?"

My God, not a *Christian!* But he went on, "I didn't come prepared, you see."

"It doesn't matter. See, I'm pregnant already."

He looked at my belly, then at my face as if he feared for my sanity. "Pregnant—are you being serious?"

"Yes. About three months."

When I had explained it all, he put his arms round me: "Poor child, poor child. Whoever he is, I'd like to punch him out!"

"Never mind about it: I can manage. Here, we'll put the raincoats down."

It was not only the freshness of the cool air and green woods that so moved me this time, it was the quality of his exploration, at once tentative and adroit; it was the pristine enjoyment of adventure on the part of a long-married man, unjaded by the adolescent's repetitive work of masturbation and defensive cynicism. He seemed to me years younger than Roger in spirit—a truer lover, greeting me at every turn and rise with equal response, equal happiness.

I did not see his body all naked until the evening, when we had gone on to spend the night in a hotel twenty miles from the city; then, when I looked I was reminded of the woods still, for his shoulders, arms and back were freckled like foxgloves with brown dappling, vivid against the milky ground of his skin. His beauty awed me almost, as if I had casually lifted a lid like one of Portia's suitors, and found an unexpected treasure. All night, even while drowsing, I remained in a state of arousal; wherever he touched me as we rested together I felt the message pulsing between my legs. I was a field, a web, trembling from edge to centre.

"Like flowers, you are," I told him in the morning. "Beautiful."

And he blushed. "Please!—what a thing to say to a man."

"I'm sorry. You also look rather like Julius Caesar."

"That's better." (And rather like my father, I admitted silently.)

"Who do I look like?" I asked.

He reached out and brushed a hand over my hair, thinking. "I really don't know."

"Nobody," I said. "At least, nobody *you've* met before."

"You're correct about that."

"We all look like this, down in South London."

255

"Do you?"

"No, actually. Just the odd few."

We drove back to Oxford after breakfast, stopping again at the launderette.

"So," he said, "is this the end?"

"It depends, doesn't it? What do you think?"

"If it depends on me, I'd like to see you again."

"All right. But I've got to see about an abortion this week."

He made a painful grimace. "I'd forgotten that. Well, I'll give you my name and college address, telephone also. I'll wait until I hear from you; if there's any way for me to help, let me know."

I looked at him one more time: today he looked like a man close to fifty (how old *had* I thought him before I knew he had four children, the oldest fifteen?—I forget), with eyes slightly pouched and bloodshot from a night of little sleep. And he didn't look so much like Dad; the eyes were hazel, and the hair darker, crisper, and the face itself more focussed and alert, and much, much luckier.

Walking up the path from the back gate, I imagined the scene as he told lies to his wife to explain his arrival back in Cambridge a day late. It must be stupidly easy for people like him: "Rhys-Jones wanted to go over some details of the *Festschrift*. . . . Yes, sorry I missed Peter's concert last night." And so on. The wives were used to putting up with things; he needn't twist about and invent cover stories with details matched to reality at all sorts of interlocking points, as I would with Roger if we were to get married.

I supposed I might ask him, if we ever met again, what philosophers thought about the lies they told. The question would annoy him, surely, and he very likely did not behave well when annoyed: that immense sweetness and gentleness could not possibly extend itself throughout ordinary life. True, he had good friends, if Beckworth was an example, but then again one did not become an advisory editor of *Greece and Rome* precisely in that mode. He must be at best *partly* nice, and never mind, what mattered to me was the goodness in the touch. It was curious that I had come across two men in the past few months with whom I could make love, when for years before all the passes that were made at me by random men (Sean included, last summer) caused an immediate refusal on my body's part, a drastic *No!*—which I was hard put to soften by polite temporizing. For Shirley there was a middle ground: men who were nothing particular but all right. But I knew nothing of it.

Here I reached the outer door, and the end of speculation. I went upstairs to my room, found the aspirin bottle in the sink alcove and took three tablets, threw Saturday night's clothes off the chair, and sat down to work.

Shirley and I went to see Linda after dinner. She produced the desired list of names and addresses at once, handing it over at the cost only of a short discussion of the company I kept.

"I was rather surprised," she said, "knowing Trevor and company, that you didn't get rid of Roger when you had the chance. I find those people utterly selfish. Not that I ever really *met* Roger, of course—Trevor kept his friends to himself like everything else. Almost everything else."

"It wasn't a simple situation. As to selfishness, I don't know—who's different?"

She stared out of her window for a moment and pulled her fingers through her long dark hair. It was easy to see that she was altogether out of Trevor's class, with her cameo-pinned white shirt, and this room too—the pied pony skin on the bed, heavy bronze-coloured

257

cotton spreads, and filmy white curtains belling inwards from the open sash.

"I suppose," she said, "I thought someone with Trevor's background would understand certain things better. For example, prejudice against women—after all, State-school people have to deal with a certain amount of prejudice against them here. But he hadn't a clue—he was worse than any of them."

"Prejudice?"

"I mean, the way women aren't taken seriously here. And in general, the way they're held back in this country: lower types of jobs and so forth."

"But surely all that is past history—surely it's not nowadays," I said.

"Oh no. But I'm not going to labour the point. I'm just observing that these grammar-school types are appalling conservatives when you come down to it."

At once something that had been long suppressed in my memory came to mind: Roger's surprise, when he told me how he and Sean had belonged to the Young Conservatives, at my indignant reaction. "Hold it—" he'd said, "we weren't actually Tories, although Sean *is* I think a bit drawn that way. It was a social thing, to meet the better-looking girls, and part of the business of getting to the top—I'm not denying that."

"That isn't surprising," I answered Linda, "when you consider that the working class has always been told they aren't fit to understand anything. Of course a lot of them believe it, including some of the cleverest ones. So the way up is to join the other bastards."

"Well, it's a pity." And Linda got up to let us know we should leave. "I should mention, when you phone up any of these people on the list, that if you can't get it done right away you'd better leave it till after Schools:

258

it's going to take you a couple of weeks to get over something like this. At least, so they say."

"Wouldn't that be leaving it rather late, though? I mean, it'll be practically four months by then."

"Yes, well with luck you could get it done this week."

But there was no luck—no appointment earlier than the last week in May, and I must settle for a date almost a month later. Already my waist was thickening, and I should have to move the button on the skirt of my black examination uniform to its farthest edge. The delay would give me time to collect some money together, however, and perhaps see Stuart again also.

I sent a letter to Stuart's college suggesting a choice of two weekends in late May for a meeting, and the reply by return post asked for both.

Of our next encounter I remember terribly little, since out of nervousness I began drinking in the train to Bletchley, and continued through dinner at the small inn he drove us to, and after. Of that night, only the trembling moment of first nakedness, and the recognition immediately afterwards of an unforced, perfect rightness of fit between us comes back. Perhaps we didn't talk much; or perhaps he remembers what we talked about.

Next morning, though, he had an apology to make: he had thought me that time in Oxford a kind of young Apache, an amoral primitive of the new democratic order, without a recognizable sensibility. Now he conceded his mistake.

"So you believe I'm human—how kind of you, and when did that begin?"

"Don't put it in that way—I'm not so atrocious," he said, blushing. "Granted my blindness at the time, I did notice some things. You were very kind, very considerate in the things you said to me, and the things you didn't say, and in kissing me good-bye. I came away feeling intensely grateful."

"That's all right. The benefits aren't all on one side."

"What I want to convey is that the terms of our being together are entirely up to you. And that I'm incredibly happy making love to you."

"So am I, to you."

We arranged to meet in the same way the following Saturday, and on that occasion drove south to a village on the northern edge of the Chilterns where he knew the name of an inn. I thought it likely that he had been there before with his wife, but not recently or often, since he would not care to be recognized. Staying away from that subject, as we drove through Leighton Buzzard, I mentioned last night's party to him, at which Singleton was present.

"John Singleton?" His moment of uncertainty made it clear that novelists did not figure largely in his scheme of things. "Writer of some sort, isn't he? Cantankerous fellow too—I remember he came to one of our dinners, and asked for ketchup in a rather pointed way."

"Yes, well that would've been for effect."

"Were you impressed?" he asked, keeping his eyes on the winding road ahead.

"Difficult question. He's got to mean *something* to people like myself, upper-working, lower-middle; by the by he isn't really from the back streets of Warrington—doesn't even have an accent—but it's more a question of the other things he isn't."

I stopped here, with the sense that I had already gone too far for Stuart's comfort, and side-tracked. "Anyway, I'm sure you've noticed that sort of *glaze* that people who are public figures acquire. Just a little more

260

of it, and you could stick them on the mantelpiece."

The place we were going to stay at turned out to be a hotel of some size, with a baronial doorway from which the porter immediately stepped out with an offer to park the car. I took my suitcase from the back seat and carried it inside; Stuart followed me, and as soon as we were alone upstairs scolded me for the indiscretion.

"A married woman doesn't *ever* say 'I'll take mine myself.' Her husband takes the luggage."

"Sorry, I didn't think. Were you embarrassed?"

"Of course! You made it perfectly clear that we weren't married."

"Well, how would I know how a wife behaves? I think it's a bit bizarre to criticize me on those grounds."

"It's a matter of common sense—behaving as any normal adult woman would behave. There are conventions which it's simplest to accept. To fit in."

"Well, fuck that."

"And that's another thing. You do talk like an absolute fishwife: face it."

The retort *Well, piss off then if you want to!* was ready on my lips, but I didn't utter it: seeing him hovering between desire and disgust, I couldn't take the risk. For it was that body standing across from me that I wanted today, and that prick: never mind the words, let them go. I threw myself face down on the bed and waited. He *must* come to me; and in the end he did.

At five-thirty he got up and bathed (it amused me, then, that he locked the door of the bathroom); I poured myself a glass of whisky from the bottle he had brought, and when he had finished I too got myself ready for dinner. We were happy again, secure in that weightless temporal bubble, floating on the margin of the stream.

"Here: this is for you. I think the colours might go well."

261

I opened the narrow box and unfolded a diaphanous square of silk: its wide border was leaf-green, and the centre printed with a small paisley pattern on light gold.

"Oh yes! *Thank* you—could I wear it now, d'you think?"

"Let's see." He watched critically as I tied it loosely over my new yellow dress from Marks and Spencer's, and I guessed his thought—was that how his wife wore such things? "The knot to one side more."

"There." And we went downstairs to the bar.

At dinner he asked me for the first time about Roger. "Who is this man? And why haven't you told him about the child?"

I drew Roger's portrait—bright enough, I summed up, but in the long run impossible—and added: "He wouldn't want *this* any more than I do. I'm just making sure, though, there won't be any question of marriage because of family pressure and so forth."

"And you intend to break it off, when he gets back from Berlin."

"More or less then."

"I suppose I don't understand," he said, "why you haven't broken it off already."

"Why?"

"I mean that after all you're *engaged* to the man, and you've changed your mind—one ought not to play about with what is really a serious decision."

"Well look: he probably wanted us to be engaged so as to have a bit more control of me. It wasn't my idea. And it's more the friendship that means something to me; I don't care about the ring business."

"I see."

"Well, and what about your wife? Are you serious about her?"

"Absolutely," he said at once. "I have *no* intention

262

of leaving her—she's my wife, and I care a great deal about her. I don't want her to be hurt."

"I think that's admirable."

He pushed his dinner plate away from him and rested his elbows on the table, cupping his wine glass in both hands. "Even though you probably wouldn't think it was much of a romance."

"Well come on, why not?"

"Well. When I was first at Cambridge, I didn't know any women. I had the usual public-school background, obviously, and no sisters or girl cousins, as it happened, so the normal opportunities didn't arise. I'd never really developed an interest in girls—all that seemed utterly remote."

Here the waiter came to remove the disarticulated bones of duckling and lamb from in front of us, and I held back my comment until he left.

"Well, be honest—you were all queer as coots, weren't you?"

"That would be the vulgar view." He got his pipe out of his pocket and put it in his mouth (for reassurance?), then set it down on the table. "Certainly there were very intense friendships among us; and some of those have remained very important to me. But that's by the way. At any rate, when I was putting in for fellowships my tutor suggested to me that I ought to think about marriage. He was happily married himself, and recommended the idea to me."

"So you just—got married?"

He rummaged for his tobacco tin, filled the pipe from it, tamped it down and lit it.

"As I said, I didn't know any women. However, a close friend of mine who had gone to the Treasury had a sister, and introduced me; I thought she was nice—pretty, too—and we rather hit it off. Nigel was and is quite a brilliant man, and I knew something of the

263

family: evidently there are some distinguished genes about. At any rate, I invited Nigel and Joanna up to Harrogate to stay with my mother (my father had been dead for some time), and that went well, and in due course we got engaged. I'm sure you don't approve of that way of doing things."

"Why ever not? People have to get married, it seems, and that's one way of doing it."

"I wonder how you would do it," he said, putting down his glass as the coffee was brought.

"I've no idea."

"But if you were seriously interested in some young man, you'd take him home to meet your family, wouldn't you?"

"Eventually, when everything was settled."

"Then whose judgment would you consult, in deciding?"

"Nobody's, Stuart. Who *is* there?"

"Your friends perhaps?"

"Only up to a point; they're about as clueless as I am. Or too busy taking care of themselves."

"You'll need a great deal of courage, then."

Later, in bed, he poured us each a final glass of Scotch, and talked some more.

"I'm not an old hand at this sort of thing, as I'm sure you realise."

"Neither am I. But let that pass: what were you going to say?"

"Only that a year ago—six months ago—I should never have believed I would be in this situation now. I was in an affair with the wife of a colleague of mine, and that was the first time I really understood, *really,* the kind of sexual power a woman can exert. She'd got hold of me—"

"By the balls, you mean to say."

"In effect, yes. And then she told me the whole

thing was an exercise in revenge against her husband. She had a great gift for cruelty. Certainly she'd been ill-treated by him, but I really think she enjoyed taking it out on me."

"When did you get out of this?"

"I didn't, exactly. It ended when she told her husband about me—in detail, I gathered. *That* finished it. And she got her reconciliation with him, became pregnant again soon afterwards, and I assume that they're very happy."

"Did your wife never find out?" I asked.

"No. That was the one consolation. But there I'm being unjust—in a sense, I owe this present state of things to her too. Pamela, I mean."

"To her, perhaps; also to the Education Act of what was it, 'forty-three or 'forty-four? Without that I should never have been within range: I should have been a—secretary in an estate-agent's, with a beehive hairdo."

"Unimaginable!" And he lifted my glass away, and turned out the light.

In the morning we did not talk much, rehearsing in our silences the separation to come. We drove back through the pretty villages in sunshine, looking absently past rustic porches and fences overgrown with bridal trails of roses and jasmine.

"Where will you be," I asked, "around the end of June?"

"At the cottage, quite a lot of the time. It's near Aldeburgh, on the coast. There's a boat; the children like to sail it—just a dinghy."

"What are their names?"

"The boys are James and Mark." He paused before mentioning the girls' names, as if struck by some awkwardness. "My daughters are Cressida and Helen."

"And you've got a dog."

"Yes—how did you know?"

"The car smelled of it yesterday, when it was damp."

"Of course. Sharp of you."

A picture of the Underwoods' summer drew itself spontaneously out of my memory of Arthur Ransome's *Swallows and Amazons*, a book whose details had teased and baffled me so that I could never, in the end, be sure about what had happened; but here, certainly, were tanned boys in jerseys hauling up sails, and flags; here were athletic girl-children with the beginnings of a firm jawline; here was their mother, a good sport, wearing canvas shoes and a pullover and gored skirt; and there in the background was their cottage where on cool nights they lit driftwood fires in the fireplace and sat round with their cocoa and family stories.

"In August the children go to stay with their grandmother. Joanna and I usually go to Greece."

I could imagine that, too: why, then, could Stuart not imagine the life of a secretary in an estate-agent's office?

V

Quad 16

It's been a night and a morning, and nothing has happened aside from a slight, recurrent ache. I think I shall have to telephone Nanda and ask what to do. I think it's failed.

Shirley and Linda are among the thinly scattered group at lunch, and I tell them the bad news.

"Wait a bit," Linda says. "I don't suppose they're always accurate about the time it takes."

"What should I do, then, run up and down stairs?"

"You could try that."

Quad building is deserted, so I can fling myself into action with abandon, leaping up the stairway by threes and pounding furiously down by fives. And again, and again—I know my body's holding on dumbly there to its fate, but I'll *make* it give up. It's mind that has to rule here: again, up the stairs, again down, panting and jerking. When I'm completely out of breath, I sit down heaving and think: if everything else fails, I'll hang myself from the top railing. Tomorrow the college closes, and nobody will find me until they come to clean.

But for the moment I drag myself along to my room, and am quickly rewarded by a clutching of the muscles inside, at the involuntary level. It repeats itself after five minutes—now I can begin to be happy!—and by late afternoon the spasm is turning over methodically as a wheel, with increasing power.

"It hurts!" I say to myself aloud, in surprise. And soon I am grasping onto my hair when the pain comes, and sweating as much from the beginning of panic as from the cramps. I have refused from the very outset of all this to get any information about what my body is up to, for I never for one moment agreed to it; and now I find myself ambushed, drawn into a programme whose precise nature is a tormenting mystery. *What* is going on?

The pages of *The Brothers Karamazov,* which I have started reading again, are becoming marked by my damp fingers. I continue to read, however inefficiently, with trust in the book as a talisman still, keeping death away from me so long as the story lasts. But each time the contraction gathers force so my eyes travel faster along the lines of print, racing until at the height of pain I can no longer take in the sense, and let the pages close on my thumb; in this way characters and events zoom unevenly by me—the old man, Dmitri, and these detestable women: Grushenka, Katerina, like cancers on the human race, the first an opulent tumour, the second a cruel sarcoma in the bone. They only crawl, and suck, like slugs. It is the men who are the people in this world.

Eight o'clock. Is that all it is? I get up for a drink of milk and am relieved that I can still walk about, in these intervals. It must be time to put the plastic sheet in the bed, and the towels nearby.

Across the quadrangle there is only one window with a light showing, under the mauve evening sky. It was curious, at lunch, how with only three tables set in the entire hall, people managed to sit distinctly apart from one another, preferring loyalty to their departed groups to the random company of those left behind. People who haven't spoken to the likes of Shirley or me in three years are not going to change their minds now. In any case, it's over.

With the onset of another pain I get back into bed, and remember despite myself Stinking Lizaveta and her speechless agony of childbirth in the bathhouse. That was the old way. And with the fading of pain I'm reminded also of the story Auntie Vee told me once, as a result of which we could claim to have drops of "noble blood" in our veins. That was the story of Grampa's father being the son of a village girl near Faversham, who got pregnant by the son of the family at the big house nearby. Was she a field hand, or in service? I never thought to ask. But she would have got the sack, inevitably, and Auntie said the young man was sent out to India. His father's title, she said, was from India—and so much for "noble blood," since it originated with one of Clive's petty warlords no doubt. More of the old way. Vee is a *stupid* woman, I gasp to the wall, proud of a mass of atrocities! And meanwhile the pain rings through me like a terrific bell, enforcing the rule of necessity, denying change.

I wipe my face and pick up the book again, to search further into this world in which all terrors are fulfilled. I turn the pages of Dmitri's humiliation, and feel myself a part of the vast misery-producing system, the satanic mill in which everything is ground, turn by turn. It all seems of a piece throughout.

Shirley and Linda come in at eleven-thirty. They are wearing party clothes—Linda in taffeta like a beetle's wing, and Shirley in a tight black dress that shows her pale pink knees to advantage.

"It's happening, then," Shirley says. "Thank God, I was worried."

Linda brings me water, and offers some codeine

271

tablets which I take. They sit down across from the bed on my two chairs, and adjust their skirts.

"Look at this, d'you know it?" I wave *The Brothers K* at them. "They haven't got any self-respect, these Russians—it's extraordinary how they carry on!"

"I haven't read it yet," Shirley says.

It's clear that Linda *has* read it, but she hesitates before speaking: one does not make casual remarks about *The Brothers K.* "Yes, the behaviour *is* more extreme—it's the absence of an influential bourgeois class in Russian society, partly. And no Protestant tradition either."

"I see—I see."

"Tolstoy's people are much more Westernized."

"Well, but I'm up to where the old father's been murdered," I say, and for the moment am unable to go on. They look anxiously at me, then at one another, while the pain takes over. "So," I pick up slowly, "so it is obviously not Dmitri who did it, but who did?"

"Well I don't think I ought to give it away," Linda says seriously.

At this I want to shout *Tell me—I may die before I get to the answer!* But that would be unfair.

I do not know whether the pain now is really worse, or whether the presence of sympathetic people makes it harder to bear, but I am suffering more acutely—must twist and turn, and bite my hand to keep from crying out. And I see that this embarrasses them; I urge them to go away and sleep, but they won't.

Towards one in the morning (my alarm clock is in the direct line of my vision, on the floor beside the electric fire) I begin to vomit, and Shirley runs for a saucepan from the kitchen just in time. From this point on I cannot pretend to bear the wrenching belly pains with decency, and only try to stifle the noise in a towel. Then voices are heard at the door where Shirley keeps guard; someone offers me a strong sleeping pill, it appears. And I take it, but when I have another bout of retching we see flecks of the thing appearing among strings of greenish bile. It is no good. And crazy Henrietta pushes her way in and sits on the floor, staring at me with excited eyes.

"D'you mind her here?" Shirley whispers, bringing me a wet cloth. "She gave us that pill, but we can make her go."

"I don't care."

Every minute now I am getting dragged past the limit previously imagined of pain and exhaustion—and then thrown back. Surely I'll die of this if it goes on much longer. Yet through it all my head's clear; and I ask again, who killed the old man Karamazov?

"What?" asks Henrietta. "Oh, Smerdyakov, of course."

"Of course." I am bitterly disappointed—bitterly.

Henrietta leans forward: "Well, but that isn't the whole point—Smerdyakov did it, but it was Ivan's influence behind him."

"Oh yes." It doesn't surprise me any more. "The servant has to do it, naturally—the dirty work. Why can't books ever say anything different—why not?"

"But you didn't guess the plot beforehand," Linda objects. "She had to tell you."

The onset of pain saves me from having to answer immediately. Now it fades again, and I take a breath: "I expected Dostoevsky to be different. But why don't you go off to bed, the three of you—nothing's happening here."

It irritates me to see them, like an audience of Fates: Shirley sitting there smoking and rubbing her eyes, Linda pacing to the door and back nervously, and Henrietta on the floor leafing curiously through my stack of examination notes.

"Somebody's got to stay with you," Linda says firmly.

Henrietta pays no attention. "Are you going to keep all your notes?" she asks.

"No—throwing them out."

She is appalled. "I'm keeping *everything*. Otherwise what would it all be for?"

"But I'm not going to teach."

"No, I mean one would keep them for oneself."

"Me Ma hasn't got the room," I say at a venture, and then the pain is here, raging, and again letting slowly go.

No, I shan't keep them. One is bent enough by this place. On the other hand, when will I start building and preserving my piece of the world, as even the mad among the middle class do? Why is that impossible to think of? But then I remember the middle-class faults, and how badly the English group (except Joan from Crawley) behaved in the past few weeks, quarrelling over the possession of library copies of Bush on the seventeenth century and Lewis on the sixteenth, inventing pretexts for coming into one's room to see what books were on the shelves, comparing day after day their progress in revision, and repeating in overbearing tones the tutors' words of praise: "Villiers says I'm among the top three of this year," "She said my last essay was *definitely* at the First Class level." They were suspicious because I kept away from Villiers' sessions—what was I *doing*, by myself? I was keeping away from Villiers, simply, and taking refuge in Wordsworth.

The electric fire has been on for hours, since I first felt cold; I can tell the air in the room is hot and stale, but the shivering inside me is undiminished.

"I'm too tired—I can't stand much more of it. Have to telephone the Radcliffe soon."

274

"Try and hold out for another half-hour," Linda says. "You must be awfully close now. After that we'll help you get there, all right?"

"All right."

A ragged chirping sound begins outside from the sparrows in the eaves; we all look towards the window and see grey light behind the roof opposite. Morning, then, but no hope in it at all; I haven't any courage left—I put a pillow over my face now, hard, as soon as the clenching starts, and it is sodden with the spit from my open mouth and the tears that are forced from me.

"I'm going to the hospital now—had enough."

So I reach for a pair of trousers lying at the end of the bed, and sit up to put them on. But with the sudden change of position something inside me gives way, and a flood of water runs out onto the plastic sheet under me in the bed. My feet are trapped in the trousers; still, I pull my knees apart and see the puddle tinged with red.

"Oh *God!*" The pain has focussed itself, sharp like a cut, and a second later I feel the warm shape of a different flesh easing out between my thighs. My victim, it is, a dark-red miniature of a person, tiny thin arms folded together across its chest, legs folded across its hidden sex. I push myself up on my elbows. It doesn't move. Linda has brought a towel to hide it in, but holds back, seeing the bluish-white spiralling cord still attached.

"I've got to piss," I say suddenly, and utterly helpless see myself letting go, urinating over the edge of the bed and over the dead child. As I do so, a bloody sponge pulses out of me.

"O.K., that's it." Linda gathers everything rapidly into the towel and takes the bundle to the far side of the room.

And I raise my eyes and meet those of Henrietta staring like a fanatic—her face wears a rictus of dreadful

275

excitement. When I look down, I see what she sees: my bare streaked legs framing a bloody pool, and open cunt in full view; stained bedclothes, a pan of green vomit on the floor beside a stack of books: *Varieties of History,* Eliot's *Selected Essays,* Pound's *Personae.*

"Sorry," I begin to say, and immediately correct myself: "Oh get out of here!"

She gives an embarrassed laugh, and shrugs off to the door. Linda is going too, with a carrier bag apparently full of waste paper and rags. She'll put it in the bins at the back gate.

How shall I ever thank her for doing this for me? Who did it for her, last year, and for whom, one day, shall I do it in my turn?

Now, to my surprise, I'm getting up—I can move all of myself—and then I catch up a towel to stop the immediate pouring of hot blood. Shirley hands me a pad; I put it on and hitch up the trousers over. We gather in the mess from the bed, stow it in a corner.

"Leave it, Shirley. It's all right—I'll manage."

She can go off and sleep; no more to be done. I turn off the light and the electric bars, and open the window to let in the cool, brightening air. To slow the bleeding, which is the only thing I'm still afraid of, I lean back in the armchair with my feet up on the bed.

Well, how strange! For all those hours I was so sure that I was close to dying, thinking that was what so much terrible pain had to mean. It was so bad, the pain, so very much worse than anything imagined, that afterwards the moment of recognition—of the child, of Roger's long shape of head—felt, and feels imponderable. Shall I even remember it? But I know as I put the question that I shall have to; and perhaps when I'm thirty, and then forty, it will be putting its ghostly hand (no thicker altogether than one finger) every morning on my lips. It will be the thing I can't mention, the thing outside of poetry.

Did Singleton have a point, then, warning me against this? One sets out to toughen oneself, to face all the obscenities of the universe with open eyes. But what if doing that somehow blunts the quality of vision? It is possible. Still, there's no reason to trust Singleton's opinion, not the opinion of a man who was so obviously wanting something.

No; this morning I'll rest, this afternoon pack up the last of the clothes and books, and go.

The sun is up now, over the slanting roof of St. Aloysius' church. When I close my eyes and the heat of it bathes my face I feel wetness between the eyelids, a tear on each side, running out to the corner. So I know the animal, at least, is intact. It's glad to have got away—it's hungry, and it wants to be happy.